Books by Delphine Boswell

Unholy Secrets	April 2018
Silent Betrayal	December 2018
Bitter Wrath	Spring 2019

Published by Jujapa Press

SILENT

BETRAYAL

A Dana Greer Mystery Series

DELPHINE BOSWELL

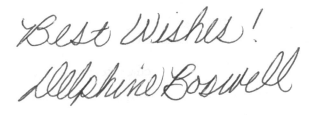

jujapa
hansville
press
washington

ISBN-13: 978-1-7321976-2-6
Library of Congress Catalog Number: 2018912209
Published by:
Jujapa Press
PO Box 269
Hansville, Wa 98340

Cover, telegram, certificate, diagram…by: Jujapa Press

Other illustrations: fiverr.com artists
        boy's portraits - reivalg,
        magazine covers - blackshoven

Acknowledgments

Someone told me once that if you're born to be a writer, you will never stop writing. Such is my story. Before my first mystery novel UNHOLY SECRETS was published, my ideas for book two were becoming solidified. But ideas come from somewhere.

When I was an undergraduate student at Wayne State University, I took a course in criminology, and although I no longer recall the professor's name, I owe my first words of thanks to this person. The class took a field trip somewhere in Detroit to a boys' prison. There, for the first time, I watched aghast as young boys, probably six- or seven-years of age, walked the dreary halls, arms clutched behind their backs. How, I wondered, could these youngsters have already entered the penal system. Hence came my idea for my second book in the Dana Greer Mystery Series, SILENT BETRAYAL.

A book usually goes on several journeys before publication where it is carefully read and scrutinized. For this, I thank my beta readers: Nicky, Deborah, Grace, Dori, and Marian.

Special thanks to Clark Parsons of Jujapa Press for not only giving Silent Betrayal a final read but also for enabling the book to go to print. His kindness, patience, and know-how made the book you're holding possible.

Thanks to my family for pushing me onward, especially, my husband who believes in me

I won't forget the friends and strangers who purchased my first book, UNHOLY SECRETS, and for the reviews they gave me that are much appreciated. They have been standing in the wings waiting for SILENT BETRAYAL, so they can continue to follow Dana Greer in her efforts to solve yet another murder.

As I've said before, a special thank you to my readers, who bring me the greatest joy knowing my words have traveled the distance to reach each and every one of you!

Prologue

March 19, 1952

I heard a high-pitched screech. The air smelled like burnt rubber. The next thing I see is the MG crash through the metal barrier and roll down the embankment. Dried weeds, dirt, and metal car parts flying in the air. Hell, the thing burst into a ball of flames!" the man in the Fedora and tweed sports coat told the police officer.

The story made front-page news the next day once identifications had been made.

Movie Star's Sports Car a Flaming Inferno

The article describing the event followed.

Movie star Chantel DeBour, one of the biggest box office attractions on the silver screen, and her chauffeur, Hamilton Jackson, were involved in a fatal automobile accident yesterday, at 3:10 p.m., on Route 1. The sports car Mr. Jackson was driving careened off the road, through a road barrier, and plunged 600 feet into an embankment, exploding upon impact. Cause of the crash is under investigation. According to an eye witness, the brakes on the vehicle appeared to have malfunctioned, and speed may also have been a factor.

Funeral services for Miss DeBour will be announced shortly. The handling of her multi-million-dollar estate will be by her executor, Theodore Prussia, Esq.

He rattled the newspaper and threw it onto the floor. "The damn broad sure got what she deserved. The plan was foolproof, appearing like an ordinary car malfunction, thanks to Max Freda. But, now, the payoff is all mine!" He danced the chicken around the small room, swinging an imaginary partner in his arms, and sang the lyrics to "Happy Payday" by Little Willie Littlefield and the Jivin' Jewels. He bent down and picked up the paper, hoping to find an address for the attorney handling the estate. There in small print at the bottom of the article was the key to his fortune:

Theodore Prussia, Esq.
One Liberty Street
Utica, New York

Suddenly, his rock 'n roll moves stopped. His inner voice screamed, "Get a grip you stupid idiot. Chantel might have been a bit ditzy, but do you think she'd be that dumb? I mean leaving her estate to you?"

Chapter One

May 15, 1953

The sound of the train rattling along the tracks and the intermittent blare of its horn became a mesmerizing pattern on its route from Maine to Texas. Dana made it a habit to read and reread the telegram, covered in creases, which she held in her hands:

PATRONS ARE REQUESTED TO FAVOR THE COMPANY BY CRITICISM AND SUGGESTION CONCERNING ITS SERVICE

CLASS OF SERVICE

This is a full-rate Telegram or Cable-gram unless its deferred character is indicated by a suitable sign above or preceding the address.

WESTERN UNION

NEWCOMB CARLTON, PRESIDENT   J.C. WILLEVER, FIRST VICE-PRESIDENT

SIGNS
DL=Day Letter
NM=Night Message
NL=Night Letter
LCO=Deferred Cable
NLT=Cable Night Letter
WLT=Week End Letter

The filing time as shown in the date line on full-rate telegrams and day letters, and the time of receipt at destination as shown on all messages, is STANDARD TIME.

Received at

MS DANA GREER C/O JAY HARRISON
CAPE PERIL, MAINE=
FEBRUARY 28 A NINE YEAR OLD INMATE WAS
MURDERED AT THE ST ALOYSIUS GONZAGA HOME
FOR TROUBLED YOUTH IN PUNKERTON TEXAS=
REQUEST YOUR INVESTIGATION INTO THE
MATTER=
PLEASE RESPOND ASAP=
ARCHBISHOP FLOYD J BORETTI=

TELEGRAMS MAY BE TELEPHONED TO WESTERN UNION FROM ANY PRIVATE OR PAY STATION TELEPHONE

Dana stuffed the telegram into her bag. Life had a strange way of unfolding. Only weeks ago, she had stood in the presence of Sergeant Logan who congratulated her on the closure of the Bernadette Godfrey case on Cape Peril, Maine. Dana would never forget the seven-year-old child whose body was found by a hunter in a shallow grave. Once the case resolved, word spread throughout the church community. She developed a reputation for being a professional investigator but also a caring individual who put the hearts of people before all else.

Sergeant Logan had announced Dana would next be traveling to Punkerton, Texas to solve a case involving a young child and a Catholic institution. There was something about investigating a child murder that brought an overtone of sorrow mixed with an urgency to solve. A job not suitable for the faint of heart, yet Dana believed it to be a calling of sorts. The only woman in the role of private investigator in the fifties, there were those who thought she should be at home raising a family, baking chocolate chip cookies, and attending to a husband's every need, but Dana was not that kind of woman. Her curiosity and innate desire to problem solve took her on a different kind of journey…a journey that gave hope to the living, provided answers to loved ones, offered peace to the survivors, and justice to the guilty.

Across the aisle from Dana, a young child bounced on her mother's lap in time with the jostling train. For a moment, Dana fantasized what it might be like to be a mother, to raise a child; after all, most women her age were doing just that. However, she had separated from her husband once she learned of his cheating, and growing up in the Catholic faith, she took seriously the church's dogma regarding divorce…until death do us part.

Enough day dreaming, Dana focused her attention on a book she had picked-up at the train station before leaving. There she found *Texas in All Its Glory,* a hard-covered book, which bore a colorful picture of the Southern flag on its front, discussed the geography, the demographics, and the remarkable climate changes of the state.

Punkerton, two hours outside of Lubbock, was a mere speck on the map as it was not even mentioned other than to say it had an active KKK group and had been the subject of a drought for the past six years.

Dana looked forward to the new adventure before her yet bore a certain amount of trepidation, knowing she was traveling to a place she had only read about. She, a white, Catholic woman heading to the heart of a small Southern town in the middle of the Bible belt and its association with an active Klan membership, made her jittery. She reached for her small Bible, which she kept hidden in her bag, and let her fingertips glide across its grainy cover. "God be with me," she whispered to herself.

Once Dana had accepted the archbishop's request to come to Texas, she was informed by Sergeant McKnight, from Punkerton, that she would be staying at the home of Eleanor Banks, the wife of a former guard at the boys' prison, and conferring, as necessary, with him. Eleanor lived alone after the recent death of her husband. Dana had no idea how long she might be there and hoped the woman would be accepting of her new live-in guest.

* * *

Monday afternoon, three p.m., Dana Greer arrived in the heat of day at the Punkerton Station. After a cross country excursion from Maine to Texas, via the Atchison, Topeka, and Santa Fe Railway, she felt relieved to set her bags down and to stretch every muscle in her weary body. A dry, brittle wind blew through her hair, the kind of breeze that does not cool but only intensifies the already existing God-awful temperature. She pulled the telegram from her bag and began to fan herself. She stared as far ahead as she could see. Miles of wheat fields lay stretched before her like a blanket of gold, and in the forefront, a weathered and rusty oil rig pumped deeply within the parched ground. In the distance, a lone farm stood…a grey wooden house; a neglected barn; and a windmill, spinning slowly. Punkerton, Texas, located midway down the panhandle, not the kind of place anyone would want to write home about but, then again, it made sense why it was the location of the Saint Aloysius Gonzaga Home for Troubled Youth, nestled about six miles out of town on forty acres. The archbishop informed her that on the grounds was a residence, a school, a prison, a gift shop, an infirmary, a garden, and even a cemetery.

As Dana waited in front of the train station, a cab pulled to the curb. A man with a straw hat and bushy beard stretched his neck toward the open passenger window. "You Miss Greer? Gotta call you needin' a ride over to Eleanor Banks' place." The grubby, mustard-colored car boasted shiny black lettering: Lubbock Transport.

"Yes, I am. Sergeant McKnight said that he'd—."

"He said he'd only seen a picture of you, but I should be lookin' for a pretty blond. Gotta be you, all right."

Dana cringed. She chose to ignore his comment. She wondered if the day would ever come when women would be acknowledged for their abilities, their talents, their intellects, rather than viewed as mere sexual objects. But it was the fifties, and most women knew their place, and certainly, it was not traveling the countryside in an effort to solve murders.

The man put her luggage in the trunk and rolled down the windows in the back seat. "Gets mighty hot 'round this time of day." As he pulled away, he cocked his neck to the side and said, "Hear you're from Maine?"

"Yes, Bay View." Dana always seemed to get the chatty type of cab driver.

"Goin' be workin' up at the pit, huh?"

When she didn't respond, he said, "The boys' home, where kids from all over the country are sent when nobody don't know what to do with the felons. . .too young for state prisons or the death penalty." He rattled on, "But I can tell you one thing, Miss, these kids ain't for messin' with. They may be kids, but they got the minds of the devil, they do. Y'all bettin' believe it."

Dana stuffed the telegram into her bag. "Think I'd like to be the judge of that if you don't mind." She wiped her sweaty brow with a linen handkerchief embroidered with the initial *D*. Her mother, while alive, had kept quite the collection of colored threads and enjoyed crocheting edges on pillowcases, making doilies for every table, and embroidering designs on linens. At other times, her mother was too despondent to even get out of bed for days and weeks at a time. Then, her father would step in and take responsibility to raise his only daughter.

Out the window, more and more fields of wheat crossed the countryside. Breathing in the dry air, she could not wait for something cold to drink. Only minutes from the train station and she already felt as if they had been driving for half an hour. The heat, the monotony of the view, and her own, as of yet, unanswered questions made her restless. In the background, the cab driver still mumbled on with his solo conversation obviously not realizing Dana had distanced herself from his words many miles ago.

The speed of the cab slowed down as the driver stopped for a red light. They had entered a town. The green and white sign out the window read:

Punkerton - Population 1,903
Home to the Punkerton Pirates

A narrow, two-story brick building boasted a sign out front of a one-legged pirate in a wooden ship. . .the high school, she assumed. There were two doors to the school. Above each, carved deeply into concrete, appeared the words *Girls* and *Boys*. Directly across from it, a group of Negroes, wearing big straw hats and denim overalls, picked wads of cotton off small, prickly bushes. They filled their baskets to the brim, their skin wet and shiny in the afternoon sun.

"That's the cop's station over there on the left," the driver said. A building surrounded by a chain-link fence stood on the corner. The driver continued, "Folks around here call this area Jesus Row."

"Oh?"

"All the churches. . .too many really for a town of this size. We got the Baptists, the Presbyterians, and the Lutherans."

"No Catholic?"

The cab driver let out a howl like a screeching hyena. "You kiddin' me lady? In Texas?" He laughed some more. "We don't believe in 'em. This is KKK country. No place for Catholics, Jews, or those queer type." The man's voice sounded proud and almost boastful. Dana wondered if the man might have an affiliation with the Klan.

That explained why the Saint Aloysius Gonzaga Home for Troubled Youth was set on the outskirts of town far enough to be out of sight, out of mind, to the panhandle people of Punkerton.

Before the light changed, Dana watched a group of men. Some huddled under a wooden roof, an escape from the blazing sun, waiting under a sign that read: bus stop. Others lined up at a city water fountain. Dana noticed in both cases there was a line for the colored folk and a line for the white folk. This would be another thing she would have to get used to. Not only was Cape Peril, Maine ninety-nine percent Catholic, but the residents were all Caucasian. Although an outsider to these parts, Dana could feel the tension in the air. People here were segregated by gender, race, and religion. She wondered how any of these tensions might play into the murder of the young boy, a white child who found himself imprisoned in a Catholic institution.

The light finally turned green. Life was going to move at a much slower pace in the South; something else she would have to get used to. A block or two later and they were out of town, once again on a two-lane highway. Behind a wire fence, some cattle grazed in the hot sun. Dry rot barns, more than likely from the severe temperatures, looked ready to tumble over from the slightest gust of wind. Dana figured they were nearing Eleanor Banks' place since McKnight said the woman lived on an isolated plot of land, out of town and not far from the youth home. No one was behind them, but the cab driver put his arm out the window signaling a right turn. A few hundred feet off the highway, he turned again, this time to the left in front of a small, yellow wooden house with a wishing well out front. A small robin posed on the rim, grooming his feathers. In contrast to the homey site, what must have formerly graced the front of the house with grass and shrubbery, now was dry patches of dirt and dead branches.

"Mrs. Banks' place," the cab driver said, shutting off the engine. He opened the rear door and went around to get Dana's luggage from the trunk.

A woman who looked to be in her early sixties came out to greet her. "Dana Greer, happy to have you here. I'm Eleanor Banks. Please call me Ellie." Unlike the cab driver, Dana immediately noticed the woman had no Southern drawl. Her salt and pepper hair fell loosely from a bun, and she wore an organdy apron over a housedress covered in purple forget-me-nots with pearl buttons, a tattered pair of open-toed slippers on her feet.

The cab driver placed Dana's things on the porch. She paid the man, and Ellie and she took the suitcases in. A small yellow canary chirped from a cage in the living room, and a calico cat rushed up and began to rub at Dana's ankles.

"Don't mind them; they're a pesky twosome." She pointed toward the bird. "That's Maize. And, that's," she said pointing to the cat, "Patches."

"Not at all. I love animals." Dana bent down to pet the cat, but he hissed, ears slicked back and ran under the couch.

Ellie smiled and in a nervous breath rattled on, "I hope you haven't had lunch yet. I made us some cheese sandwiches and iced tea." She led Dana into the kitchen, decorated in red plaid wallpaper with a border of a pastoral farm scene. Dana sat down at the white wicker table, which was already set with two glasses and two China plates. She thanked the woman for her efforts.

"I hope you'll feel welcome here, Dana. Ever since my Gary passed away, I've felt so lonely here in the middle of nowhere. It will be nice to have some company." The woman's eyes filled with tears, and she sniffled. Turning her face away from Dana's, she quickly changed the subject. "So, tell me, Dana, when do you begin your investigation at the home?" While Ellie waited for Dana to respond, she placed two cheese sandwiches on the plates and poured glasses of tea from a frosted pitcher. "It's all such a tragedy. Gary told me it would only be a matter of time."

"A matter of time?" Dana could feel her eyebrows rise.

Ellie shoved a bobby pin into her bun and rubbed her neck as she explained. "Before something like this happened. None of these boys have any support system, most abandoned by their families if they had a family. Many of them are offspring of illegitimacy, and as Gary told me, the boys are more like untamed animals than humans, most never having had an opportunity to learn basic social skills."

Without realizing, Dana had finished her glass of tea as the woman spoke. Mentally, she was already making notes.

"Here let me pour you another. You'll get used to the panhandle heat sooner than you think."

"Eleanor—."

"Ellie, please."

Since the woman appeared comfortable talking about the youth home, Dana felt at ease asking an otherwise awkward question. "Are you thinking someone from within the home may have killed the young boy?"

The woman's eyes narrowed and squinted as if looking into a blazing afternoon sun. "I wish I knew. I can say this, though; I doubt anyone cares. If you ever have a chance to look at the cemetery out back, you'll see what I mean. Gary used to say more boys got buried there than came walking in the front door. He was kidding, of course, but it gives you an idea how unsympathetic the staff is toward the inmates."

Ellie's comments left Dana speechless for a moment. How could an institution run by the church sound so indifferent, so heartless? "Your husband. . .did he know Douglas Clifford?"

Ellie nodded. "Oh, he sure did. He was a guard on G Wing, Level 1, where the worst of the worst are kept. Gary used to be an officer for the New York Police Department. He sure saw his share of crime and even was shot at multiple times. Once he came in on a burglary in progress at a large downtown bank, when one of the masked robbers pulled his gun at Gary, shooting him within inches of his heart. He was in Bellevue Hospital for over two weeks…near almost died on me. After the incident, he decided to retire but not for long. When he got bored of retirement, he learned about the boys' home, and the rest is history." Ellie ran her fingertips over the edge of her glass and with a gulp swallowed what remained of her sandwich. "Little did he know what evil lurked ahead."

"Could you tell me what he knew?" Fiona Wharton, Dana's former mentor who taught Dana everything she knew about law enforcement, used to say, "There's no time like now to begin askin' yer questions. Why wait for tomorrow?"

"The staff believed the boy was possessed." Ellie looked over her shoulder and hushed her voice. "You did know supposedly he bludgeoned his parents to death, didn't you?" Ellie emphasized the letter *B*.

"So, I was told."

"According to what the staff told Gary, the boy wrestled with demons that even a priest couldn't exorcise. Boy was adopted by an elderly couple from Los Angeles, I believe. Arrested a few times. . .petty crimes. His parents always were there to bail him out, and off he went back on the streets."

Dana intended to interrupt the woman but without success. Ellie carried on as if fearful she might lose her audience.

"You never know what you'll get when you adopt. Gary and I weren't able to have children, but the thought of adoption didn't cross our minds. Gary used to say, 'Why take on someone else's trouble?' and I believe he knew what he was talking about. Have to admit, though, there are days when I regret not having had any children to raise. It'd be nice now to have some company in my old age."

The thought made Dana ponder for a moment. In her thirties, married but separated, a church that did not believe in divorce...what was the likelihood that she would have a child? She could see the sadness in Ellie's eyes and could understand the emptiness she must have felt.

"Dana? You were interested in Douglas Clifford's encounters with the law?"

"Oh, yes, sorry. Back to the boy's crimes—."

"Mostly misdemeanors. You know, stealing and stuff." Ellie set her empty glass down. "But I'm sure you can learn a lot more than I can tell you by visiting the home. Confidential records are kept, I'm sure, under lock and key."

"I'll do that." Dana stood up and put her glass and plate in the sink. As warm as she had felt, suddenly, she felt chilled at the thought of what lay ahead of her. This wasn't going to be an open and shut case. She knew it.

"Oh, there is one more thing you should know, Dana."

Dana turned to face Ellie.

"It would pay you to eavesdrop on other's conversations. You know. . .the guards, the other boys, the cooks. You'll be more apt to learn things that way. Gary told me some tales I'm not about to repeat." Ellie moved restlessly in her chair. She toyed with two of the pearl buttons on her dress. Patches purred by her feet.

From the look on the woman's face, Dana could tell she was about to abide by her deceased husband's wishes. Yet as an investigator, these so-called tales were the very things Dana intended to explore, and from what Ellie had said, it made her wonder if those in charge of the St. Aloysius Gonzaga Home for Troubled Youth might not also have their lips sealed. No matter what, Dana knew she would find a way to solve the case of the murdered nine-year-old boy as well as the motive.

Chapter Two

Thank goodness the alarm clock in Ellie Banks' guest room blared like a horn on a ship, or Dana might have continued sleeping. The cross-country trip left her feeling lethargic, and the change in weather prompted her to fall into a deep sleep. She awoke with a start and glanced out the window, which faced the backyard of the house and overlooked acres of wheat, stretching endlessly into the horizon. A deep, royal-blue sky loomed overhead, looking like something a child might have finger-painted. Far off, jagged lines of lightning resembling shards of glass etched across the sky. A man, who Dana had met on the train, told her about the rainstorms that often followed a season of drought. He had said, the rain sometimes pours for days, for weeks, causing flooding and loss of crops.

Dana needed to hurry. Today, she was meeting with Sergeant McKnight. Ellie had offered her Gary's 1940 Chevy pick-up to get around while living in Punkerton. The only problem with the truck, Ellie had said, was the passenger window, which was stuck and would not close. With the storm moving in, Dana decided to head for Jesus Row just as soon as she could.

Ellie was already up and had brewed a fresh pot of coffee. "Won't you join me for a hot-cross bun? I just took a tray out of the oven." Scents of cinnamon and vanilla filled the air. She set her hot pads on the green Formica counter.

Dana could tell the woman appreciated her company and decided rather than be rude and rush off, she'd sit for a moment with her.

"Did you sleep well? I know, I always have trouble sleeping in a new place." She poured each of them a cup of coffee and proceeded to slice the rolls into bite-size pieces.

Dana sipped on her coffee and set her cup down. "I did, too well, I'm afraid. Thank goodness the alarm clock jolted me awake."

"If not, the storm overhead would have awakened you. It's heading our way; I just heard the news on the radio. We've gone through a terrible dry spell. Can you believe we've had a drought for six years? To some, any rain will be a blessing. On the other hand, too much and we're in for a major flood."

"So, I've heard." Dana could tell Ellie was anxious to carry on a conversation. A look of worry covered her face as she was about to say more. Dana apologized for having to rush off but explained she had a meeting with the sergeant.

"He's a good man, Sam." Ellie started to put the rolls in the cupboard, turned, and said, "You might as well know, though, Sam and Brother Donald plain don't see eye-to-eye, never have. You'll find he's pretty much washed his hands with the Douglas Clifford case." The woman sat back down and sipped on her coffee.

"I hope not, but if so, I'll find another way, I'm sure."

* * *

Dana turned the key off, and the engine of the Chevy gave an irritated rumble. She crossed the street and took a look at the Punkerton Police Station, a red brick building whose façade was painted white. A large red, white, and blue flag flew from a pole above the front door, beneath it the flag of Punkerton, a field of bronze wheat with an orange sun above it. Two planters stood on either side of the entrance to the station, their withering leaves beyond the need for water. A chain-link fence bordered the property with a gate at the front, which hung from a broken hinge.

Dana expected to meet with a receptionist as she entered the building, but no one was at the desk, where a calendar lay open to March twentieth and a cup of half-finished coffee stood. She tapped lightly on the door marked: Sergeant Sam McKnight.

"Y'all, come on in," a deep voice resounded.

To Dana's surprise, the sergeant was a young man, probably in his late twenties at most. His cheeks barely had any fuzz, and his Adam's apple bulged from his skinny neck. In large wooden frames along the wall behind him were the photographs of three men, all wearing the same tan uniforms as the sergeants with silver stars on their pockets.

"Have a seat, Miss Greer. I've been expectin' y'all." He caught her staring at the images of the men and added, "All my relatives, these fine men." Pointing, he continued, "That's my great granddaddy, my granddaddy, and my daddy. Police work here in Punkerton's been a long family tradition." He sat down in the wooden, spindled chair. "Hope y'all had a chance to get a good night's sleep at Ellie Banks' place."

Dana could tell the man was deliberately working at squelching his southern drawl, but it was obvious he couldn't take his Texas accent out of his voice. "I did, thank you again for making the arrangements. I'm sure I'll be content at Ellie's place."

Sam tossed his hat across the room, missing a metal hook on the wall. He scratched at his head. "Jist glad y'all here. Don't normally go gittin' myself involved in solvin' crimes on private property, but y'all see, this case kinda fell into my lap when I wasn't lookin'."

"How's that?" Dana asked.

"My secretary, Brenda. . .well, it was her son, Stevie, who darn tootin' if he didn't let the cat out of the bag."

Dana wondered where McKnight planned to go with this.

"Y'all see, he's a friend with one of the boys at the Gonzaga Home. Kinda a sad story, sure'nuff. Stevie's friend, kid by the name of Tim Laughton, done got arrested months before graduatin' from Punkerton High. The kid gone ahead and got in a brawl in the school cafeteria and pulled a switchblade on a freshman." McKnight reenacted the scene. "The blade went right through the kid's aorta, didn't stand a chance in hell of survivin'." McKnight put his fake knife down and started to pick at the space between his front teeth. He flipped a flake of tobacco into the air.

"How tragic."

"Tim been in the clinker 'bout five months when the Clifford kid got wiped out. Laughton done told Stevie every dang thing about the night the Douglas kid was killed."

"So, it wasn't the headmaster Brother Donald who contacted you about Douglas Clifford's murder?"

"Hell, no. Stevie done come in one day and handed me this. Said Timothy told him to give it to the authorities."

I was the first to find Douglas. I was coming back from mandatory lavatory. He was easy to see. The light of a full moon shone through the narrow, overhead window. Behind the rusted bars on the bare concrete floor, I saw his bloodied body. I screamed. Brother Calvin came running. He shoved me aside and unlocked the cell. He skidded on the bloody floor, grabbing the wall for balance. He yelled for me to get help.

I ran to the infirmary to get Doctor Hansen, but he was gone. When I got back to Douglas's cell, I saw two monks wheeling Douglas out on a gurney. Brother Calvin gave me a pail, a mop, and a bottle of Spic and Span. He called me a vulture, accused me of gawking. I scrubbed the floor, the walls on my hands and knees. All I remember seeing after that was Douglas's stuffed rabbit on his cot.

Dana read the note. "How tragic. This is horrible. The poor boy…to be traumatized, abused that way."

"Now that's out, between y'all and me," McKnight edged closer, his chest pressing against the edge of his desk, "I'm fixin' to think the Laughton kid is payin' a pretty penny for his big mouth." McKnight ran his finger across his lips as if zipping his mouth shut.

"Is there any chance I might speak to Stevie?"

McKnight ran his hand through his buzzed hair. "God knows. Brenda ain't been at work ever since this whole thing broke. Left her calendar page open to the last day she done show up here. Her and her son are keepin' a low profile. Why, they wouldn't even get up with the reporter at the 'Punketon Press.' The folks around here are none too friendly with Brenda or her son. Stevie being friends with a murderer sure don't make him very popular."

"I'd still like to meet with the boy."

"Y'all can pretty much read what you need to know right there in that letter," the sergeant said, pointing to the paper in Dana's hands, but you do what yer fixin' to do." He opened his desk drawer and pulled out a wad of tobacco, shoved it into the side of his mouth, and began chomping on it. While he scribbled something on a note pad in front of him, Dana noticed the buffalo head ring he wore on his pinkie. "Here. Take this. Tell Brenda I sent y'all.

Brenda Ames
LA 7- 4472

Think she jus' might be expectin' ya." He smiled. "Git a wiggle on; that's why y'all here in Punkerton." Saliva oozed out of the corner of his lip. He wiped it on the cuff of his sleeve.

Dana had the distinct feeling Sam McKnight had prewarned Brenda that she should be expecting a call. Dana asked to use the sergeant's phone and dialed the number. Brenda agreed to meet with her in the morning.

Chapter Three

Dana stood on the porch of what looked to be an old, one room schoolhouse. The red shingles peeled back to reveal the struts; the small overhang above the front door dilapidated and drooping with the words *Star District 56*; many of the glass panes in the window frames were missing. The white wooden door, in need of paint, opened a crack, and a middle-aged woman with curly blond hair and a pox-covered complexion peered out.

"Brenda, it's Dana Greer. We had plans to meet this morning."

"Praise Jesus. You sure enough c'mon in, Miss."

The house had one room with a worn cloth sofa; a small wooden table with three chipped chairs; two twin beds; a potbelly fireplace; and a small sink with faucet, apparently, used as a kitchen. In the corner, Dana spotted a cage with two white mice.

The woman motioned for Dana to have a seat at the table. "This here is my son, Stevie," she said, and a boy about six-foot six stepped out from the darkened shadows in the room. His bowl-cut hair made him look younger than his high school years. His freckles were sprinkled across his nose, and his acne-covered cheeks were red like ripened tomatoes.

The boy shook Dana's hand. "Pleased to meet y'all, Ma'am." Brenda and he sat down at the table.

"I'm happy, Stevie, that you're willing to talk with me. It's my goal to find out who did such a horrible thing to Douglas Clifford, and any information you might have learned from your friend, Timothy Laughton, will be most helpful."

The boy exchanged glances with his mother.

"Stevie ain't goin' to see Tim these days. Ever since he did, the boys in the neighborhood been wantin' to throw stones at him and call him names. Why, he ain't even been able to work at the feed store. He's scared silly, he is." She patted her son's hand, and he tried to smile at his mother.

"I'm sorry to hear that. Children can be so cruel." Dana found herself staring at the young boy who looked like he was about to cry.

"It ain't jus' the children. Punkerton's like that. Once someone's got a bone to chew, there ain't much kindness in them hearts."

Dana looked from Brenda to the boy. "Stevie, were you and Tim friends before all of this happened?"

Before the boy spoke, he looked first at his mother and then at Dana. "Yes, Ma'am. We been friends since second grade." The boy's voice quivered. He folded and unfolded his hands in the lap of his coveralls.

"And did he have trouble with the law before the incident at the high school?"

Brenda jumped in with, "The boy's got a heart of gold. . .always has. I don't know what set him off none. Why, Stevie and I jus' saw him at Sunday services only days before all this happened. The boy was a God fearing one."

"Do you know what might have triggered the incident at Punkerton High, Stevie?"

"It wasn't Tim's fault. The new kid was hankerin' for a fight. . .called Tim a Jesus freak. Nobody makes fun of the Lord to Tim. Next thing I know, Tim pulls out a switchblade from his back pocket. The two of 'em go rolling on the floor when I done seen blood comin' out of the boy's chest."

"Like I said, Tim's a God-fearing boy. Ain't nobody goin' to poke fun at his relationship with the Lord," Brenda said.

Dana tapped her index finder against her upper lip. "From what I've been told when the new kid died, Tim got sent to the Gonzaga Home," Dana said.

"Yes, Ma'am." The boy scratched at a large pimple on his chin.

"So, you had been visiting your friend at the home. . .I mean, before people in Punkerton became aware you were doing so?"

"Wuz until the headmaster told me I ain't welcome there no more." Stevie looked down at the floor and sniffled. The boy's forehead creased like a Venetian blind. "I never should of told nobody what Tim told me. Wish I'd never gone to the sergeant with that note."

Dana took the letter out of her bag. "This?"

A small trickle of sweat fan down the boy's face. "Yes, Ma'am."

"Beside what's written here, what did Tim actually tell you about the death of Douglas Clifford?"

Stevie focused on the floor and in a muffled voice said, "He told me the brothers weren't treatin' Douglas good, hosing 'em down in the shower with one of those power sprays; making him crawl like an animal on all fours; and when he went to git up, they done slap 'em with a long leather belt."

Dana listened intently to the incredulous tale. "Any idea why the brothers were so mean to the boy?"

Stevie shook his head. He eyed his mother, who nodded and gave him the go ahead. He continued, "It wuz right after that, that Tim wuz returning to his own cell when he seen the boy dead."

"Does Tim have any idea who might have murdered the boy?"

Stevie looked up at Dana. "Nu-uh. Jus' found him layin' in a pool of blood in his cell."

As if to add closure to the story, Brenda said, "Douglas was buried out back with the help of some of the boys. Juz dropped his wooden coffin straight into the hole. Boy didn't have no relatives, no friends."

".....Sad, so sad," Dana said. She turned to look at Stevie. "Do you think your friend is in trouble now with the brothers since he told you so much?" she asked.

Stevie stared at Dana, unblinking. Suddenly, tears rolled from his eyes as he said, "Suppose he is but ain't nothin' I can do to help him."

Brenda put her arms around her son's shoulders. "And what's just as bad is Stevie can't leave. Why, he's a prisoner in his own house. He didn't mean no harm goin' to see Tim and all, but no one's goin' believe that."

Although Dana didn't know how she could better the plight of mother and son, she realized she had already learned much about the small, dusty town they called home: Punkerton, Texas. And from what she'd learned, it did not paint a very pretty picture.

* * *

"You look like you have the weight of the world on your shoulders," Ellie said, to Dana as she returned from seeing Brenda and her son. "Let me guess. Have you been out to the boys' home yet?" Ellie asked, as she poured some hot water from the steaming teapot. "Here, you sit down and let me fix you a nice cup of hot tea. Like my mama used to say, 'There ain't a thing a cup of tea can't fix.'"

Dana only wished Ellie's mama's solution was that simple. "Guess I always feel this way at the start of a case," Dana said, trying to conceal her emotions. In less than forty-eight hours, she had witnessed racial inequalities, religious unrest, and neighborly intolerance.

"No, actually I haven't been out to the boys' home yet. Only met with the sergeant and his receptionist."

"Brenda Ames and her son, Stevie? Isn't that the most unfair thing you ever heard? People around here can be cruel; you'll learn soon enough."

"I may have already," Dana said, sipping on her tea.

"Stevie and Tim Laughton. . .well, maybe you didn't know—."

Dana set her cup down and shook her head.

"The boys. . .they're more than friends, you see. Brenda, bless her heart. She tried to cover as best she could for Stevie, but most people around here are aware of the boys' relationship. You know how quick rumors can spread in small towns. Well, Punkerton's no different."

"Are you saying the boys were in a relationship?" Dana recalled the tears in Stevie's eyes and the quiver in his voice when he spoke of Tim Laughton. It made even more sense why Stevie would want to visit at the boys' home.

Ellie's lips trembled in response.

"Seems that might account for the town's people's treatment of him," Dana raised her voice more as a question than a statement.

"The poor kid has been called every name in the book. You see, the people of Punkerton don't tolerate differences, but it was when Tim Laughton was sent to the home that the town really turned on Brenda and Stevie." Ellie interrupted her story. "Might you like a lemon for your tea?"

"No, thanks."

In the same breath, Ellie continued, "They called Stevie a killer's fag, threw stones at the boy, and even put a pipe bomb in Brenda's mailbox. Both she and the boy are afraid to leave their house."

"Can't the sergeant put a stop to this?" Dana could feel her heart thumping as she became more enraged.

"Not a crime unless caught," Ellie said. "Plus, bullying the boy's not on the books as any offense. No, everyone around here believes boys will be boys."

"But this is well beyond boys just being boys."

"Granted," Ellie said.

"Seems so sad Brenda has no recourse," Dana added.

"To make matters worse, ever since Stevie blew the whistle on what he'd heard about Douglas Clifford's body being found in his cell, not only is all of Punkerton against him, but the administration of the youth home is fit to be tied. He was told he's not to come back to the home ever again." Ellie twisted the gold band around her ring finger.

Dana found herself speechless at the small mindedness of these actions.

Ellie tugged on the edge of her collar. She looked off into the distance. "Gary told me stories about the home. I couldn't believe my ears. Some not so nice things go on up there."

"Between the boys, you mean?"

"And the brothers. Some rumors, I suppose."

"Oh?"

"Well, enough said for one day. You'll learn for yourself. Give it some time."

Dana thanked Ellie for the tea, wanting to thank her more for the background information she had given her. Dana went to her room

and got out her notebook. Slowly, she jotted down what her next
plans would be.

- *Gather more information on Timothy Laughton from the sergeant*
- *Visit with Brother Donald, Head Master of the Youth Home*
- *Arrange to speak with Timothy Laughton*
- *Prompt Ellie to tell me more of what she knows*

Dana paused for a moment, and as she did so, she noticed a small
pewter picture frame on the wall next to the window. She got up and
studied the photo. There was an elderly man, probably in his sixties,
and a young boy, about eight or nine with tousled blond hair, standing
at his side. The man, dressed in a green uniform, had his arm around
the boy's shoulder. The boy was dressed in a navy-blue T-shirt and
matching pants. As Dana looked closer, she saw a badge above the
man's shirt pocket: Warden Gary Banks. The boy? Douglas Clifford?

Chapter Four

The following morning before Dana left for the police station, she stopped Ellie and asked, "The photo on the wall in my room. . .your husband, I assume? But who's the boy with him?"

Ellie set her coffee cup down and squeezed her hands together. "That's Douglas Clifford. Sweet looking little thing, isn't he?"

"Pictures can be deceiving, but the boy sure doesn't look to be as volatile as most seem to make him out to be. Know anything about his background?"

"Pretty much what I already told you. The little guy supposedly was adopted as an infant. As a young boy, he never seemed to get along with the law. Committed a number of small infractions, you know, misdemeanors."

"His relationship with his adoptive parents...how was that?"

"From what I was told, the parents loved Douglas and he them."

"Any idea who the biological mother was?"

Ellie cupped her chin and thought for a moment. "No idea."

"On another note, if you don't mind me asking, your husband—Gary—what kind of relationship did he have with the Clifford boy?"

Deep creases formed in Ellie's forehead. Her expression pensive, she said, "Gary rather felt sorry for the child. The boy never caused him any trouble. The staff portrayed him differently. The contrast in perceptions puzzled Gary."

"Meaning there were those on the staff who thought the boy possessed and capable of bludgeoning his parents to death?"

"Yes. Gary never saw any evidence of violent behavior; in fact, Gary actually felt sorry for Douglas. Might say, he saw Douglas as the boy he never had. But that's something one doesn't do…develop a liking for any of the inmates. Like I told you before, the staff has no sympathy for the boys. . .might as well be a herd of cattle." Ellie bit down on her lower lip.

"You're saying the staff is not allowed to get too close with the boys?"

Ellie nodded, fiddling with a blue satin ribbon on her robe, running her hand up and down the length of it.

"Please excuse me. I don't mean to pry, but did your husband's bonding with the Clifford boy cause him trouble at work?"

"It didn't make his life any too easy. Brother Calvin, the head warden on G Wing, wrote my Gary up a few times. Said he was fraternizing with the inmates. Said he wasn't maintaining his professionalism. I told you before, Gary wasn't all too fond of the brother."

"Do you think the tension might have affected your husband's health?"

Ellie looked puzzled. She pondered the question for a moment. "Oh, his heart attack. . .quite possibly. The man never had any symptoms, though. I was told Gary dropped dead . . .just like that."

Something about the way Ellie looked and the way she chose her words made Dana wonder if the woman was telling her the truth. "Was this what you were told by the brothers?"

"Uh huh. Passed away on the job."

Dana told herself to make a note to meet with the coroner in Punkerton.

* * *

Eight o'clock in the morning and Dana could already feel the humidity in the air. She rolled down the driver's window of the truck, but soon realized she was only bringing in the dust from the fields. A plow, nearby, pulled by two work horses cultivated the soil in preparation for the sowing of seed. Dana flicked on the radio to hear a woman and man belt out the words, "Dang, dang me. They ought a take a rope and hang me." She couldn't remember the title of the song or the artist but soon found herself tapping her fingers to the beat on the steering wheel.

When she entered the Punkerton Police Station, the reception area was empty. The door to the sergeant's office was ajar, and Dana could see he was sitting at his desk half asleep. A trickle of saliva oozed from the corner of his mouth. She tapped gently, and he jumped slightly when he heard the knock on his door.

"Good mornin', Miss Greer." He tipped his hat. "I'd get y'all a cup of coffee, but Brenda's not here."

Dana put her hands on her hips and narrowed her eyes. Was Brenda the only one around who could make coffee, she thought but decided to keep her comment to herself. "Speaking of which, I had the chance to meet with her and her son yesterday." Dana sat down across from McKnight.

"Nice family, ain't they? The mister got killed in a tractor accident 'bout six years ago, and Brenda is raising Stevie all by her lonely."

"Sergeant?"

"Call me Sam, why don't y'all?"

"Only if you call me Dana."

Sam smiled, his bottom tooth chipped and his incisors black as coal.

"Sam, I did have some questions about Brenda's son."

Before she went any further, Sam said, "Think I know what y'all 'bout to ask. You mean Stevie and Tim Laughton. . .them being queers and all? Pretty common knowledge in Punkerton. If it weren't for Brenda workin' for me, I say the town's folk would have killed the boy by now."

"I hope you're not serious."

"Most certainly am. 'Bout two years ago, one of those queer guys went and got himself murdered."

Dana's shoulders tightened. She sighed heavily.

"Don't look so shocked. It's common in these parts. Ain't got too much room for differences in this neck of the woods."

"Tell me. . .what happened to this young man you mentioned?"

"Some teenagers got ahold of him, tied him to the back of their pick-up, and dragged him down the highway some. Case went to trial and all, and the boys went free."

Dana put her hand to her mouth and gasped.

"The longer you've been around here, the less shockin' this kind of news will be to y'all. Like I said, Punkerton ain't got no room for no misfits."

His words were so cold, Dana felt as if she could have chipped them with an ice pick. "And Stevie, Brenda's boy?"

"The only thing keepin' him alive is that his mama works for me. No one dare wanna take a chance messin' with Stevie."

Not the exact story Brenda had told her, Dana thought.

The sergeant bit down on his lower lip. "Now that the Laughton kid went and killed the Punkerton High boy, the locals don't have much patience for Stevie being in love with a murderer no less."

"The Laughton boy? What can you tell me about him?"

McKnight ran his fingers along the corners of his mouth. He opened his desk drawer and pushed a small piece of tobacco into the corner of his mouth. "Nice kid. . .why everyone wuz so surprised to learn he pulled a knife on a classmate. Kept to himself most of the time, though. Tried to keep his relationship with Stevie a secret, but that don't much work around here. Punkerton's a small family town, a praise Jesus kind of place, and there ain't much one can hide."

The more Dana heard about Punkerton, the more out of place she felt. The town reminded her of the short story "The Lottery" by

Shirley Jackson. . .a weird little out of the way kind of place, where strange behavior was the norm, never questioned or challenged.

"I'd like to talk to the boy. What do you think would be the best way of getting to speak with the head master, Brother Donald?" From what Ellie had told Dana about the tension between the sergeant and the brother, Dana wanted to make sure her entrance onto the scene was handled as delicately as possible.

"Brother Donald done know someone wuz comin' to solve the case, so guessin' he'll be expectin' y'all."

Dana wished she had known about the status between the brother and Sergeant McKnight before she had accepted the offer to come to Punkerton. She could tell more than one hurdle lay before her. She would have to find a way to make her visit as non-disruptive as possible yet allow herself enough room to explore exactly what happened behind the locked doors of the youth home. It was more than clear McKnight's intentions were to bow out of the picture until the time the case was solved.

Chapter Five

Dana could tell her anxiety would only escalate the longer she postponed getting involved in the case. She had no choice but to plunge right in, even though it meant doing it alone without the support of the sergeant.

For moments, she sat in the truck outside the St. Aloysius Gonzaga Home for Troubled Youth. From what she had been told, boys, as young as six years old and as old as eighteen years old, from all over the country, were sent to the home in hopes, not so much of rehabilitating them as to keep them away from the society they were convicted of hurting. It all sounded so hopeless and depressing.

She pulled the brochure from her bag that the bishop had mailed her before her arrival. The home looked exactly as it did on the cover of the flier: a three-story brown brick building with six dormers across the top, symmetrical rectangular windows, and a bell tower with a crooked wooden cross. A circular drive led up to the double front doors, which were surrounded by Doric columns and an arched window on each side. Dana wouldn't describe the building so much as stately as it was ominous. Surrounding the home were fenced-in fields where crops grew, and cattle grazed. From what she had read in the brochure, the boys learned to farm and lived off the fruits of their labor. She shielded her eyes from the sun and noticed a group of boys leading some cows toward a metal shed. The flier mentioned the inmates were also trained in woodworking, making crucifixes and carving statues as well as creating other sacramentals, such as rosaries.

The money raised went back into the running of the home. Dana scanned the pages of the flier; the statistics and graphs were shocking.

The home housed, at any one time, as many as two hundred forty children, accounting for every state in the union with the median age of resident being ten years of age. The home not only trained the boys in making a living but also educated them until twelfth grade. Once a resident's formal training was completed, he was extradited to the state penitentiary, where the original crime was committed and where the boy, under most circumstances, was given a life sentence and, in some situations, awaited the death penalty.

Dana shook her head. How difficult to believe the future of these children lay in the hands of a judicial system that had already committed them to a life of doom. She put the brochure back in her bag and found the miniature Bible she always carried, the one she received on her First Communion Day. Her uncle had given her the book on that happy occasion to remind her of her unfailing faith in the Lord. As much as she loved the Bible, she would soon come to hate her uncle. Her heart beat quickly as she recalled the fateful late afternoon when her uncle insisted they take a boat ride around the lake. In less than an hour, a storm arose, and Dana became frightened and insisted they go back to shore. Her uncle forced her to serve his needs first. The boat rocked from side to side; the sky lit up like fireworks; the thunder banged in the distance. The boat tipped, and she had fallen over its side. Her uncle grabbed her by her long, blond hair. He promised if she ever told, he would see to it she would never read her Bible again. She ran her fingers across the book's grainy white cover. She had never told, and the book provided her comfort as nothing else could.

She pulled into one of the *Guest's* parking spots, threw her bag over her shoulder, and made her way to the front doors. An elderly man in the habit of a Franciscan monk met her on the concrete steps leading up to the building.

"Your identification, Miss," he said.

She removed her investigator badge from her bag and introduced herself.

The brother stared at the photograph on Dana's card and then at her. "The purpose of your visit to the Gonzaga Home?" Rather than a customary rosary at his side, Dana was surprised to see a small pistol attached to his belt loop. He fingered the gun in his holster. She got the distinct feeling the man was more than accustomed to using the firearm if needed.

"I had hoped to meet with the head master, Brother Donald." She did not feel the need to explain any details.

The monk raised his eyebrows and pulled a pad and pencil from the pocket of his habit. He jotted something down. "Here, take this to Room 141. It'll at least get you inside."

Dana started to push the wooden door open when the guard cleared his throat and yelled back over his shoulder, "You happen to be here about that Clifford kid?"

"Is Room 141 Brother Donald's office?" Dana asked.

The man smirked but refused to answer.

The sound of Gregorian chant met her as did the smell of incense in the rotunda, quite an impressive entry for what was a boys' prison. Light pink marble tiles covered the entire floor, making it appear more like a ballroom than an institution. The walls painted an off white seemed to reflect the color of the floor, adding a warm ambience to an otherwise cold place. On one wall, a large painting of the holy family was hung. On another wall a museum-like display featured all the popes of the Catholic Church from St. Peter to the present Pope Pius XII. Two sculpted life size angels graced the entry to the chapel, their hands folded upright in prayer. Nearby, glass windows showcased religious artifacts. A monk in a brown habit and sandals approached Dana rather abruptly. With the palm of his hand out, he ordered, "Your entry pass, please."

She showed him what the guard had given her.

"You're planning on seeing Brother Victor?"

"Actually, I was hoping to meet with Brother Donald."

"Brother Victor oversees clearance. It's up to him. Room 141 is to your left, down that corridor, next to the painting of the Sorrowful Mother."

Dana turned abruptly and bumped into a young, handsome man dressed in a black shirt and pants. "So sorry. I'm new here and don't know my way around."

"Happy to help. The name's Carl Fenton."

"And, you are?"

"I'm an intern here, studying for the priesthood. Overheard you're looking for Brother Victor's office?"

"Next to the Sorrowful Mother," Dana added.

The man smiled. "And, I might add, right across from the portrait of St. Aloysius, patron of troubled youth."

"So, I've heard. . .about Aloysius." Dana decided not to bore the man about her hobby of collecting holy cards, but she must have had at least a hundred by now, if not more. Been saving them ever since she was a child in Catholic elementary school.

Dana thanked the seminarian for his help.

"My pleasure. By the way, on your way out, why not stop at our gift shop?" He pointed toward the end of the rotunda. "You'll get a chance to see some of the incredible work our boys do. We've got some budding artists."

Dana smiled. "I'd like that," yet she wondered from what she had read, how the boys could look forward to any future careers when it sounded as if they were doomed to a lifetime of paying for their sins. Before she knocked on the door to Room 141, she bowed her head in front of the painting and whispered a prayer to Mary.

A meek, almost feminine voice asked her to come in. "I'm Brother Victor. And you?" The monk stood to shake Dana's hand, his grip weak. "Please, have a seat." The monk, who Dana assumed would appear arrogant in his role of superiority, came across as waif-like, his body thin and his cheeks gaunt.

"Thank you. The name's Dana Greer. I recently arrived in Punkerton at the request of Archbishop Boretti."

"Boretti, right, right. The archbishop told me you were a private investigator. Your plans are?" He ran his hand across his bald head and straightened the hood of his habit, which lay crumpled on his shoulders. His deep brown eyes stared at her as if riveting through her soul.

Dana felt ill at ease telling the brother more than she needed to since she was aware of the tension between Sergeant McKnight and the brothers running the home. "I thought, initially, I might be able to speak with one of the boys. . .a Timothy Laughton."

At the mention of the boy's name, the friar gulped. He yanked a large linen handkerchief from the folds of his habit and wiped at the corners of his mouth. He turned and opened the cabinet next to his desk. He pulled out a file and, upon opening it, leafed through several typed forms. "I'm afraid Timothy Laughton, just as I had expected, is not in his cell."

"I'm not sure I understand."

"Were you aware, Miss Greer," he said, gesturing with his arms, "that in addition to a chapel, a school, a residence, and a workshop, the St. Aloysius Gonzaga Home for Troubled Youth also has an infirmary on its acreage? Indeed, twenty beds."

Dana feigned her answer. "No, no, I had no idea."

"Doctor Hansen attends to the boys' physical ailments on a bi-weekly basis or as called upon."

"Is Timothy Laughton sick?"

The brother attempted a smile that quickly faded to a scowl. "I'm not at liberty to release such information. All I can tell you is the boy is not in his cell and is in the infirmary as we speak." He stood and pushed his chair away from his desk as if indicating the conversation had come to a close.

"Might you know if I could visit him there?" Dana realized the question bold, but she could tell the warden wasn't used to people beating around the bush.

The man spread his hands out on his desk until the veins stood rigid and purple. "Hardly. You must understand the infirmary is for those boys who are significantly in need of Doctor Hansen's care; we're not speaking of the common cold here."

The sergeant's words suddenly came to mind, "I'm fixin' to think that Laughton kid is payin' a pretty penny for his big mouth." Might the price he had to pay relate in some way to his stay in the infirmary?

Dana nodded. "Might I speak with Doctor Hansen then?"

The man's face reddened as he sucked in his breath and heaved a sigh. "Let me ring his office and see if he is in."

He picked up the phone on his desk. "A Dana Greer," he said, speaking into the mouthpiece and squinting his eyes, "a private investigator." He listened for a moment, and said, "I know. No, Brother Calvin has not been notified." After a few more seconds, he said, "I'll let her know. Thank you, Doctor." The brother set the receiver down and nibbled on his lower lip. "Seems Brother Calvin ordered immediate surgery on the Laughton boy. From Doctor Hansen's report, the boy is still in recovery."

"Brother Calvin? Why would he be ordering surgery on the boy? Isn't he the head warden?"

"A brother is assigned to oversee each wing; Brother Calvin attends to G Wing."

G Wing. . .Dana recalled Ellie telling her Douglas Clifford was formerly on G Wing, Level One. "Where the worst of the worst are housed?" Dana asked.

Brother Victor smiled and chuckled under his breath. "So, you know," he said, his voice rising. "That's correct." His eyes widened. "Some like to say it's the ward of the possessed."

"Then, perhaps, Brother Calvin is the man I should be speaking with. Is he available?"

No sooner had Dana posed her question, then there was a knock on the door. Brother Victor asked, "Who's there?" when the door opened a crack. "Speak of the devil. . .Brother Calvin, come in and have a seat." A tall man with a full, black beard and only a ring of hair on his head took a seat, scrutinizing Dana from her red high heels to the blond curls resting on her shoulders. "Miss Greer is a private investigator sent by Archbishop Boretti. She was just asking if she might meet with Timothy Laughton." Brother Victor sat back down.

Brother Calvin's face, hard and cold like a porcelain statue, replied, "He's in recovery."

Dana's frustration at having been in Room 141 for so long and seemingly getting nowhere began to show. She could feel her jawline tighten, and she imagined her forehead a line of wrinkles.

The tall man glanced at Brother Victor. "Brother Victor is in charge of clearance at this facility. No unauthorized visitors get beyond this point without his approval."

An unspoken tension filled the office; the silence, of which, intensified the moment. Finally, Brother Victor tried to ease the situation. "Maybe Miss Greer would like a tour of the home. And somewhere around here," he said, fumbling in his desk drawer, "I believe, I have a map of the facility."

"Brother Calvin, you must have known Gary Banks quite well then, correct, since he was a guard in your Wing?" Dana asked.

"Somewhat. Each cellblock has its own guard. Mr. Banks was one of three."

Brother Victor cut in, "Let me guess. You're going to ask how many floors there are to each wing, correct?"

Dana smiled at his assumption.

"There are three, consisting of ten cells per floor. At any one time, we can house as many as two hundred and forty inmates in this facility if the boys are doubled up. Since G Wing has the worst of the worst as you put it, Miss Greer, we try to place as few boys as possible in these cells. Well, here's what I've been looking for." He handed her a sketch of St. Aloysius Gonzaga Home for Troubled Youth. "Ah, hah. Here's the list of the guards under Brother Calvin in G Wing."

Dana quickly scanned the list:

Level 1: Gary Banks

Level 2: Walter Robinski

Level 3: Martin Lloyd

Dana questioned why Brother Calvin had said he only knew Gary Banks somewhat. If only three guards were under the brother, it seemed more than likely he should know his men. "About cell block one—."

"Mr. Banks?" He raised and lowered his hand as if chasing a fly. "Yes, he went to the Good Lord, and we haven't been able to find a replacement," Brother Victor said. "Mr. Banks, such a good man, but working as a guard is not easy when it comes to the boys here. Most are incorrigible and volatile. Over time, they certainly can take a toll on the best of us."

Brother Calvin never volunteered a word, rather his eyes shifted back and forth between the other friar and Dana like watching a tennis match.

The man made her feel uncomfortable. Something about his presence exuded a sexual energy that did not befit a person of his religious status. She went on with her questioning, "When did Mr. Banks die?" she asked.

Brother Calvin cleared his throat, nodded his head, as he cocked his neck in the direction of Brother Victor. His thin fingers ran along the roped belt at his side, his rosary beads jingling.

"A few months back. . .dead of a heart attack. He was only fifty-six years old."

So far, that matched what Ellie had told Dana. But her intuition suggested she do some digging to see how much truth there was to their reports.

"Now for the tour, Miss Greer. Brother Calvin, Miss Greer has my clearance approval. Might you like to show her around?"

Brother Calvin's face reddened. He rolled one of the brown beads of his rosary between his thumb and index fingers, the bead shiny and wet with perspiration. Dana sensed the man's irritation in her presence. She figured it had something to do with him taking orders from a woman. His lanky body spoke of an uneasiness and reminded Dana of an eel, a slippery kind of character.

"My pleasure," he said. He stood. "Right this way." He threw his palm outward.

Dana's sixth sense felt the man eyeing her from head to foot.

From the rotunda entry, there were six concrete doors that Dana had failed to notice when she had entered the home. Brother Calvin pulled a silver ring of keys from under the layers of his brown habit. "This is G Wing." The solid door banged shut behind them.

No sooner had Dana entered when she involuntarily covered her nose with her hands.

"We get used to it after a while," Brother Calvin said.

Much like a gymnasium after athletes have left for the day, body odors permeated the space. If not bad enough, a strong scent of urine and feces filled the air along with smells of fresh vomit. Suddenly, Dana felt nauseated.

Brother Calvin took one look at her face, smirked, and said, "If you want to work here, better you get used to it now. Boys will be boys."

Dana had gotten so engrossed with the smell in the wing she hardly noticed the banging on the bars of the cells, a cacophony of voices screaming out unintelligible sounds.

"The natives are restless as is the case whenever someone new arrives, particularly, a". . .Brother Calvin coughed into the palm of his hand. . . "beautiful woman such as yourself." His eyes peered down at her, his gaze landing on her double-breasted jacket.

"Hey, up here, Lady. Look up here," one of the boys called.

Dana directed her attention to his voice and was mortified to see the boy standing backward with his bare derrière pressed against the bars of his cell. She reminded herself this was a correctional facility, however, innocent the name of the institution might be.

Whistles and hoots carried through the air.

"Hey, gotta date tonight?"

"Welcome in my cell anytime."

Another boy blew kisses at her and made smacking noises.

Brother Calvin attempted to speak over the racket. He pointed upward. "Level Two is presently used for boys who are recuperating from the infirmary or are contagious. It is necessary each of the boys has his own cell."

Dana tried to catch the brother off guard and asked, "So, let me guess. Did Timothy Laughton have a tonsillectomy?"

The brother laughed. "Actually, not a bad idea. It might cut down on the bedlam around here." He gracefully skirted her question. "Seen enough for one day?"

This time Dana ignored the monk's question. "What are the other wings used for?"

Like rattling off the song the "Twelve Days of Christmas," he said, "The other wings, Wing J and K, are where the kitchen, dining hall, infirmary, classrooms, library, and the brothers' dormitory are housed." He took a deep breath and continued, "Three of our brothers are cooks, six are teachers, six assist in the wood shop, and three are gardeners. From these, four also serve as wardens overseeing the guards on each wing."

Dana was never fond of math, and all the talk of numbers was making her head spin. All she could think to add was, "Sixteen men sound a bit shorthanded for two hundred and forty troubled youth, wouldn't you say?"

"That's not the norm; we usually have one hundred and twenty inmates. Brothers Donald and Victor help out as necessary should we have a full house. When the place gets overrun with boys, we sometimes do have to double them up in a cell. Our motto is: No Boys on the Streets. Seven of our brothers are retired but also live on the grounds. They do miscellaneous things around here. You might have met a couple when you first entered the Gonzaga Home. They greet and direct people to clearance."

"Yes, I believe I did meet one," Dana said, remembering the monk with the gun at his side. She could sense her patience waning and grew tired of waiting for the perfect time to ask about the boy's files...the real intent of her visit. She decided to blurt out what was on her mind. "The boy's files...on what wing are they housed? I'd like to take a look at the files from this wing."

"Up to Brother Victor." The brother ran his long fingers through his rosary beads, his eyebrows raised like two pointed arrows. "What exactly are you hoping to find, Miss Greer? I believe, Brother Victor made it quite clear to you the hardened status of these inmates, did he not? I should hope that would be more than sufficient." His deep-set eyes roved over Dana again. "On second thought, I question whether you'll be strong enough to endure this wing...period."

"I'd prefer to be the judge of that, Brother. After all, my job is to investigate murders; in this case, I intend to find out who took the life of Douglas Clifford. That should more than qualify me for the job." Dana hoped the brother might provide more information on the boy beyond what Ellie had already told her. "By the way, did he have any family, next of kin?"

In a matter-of-fact voice, Brother Calvin said, "The boy was adopted. After he bludgeoned his adoptive parents to death, I'm afraid he was nothing more than an orphan, a ward of the court, before he was sent here." He stopped speaking for a moment. With his long, spindly finger, he pointed at Dana's face. "As you probably have already realized, Miss Greer, these boys aren't your typical next-door neighbors. I'll be the first to caution you."

"So, you have, but I have no interest in leaving this place until I have the answers I've come looking for." She backed away from the brother.

* * *

On her way out of the youth home, Dana made it a point to find the gift shop the seminarian had told her about. Windows, facing the rotunda, were filled with religious artifacts. While Dana stood looking through the glass, admiring the rosaries of a multitude of colored beads, crucifixes on silver chains, and small wooden boxes with carved lids of various saints, a small voice said, "Impressive work, isn't it?"

Dana jumped slightly and found Carl Fenton looking over her shoulder. "Quite."

"Proves beauty can be found in even the darkest of places." Before he turned to enter the shop, he placed something into Dana's hand.

When she opened her palm, she found a holy card with the image of St. Aloysius on it.

Before Dana could thank the man, he entered the store. Dana glanced at the holy card one more time. Strange, she thought, the saint has a striking resemblance to Carl Fenton. Further, the dark, good-looking features of the man reminded her of a singer whose name she couldn't recall. She smiled and put the card in her bag.

* * *

When Dana got back to Ellie's place, she could smell a chicken roasting in the oven. Scents of rosemary and parsley greeted her as soon as she entered. Ellie's calico cat circled around Dana's feet, purring. She picked it up and kissed it softly on its head. The animal hissed and leapt from her arms. He skirted toward Dana's room.

"Never mind Patches. That creature has an unpredictable personality," Ellie said. "Here have a seat by the table. Gary and I used to eat supper early, around five o'clock. The poor man had to get up at six a.m. to cover his shift at the boys' home."

Outside the kitchen window, a noisy wind blew, rattling the wooden frame. A couple of tumbleweeds flew through the air. "Storm's been trying to come this way for the last couple of days and hasn't quite been able to make it over to these parts, but when it does——." Ellie slammed the pane shut.

All Dana could think was life was sure different in the middle of an isolated prairie than it had been on the Cape. She wondered how Ellie survived out here amid acres of fields, no human contact within miles. She sat down and admired the crocheted tablecloth. "Beautiful handwork," she said.

"Love to do crafts. Keeps me busy in my idle hours."

Ah, Dana had her answer. Ellie kept herself amused making handmade things. While Ellie checked on the red potatoes boiling on the stove, Dana said, "Ellie, I spoke with Brothers Victor and Calvin today."

"Oh, I'd love to hear what your impression was, dear."

"How well would you say your husband knew Brother Calvin?"

"Hmm." She set a green potholder down on the counter. "Probably better than he would have liked."

"What does that mean?"

"Gary never cared for the brother. My husband found him, well, peculiar, if you know what I mean."

"And Doctor Hansen?" Dana asked.

"Don't really know him well. Gary said the man came into the infirmary a couple of times a week." Ellie removed the organdy apron tied around her waist and hung it from a hook on the wall. Looked as if the woman wanted to say more but hesitated to do so. "I'm sure with so many boys in the facility, there are the typical colds and such things." Ellie combed her fingers through her hair, which fell loosely onto her collar. "Sometimes it's better knowing less than more, Dana. That's what Gary used to tell me. He didn't stick his nose where it didn't belong. That is—." She scratched at her upper lip. "I'm afraid I've already said more than I should have."

The brother had already questioned Dana's abilities. She felt the need to expel any further doubts. "There's something you must know. I've been sent to Punkerton and the Gonzaga Home to do just that. . .stick my nose where it doesn't belong. It's what investigators must do to solve crimes." As if an echo, Dana heard her words repeat back to her, a sting of sarcasm in them, something she had not intended.

Ellie pierced the red potatoes with a fork.

"It's my job to pry into matters until I find the truth. In this case, who murdered Douglas Clifford."

Ellie only nodded, but Dana could tell by the frightened look on the woman's face something caused her to be guarded. Like Brothers Calvin and Victor, Ellie wasn't telling her all she knew.

Dana and Ellie only made small talk as they sat down to dinner. Thunder pounded overhead, and the kitchen curtains swayed from side to side.

Chapter Six

The room at the end of the hall on J Wing had never been occupied. All the brothers knew this; none bothered to enter, that is with two exceptions: Brothers Donald and Vincent. And even they used caution when opening the door to Room 39. They guarded their secrecy, and although there were those who gossiped about the men, none ever went so far as to investigate the happenings or to confirm their rumors. It was easier to say it was none of their business, to look the other way, even to deny.

When Brother Donald took over the head master position of the boys' home, it became his responsibility to replace the brother in charge of clearance. Since this would be a job next in command, Brother Donald wanted to ensure he found someone who he shared a friendship with, someone he liked…liked more than just professionally. Immediately upon interviewing Brother Victor, he sensed he had found just the man. Brother's eyes spoke of an intimate softness; his hands motioned delicately; and he walked with a certain ease. Of course, none of these traits spoke to the man's work ethics, but that is not what Brother Donald based his decision on. He looked to make a close friend; to find a confidante; and, eventually, to share his love with the man. After working side by side for the past ten years, Brother Donald had found the relationship he desired.

Room 39, locked with keys only available to the two brothers, had one small window, which overlooked the farmland the boys maintained: a few cows; a couple goats; a small hen house; plus, plots of land to seed, rake, and hoe. No one questioned what went on in the upper room on the third floor of J Wing, and it was the exact way the brothers liked it.

Sometimes, the space housing one bed, two wooden chairs, and an adjoining bathroom was used for mere innocence—the two brothers whispering their inner thoughts to each other. Brother Donald shared memories from his childhood, a mother who had given birth to six sons, three of whom deserted the family as runaways at the age of sixteen, a father who spent more time in church than at home, involved in every ministry possible. His mother spent these hours involved with a married man from their parish. Donald wondered if they were good at keeping their relationship quiet, or if others purposely chose to look the other way. Donald often joked among friends that the parable about the woman caught in adultery was, by far, one of his favorites. Brother Donald's past provided many hours of conversation, and Brother Vincent never tired of listening to the tales.

Brother Vincent, on the other hand, was an only child, coming from a home of two loving parents. Once Vincent's father learned of his son's sexual preference, he threw him out of the house only two days after graduating high school. His father had found Vincent in the alley behind his home with a boy from his senior class. Vincent tried to explain they were only talking, but his father would not hear it. Vincent spent years wandering on the streets, not able to find the niche he was looking for. He, eventually, became involved with several different men he met at public parks or bathhouses. It was not until he met Father Bernard Phillip, a street missionary in Austin, Texas, that he realized he had always been a son of God and loved by him. When his life turned around, he, eventually, entered the seminary.

Besides sharing their personal stories and offering each other emotional support, the two men shared many hours in the arms of each other, finding companionship, love, and peace.

It was the other times the brothers craved to share themselves physically that the privacy of the room meant the most to them. There were nights with the work of the day put aside, the two, immediately upon finishing their dinner meal and evening offertory prayers in the chapel, would secretly escape to Room 39, and in the silence and darkness, they made love.

Chapter Seven

Gettin' into any files at Gonzaga, Dana? I'm tellin' y'all, Brother Donald runs a tight ship." As if putting an exclamation point at the end of McKnight's sentence, a bang of thunder roared overhead. As of yet, the storm had not arrived in Punkerton, but it beckoned to be heard.

"So, you told me, but if I'm to get to the bottom of this case, I'm going to need all the information I can get my hands on."

"Understood but try tellin' that to the brother. Like I said before, the man don't want no publicity 'bout the place. Well might you understand?" The sergeant stopped speaking as a piece of tobacco fell onto his lower lip. He pushed it back in his mouth and swallowed hard. He stared at Dana as if she was a fifth grader struggling over a simple addition problem.

"It only makes sense the institution would much rather look the other way over this incident. We are, after all, talking about a murder, aren't we?"

"Say what you will, Dana. I'm only tryin' to tell y'all what yer up against." The sergeant pulled a toothpick out of his desk drawer and busily plucked at one of his blackened incisors.

"What about bringing in an attorney? Petitioning the courts for a subpoena?"

"You're most welcome to try that, but in a town like Punkerton, I wouldn't go countin' my chickens."

"Meaning what?" Dana asked. She could hear the frustration in her voice.

"Meaning you might jus' have a hell ova time findin' one. You see, Dana, Punkerton folks might well know what's goin' on in their neighbor's yard, but we all prefer not to git involved. It's jus' better that way."

This was beginning to sound like Ellie and the brothers all over again. Mind your own business, look the other way, and don't ask questions. "Unfortunately, Sergeant, that goes against not only my nature but my job description, as well. Furthermore, I don't live in Punkerton!" Dana stood up and threw her bag over her shoulder.

"Don't mean no offense, Dana. It's jus' the way things is aroun' here."

"Not for long, I hope."

* * *

Dana might have only been in Punkerton a few days, but the expectations she had set for herself were far from what she had achieved. There was no doubt Brother Donald would be difficult to speak with, but he would also be more than reluctant to want to reveal any of the boy's records. It didn't matter that a murder had occurred in one of his cells. Brother Donald believed it more important to keep a spotless record than he did to help with the investigation. Dana would give it another try and visit the boys' home. If her efforts to get an audience with the brother still failed, she would have no choice but to subpoena the boy's records.

In the meantime, Dana hoped Timothy Laughton was released from the infirmary, so she might speak with him. Since he found the body of Douglas Clifford and relayed the news to his friend Stevie, he should be able to provide her with the preliminary information she needed. From there, she planned to speak with the coroner. Something about the way Ellie's husband, Gary, had died made her curious. Gary's relationship with Brother Calvin sounded wrought with tension, and the brother sure did not appear to want to befriend Dana.

She rolled down the driver's window of the old Chevy and started up its noisy engine. Her eyes scanned the countryside as she made her way to the boys' home. Acres and acres of flat land in colors of gold and brown went on forever into the horizon. The heat from the dusty road rose and left a wake of white haze in her rearview mirror. She tried to find a station on the radio, but all she got was a piercing sound of static. She wondered how people managed to live in such an environment whose soul spoke of isolation and emptiness. Dana found herself wanting to talk to the empty space in the passenger seat. The solitude and loneliness were already getting to her, and she had only arrived in Punkerton—a town that didn't seem to want it any other way.

Dana turned the steering wheel and found a parking spot right out front of the youth home. A brother in the brown habit of the Franciscans strolled along the sidewalk, reading from his book of afternoon prayers. Loud chiming rang out the noon hour, the ringing of the Angelus bells. Dana managed to make it to Brother Victor's office with ease this time and without needing a pass. She wondered how stringent the security of the place was that she had been able to walk to Room 141 without any scrutiny. She knocked, and the bald man opened his door and stared at her with his brown eyes. "Dana Greer," she said, attempting to jog his memory.

He cleared his throat and motioned her in. His desk appeared cluttered with papers, file folders, and books.

"Looks like you're busy, brother. Thank you for letting me speak with you."

The last of the bells chimed as brother closed a small, black book, which he clutched toward his chest. "The afternoon vespers," he said, bowing his head and making the sign of the cross, his fingers fluttering like a butterfly landing on his right shoulder. Dana noticed the delicacy in the man's movements.

"I am sorry to——."

Brother Victor sat back in his chair, nibbling on the tip of his index finger. "What is it you desire, Miss Greer? I had hoped Brother Calvin had addressed your concerns the other day."

Just as she figured. The brothers were hoping to sweep her away like dust under the carpet. Little did they know it wouldn't be all that simple. "Oh, yes, he did. He gave me the tour of the facility, but I'm hoping to speak with one of the boys, Timothy Laughton."

"Back to him again, are we? You seem to have such interest in the boy. Let's see. . .ah, yes, 458-39-2061."

"His social?" Dana asked, surprised the man could recite the number from memory.

"No, his number upon admittance here to St. Aloysius Gonzaga."

"Fascinating you know the number by heart. Any reason for that?"

The brother tugged the narrow cord on the hood of his habit, "Only of those who cause trouble here." He pursed his lips.

"Are you speaking of Stevie's visit with Timothy?"

"Hmm. So, you've heard. The boy has a big mouth and doesn't know how to follow the rules. He speaks when his lips should be sealed. He'll learn. I'm sure."

"What rules?"

The man turned in his swivel chair and glanced out the window. "Ah, I see the storm's moving in. Been needing rain for so long. Everything is so brittle, dry, and near death. Praise be God."

The two looked out to see ebony clouds rolling and tossing about like large balls of steel wool. The trees outside the brother's office swayed from side-to-side, a long branch tapping at the window and a crow cawing endlessly.

Brother Victor's squeaky chair turned toward her. "Can always tell when nature's awry. The birds of the air, the fish of the sea, and the animals of the land sense something is not right. Yes, indeed, like them, I sense a storm."

Dana knew exactly what the man was hinting at but chose to ignore his comment. "So, I've heard. . .about the storm, I mean." Dana had seen this tactic once too many times—an effort to distract the conversation. "But, brother, what were you saying about the rules?"

"Oh, yes, the rules. This institution is governed by a board who develop a code of conduct for the boys. One rule is we don't allow the boys revealing the goings on in the home to outsiders." He bit down on his lip. Then, he smiled. "Certainly, you can understand that, Miss Greer. We like to handle things ourselves here. . .our way. There's no need for the boys to take things outside of these halls."

"Are you telling me I won't be able to meet with the Laughton boy?"

He flipped the palm of his hand toward her. "Don't be silly. Of course, we allow the boys to have visitors." He chuckled to himself.

"It's just I can't make conversation. Is that it?" Dana could feel her adrenalin pumping and was sure her face gradually changed to a hot pink. Her irritation at the cat-and-mouse games the brothers seemed to play left her short tempered.

"I think you're making a bigger matter of this than is necessary. Our procedure is we expect a written list of topics that you wish to breach with a boy. Once they are approved by Brother Donald, you are free to visit."

"And I assume someone oversees the visit?"

The brother nodded. His lips curled on the ends in a motion of satisfaction. "Exactly. Why, of course. It's the way we do things around here. . .the rules."

"When might I see the Laughton boy?"

"When might you submit your written inquiry?"

Dana waited a moment before responding. She moved about in the leather armchair. "Let's just say after I've had a chance to speak with my attorney." She said no more. She had been brought to Punkerton to solve a murder case, not to play these elusive games. On her way out, she pulled a brochure from the rack by the door and stomped out of the office.

Trustees of the St. Aloysius Gonzaga Youth Home

Maybe the folks on the board would understand her dilemma and offer to assist her in some way. She also grabbed a holy card of St. Eustace, patron saint of difficult situations or so it said on the back. Dana was never against finding a new saint for her card collection, especially, if his specialty might offer her some help.

When she got back in the truck, she pulled out her miniature Bible and squeezed it tightly in the palms of her hands. Its gritty cover, like warm sand on a beach, offered her solace. Out of the side of her eye, she noticed a black car parked nearby. Its engine running but no one inside. Odd, she thought. Looking over her shoulder, she noticed the hubcaps of the automobile were missing.

* * *

Ellie cocked her head. "Home so early, Dana?"

Ellie's canary chirped loudly and fluttered in his cage in the living room.

"Guess I feel like your bird."

"Maize?"

"Yes, trapped, flapping my wings with nowhere to go."

"Some way I might help?" she asked. Her hands busily worked on a red piece of fabric as she continued to speak while embroidering a white lily, her needle meticulously going in and out of the cloth.

"Maybe, you just might." Dana pulled the Gonzaga brochure from her bag and sat on the couch with Ellie. "I found out the youth home has a board. Listen to this:

The Board Members of the Saint Aloysius Gonzaga Home for Troubled Youth consists of a group of men and women whose primary mission is to assist the Brothers of the First Order of Francis primarily in matters of visitations to the home's facilities and grounds.

"Let's see," Ellie said, as she took the brochure from Dana's hands. "Shirley Mitford. . .just moved to Punkerton a few months ago. Nancy Adams. . .she's a teacher at Punkerton High School. Joe Bender. . .he runs the local coffee shop." Ellie began to speak again when Dana stopped her.

"So, you know some of the board then, I see."

"Know of them, I'd say. Can't say any of them are my best friends or anything."

"That doesn't matter. As long as you know them, you might be able to introduce me to one or two of them."

Ellie's eyebrows rose. "I suppose. I mean, I could."

"I need to get to the bottom of these rules. Seems the boys aren't allowed to speak to outsiders unless a list of topics is given to Brother Donald. Even then, the visit has to be observed."

"Pure nonsense. That's what it is. . .pure nonsense."

"Anybody on the board who you think might be willing to speak with me?"

"Definitely Shirley. Like I said, she's new to Punkerton and, more than likely, won't be of the same closed mindset as the folks who have been around here for awhile. It's worth a shot."

"Sounds like a good possibility," Dana said.

"Let's give it a try. I say, let's call Shirley."

Ellie did the dialing, explained who Dana was, but deliberately left out the reason for their visit. Shirley invited them to come. Before Ellie had a chance to hang up she heard a loud buzzing in her ear. She shook the receiver. Shirley had hung up. A bolt of lightning lit the room; a clap of thunder banged; sheets of pouring rain followed. "Guess our long-awaited guest has arrived," she said.

After dinner, the two women ran out to the Chevy, juggling their umbrellas in a fight against the wild gusts of wind.

Ellie helped Dana stuff an old piece of cardboard in the passenger window of the Chevy. The rain, more like zig-zag lines, had already dampened the passenger seat. Dana turned the wipers to full speed as they click-clacked loudly, not able to keep up with the splashing downpour. She peered through the beaded windshield, her vision only a few feet in front of her. After driving for about fifteen minutes, the two stopped in front of Shirley Mitford's place, a silver Air-Stream trailer with a patch of brittle flowers out front, which were soaking up the rain after long months of drought. Shirley's home sat in the middle of an empty field like a shiny coin stuck in a plot of what was once crusty, dry soil, now quickly turning into a field of mud.

"Come on in. Bless your hearts. Get yourselves out of the storm." She grabbed the womens' umbrellas and directed the women to a small table only a few feet away.

Smells of fresh baked apples, cinnamon, and vanilla wafted through the narrow hall of her trailer. "Sit yourselves down. Got some apple dumplings fresh out of the oven." The tall woman with a black bun perched atop her head sliced into the dessert and placed a V-shaped portion for each of them onto a paper plate.

"Smells delicious, Shirley," Ellie said.

"My favorite," Dana said. The brown cinnamon oozed from between the golden apples. She blew gently upon them and let their taste melt in her mouth.

"Ellie's telling me you're new to town," Shirley said. Without asking, she poured Dana and Ellie a cup of steaming coffee.

"Arrived a few days ago. Ellie's been gracious enough to let me stay with her."

"Figures. I've heard Ellie's got a way about her."

"Hear you're relatively new to the area, as well," Dana said.

"Came from out West. I'm loving the hospitality of the South." Shirley set her fork down and eyed Dana sternly, suddenly changing her persona. "So, you're some kinda detective?" Her emphasis was on the middle syllable. She narrowed her eyes.

"An investigator here to solve the murder of Douglas Clifford."

Shirley kept piling chunks of apples into her mouth until a brown trail of juice ran over her chin. She swiped it away with a paper napkin.

"I was hoping you might be able to give me some advice. Ellie tells me you're on the board of the Gonzaga Youth Home." Dana deliberately left the part out about the brochure, thinking it sounded more personal to say she had learned of Shirley's connection from Ellie.

"Sure am. The brothers depend on our support. There's only so much they can do. Good, holy men of God, they more than have their hands full."

"So, what is it exactly the board does?" Dana asked.

"We go to meetings; basically, help the brothers run the place in the best interests of all."

"By best interests, are you referring to the rules for the home, by chance?"

The woman nodded and shoved some more of the dessert into her mouth. "That's part of it, yes." Her dark eyes shifted between the two women.

"Dana is wondering about one of the regulations in particular," Ellie said.

Shirley squinted her eyes, looking like a crow ready to hone in on some road kill.

Ellie completed her thought with, ". . .the one about the boys not being allowed to speak to outsiders. Seems nonsense to me, don't you think?"

Ellie surprised Dana with her forthrightness. She wished the woman would not have been quite as abrupt.

Shirley shot Ellie a look that spoke for itself—a look of who are you to question the board. "That rule. It's a new one. Brought up at our last meeting. Voted upon unanimously." Shirley shoved her plate aside. "After the whole thing with the Laughton boy squealing to his queer friend, Stevie, the board agreed it had no choice but to take action. The home doesn't need any gossip. It's a fine institution, is held in high esteem, and the board wants to keep it that way." Her narrow lips smiled into a straight line. One could say her words brought pleasure to her face.

Just as Dana figured. The brothers were fearful what the news about the murdered inmate might do to their reputation.

"Doesn't that go against the First Amendment?" Ellie asked. "The whole freedom of speech thing?" She put a forkful of apple and crust into her mouth.

Dana could not believe it. Ellie sure didn't fear speaking her mind any.

"The St. Aloysius Gonzaga Home for Troubled Youth is a private institution, Ellie, run by its own rules, I'll have you know. The government doesn't have any say in what we do and rightly so. They've got their nose in enough of our business."

Dana couldn't wait to speak her mind. "The government might not be able to have any say in what you do, but isn't there someone above the brothers? Do they not report to someone? What about Archbishop Boretti? Frankly, your rule sounds unreasonable; it makes no sense at all. Furthermore, isn't is expecting a bit much from the boys?"

Shirley's face turned a bright red. Even the tips of her ears turned crimson. Her breathing quickened, and her right cheek began to twitch. "Unreasonable, you say? Expecting too much of the boys? Let's get serious here. These are hardened crimials we're speaking of. Why should we care what they think of the rules or if they find them fair?"

Dana thought it best to clarify things from her perspective. "Who is it that finances the institution? I would think they might be interested in what the board decides." Dana did not wait for Shirley to respond. She continued, "Furthermore, this ruling does present a problem to someone like me, Shirley. My job is all about asking questions."

Shirley pursed her lips like a clasp on a clutch purse. When she began to speak, her words sounded like staccato notes on a piano. "I'll have you know, that is a problem now, don't you say?"

"All problems have solutions, I believe, if one is willing to look hard enough."

The woman set her fork down with a bang. Something about her tightly wound black bun perched atop her head made her look devious. "Not this one, I'm afraid. The vote by the board was unanimous. It is in the interests of the boys."

"Is it?" Dana asked and stood up ready to leave. "Or, is it in the interests of hiding the truth?"

Ellie also got up.

"You needn't show us to the door," Dana said.

"Thank you for the desert," Ellie said, as the two women stepped into the rainy night.

On the way back, Ellie said, "I can't believe Shirley is being so unreasonable. There has to be a way someone can help you, Dana. I mean would Sergeant McKnight ask for your services only to have you find out the brothers would not cooperate with you?"

Ellie had read Dana's mind. She wished she had the answer, but she didn't.

Chapter Eight

Shirley took the dishes to the kitchen sink and watched as Ellie and Dana got into the Chevy truck. She pulled the greasy white curtain shut and shook her head. "Those two damn broads have got no business around here. I purposely move in the middle of nowhere. I don't need their trouble." She cupped her hands together and squeezed her knuckles tightly.

"What you mumbling about?" Out of the bedroom shadows came a man with a grubby, beard in need of a shave. He wore a white T-shirt and pair of men's shorts. He rubbed at his sleepy eyes. Around his neck, he wore a scapula of the Virgin Mary. On his left bicep, he bore a tattoo of a large cross, the base of which was covered in flowers. From one end of his arm to the other was the word: RESURRECTION.

"That detective's got no right coming around here."

"What'd she want?" he asked, as he picked some leftover apple dumpling out of the baking dish in the sink. He plopped down on the torn, brown sofa in the narrow space called the living room and hung his bare feet over the side of the couch.

"Wanted to know how legal the board decision was. You know about not letting the boys speak to visitors unless their questions are reviewed first. It's none of the bitch's business."

Calvin licked some cinnamon sauce off his right hand and wiped it into his shirt. "What'd you tell her?" Calvin ran his fingers over the top of his bald head being careful to miss the ring of hair that encircled it.

"What do you think? I told her St. Aloysius is a private institution and is not required to follow the first amendment."

Shirley always had had a problem with people questioning her decisions. Her mother used to tell her she grew up with a bull's head. Her sister had told her it had something to do with her being a Taurus. Besides being stubborn, Shirley's outspokenness made many an enemy. She said it like she thought it—bold and forthright. If people didn't like it, they didn't need to like her. Shirley recalled her days as a nurse in Utica. There was a particular doctor who she had a crush on. For months, she flirted with the man, caring nonetheless the man was married. The day finally came when she was to meet the man at a motel in Niagara Falls. She arrived at the Starlight Motel only to find the doctor with an attractive brunette.

"What are *you* doing here?" the woman asked.

Although Shirley felt mortified, she held her head high and replied, "How dare you, Dale, lead me along the way you did. You're a good for nothing two-timer, and I am glad to tell you that." Shirley remembered the lady's face blushing.

In a stuttering voice, the woman said to the doctor, "Dale, is what this woman's saying the truth?"

The doctor put his clothes back on and left.

Calvin interrupted Shirley's thoughts with, "Good, girl, my little pumpkin. You gave that investigator just what she needed to hear.

Since when do we have to follow the law...the first amendment? Though, I have to admit, I find it interesting you were so nice about it."

Shirley smirked in disgust.

Calvin kissed her on the forehead and began to paraphrase the first amendment. "Congress shall guarantee free speech, free press, the right to assemble—."

Shirley put up her hand and pushed him aside. "Stop right there, you blundering idiot. It's not funny. We sure as hell don't need to take orders from James Madison."

Calvin swatted Shirley's butt. "Impressive you even know the author!"

"Are you even listening to what I'm saying? I tell you that woman is going to be nothing but trouble." Shirley wiped her hands on a ragged towel hanging from the cabinet knob.

Calvin gave Shirley a wink.

"She is an outright snoop. There's something about that Greer woman I don't like."

"I met her. Didn't seem bad to me. Shapely little ass and those blond curls. . .pretty snazzy to me. She's a hot number in those red heels of hers."

Shirley reached for the towel and swatted Calvin's butt.

He pretended to run back into the bedroom, laughing. "Seriously, though, Shirley, she's a nosey little bitch. It's her job after all. . .asking questions. Just doing her business."

Shirley stared at Calvin sternly, her hands on her hips. "Why are you defending her? Don't get any ideas, Cal." Shirley knew she had not been the first woman in Calvin's life since he joined the brotherhood and became the warden of G Wing. There had been plenty; in fact, he had an issue with keeping his hands off women as did *his* father. Calvin had no problem telling her about Wendy, Jane, and Marie, all women he had met at honkytonks outside of town. And, she wasn't going to let Dana be the new Eve in his life.

"Who me?" he laughed again. Then, he put his arms around Shirley's waist. "Wouldn't think of it. A blond with a shapely little ass and some big knockers to boot? She doesn't interest me in the least. You and me, baby? We're a team."

Shirley planted a kiss on his lips. "And, that's just the way I like it; don't forget it."

Calvin ran his spindly fingers up and down her back until they landed beneath her pink blouse. He shoved her gently down the hall and toward the bedroom. He kicked the door shut with his bare foot. He pressed her onto the floppy mattress and began to plant wet kisses up-and-down her neck. Suddenly, he stopped. "By the way, you don't think those two broads had any idea I was here, do you?"

"Not unless they're mind readers. Aren't you glad I told you to park your old Dodge in the shed out back?"

"You said it, baby."

Clothes quickly fell to the floor, and the two forgot there was a world outside the Airstream.

Chapter Nine

Dana kept thinking about the clichéd expression, "When one door closes, another one opens," but things appeared double bolted no matter where she attempted to enter. Ellie had secrets she didn't feel comfortable telling her, Brother Donald ran a tight ship, and the board voted against letting any more information leak to the public. Looked as if Dana's last resort was finding an attorney. She got up before Ellie arose and headed for Jesus Row. Dana recalled seeing a coffee shop mixed among the churches. She didn't need or want the coffee, but she did need legal advice, and she was ready to get some no matter what opinion the sergeant held.

Dana pulled to the back of Jesus Saves Baptist Church and parked between two large puddles. A man in sandals, a ripped yellow striped T-shirt, and soiled pants, dripping wet, stopped her.

"Jesus loves you," he said. "Got a dime for a coffee?"

Dana juggled her umbrella, reached into her bag, and placed a quarter in the man's dirty hand.

"God bless you, lady." He dug into his side pocket, pulled out a small brown bag, and took a long, hard sip on the bottle within. He burped loudly, put the coin in his pocket, and said, "All for a good cause."

Dana shook her head and entered the Bean Grinder, its windows covered in steam. On the glass, a small child had drawn a heart with the word *Mom* in the center. She smiled up at Dana obviously proud of her accomplishment.

"What can I get y'all, Ma'am?" a waitress in a pink and white uniform with a lace doily for a hairnet asked, before Dana had a chance to take a seat.

Dana found a table by the window and propped her umbrella against the leg of the table. "Coffee, please. . .black. And, oh by the way, might you have a phone book I could look at?"

"Sure thing," the woman said.

Her mind made up, she would jot down the numbers of every lawyer in Punkerton; someone had to help her.

"Here ya go, Ma'am," the waitress said. "Anythin' else y'all be needin'?" She put the cup of coffee on the wobbly table and, from under her arm, slipped Dana the city's phone book about a quarter of an inch thick.

"No, thanks." She opened the book to the yellow pages and glanced under *A*.

Baylor Fennings, Attorney-at-Law

Michael Gates, Attorney-at-Law

Howard Rhodes, Attorney-at-Law

Guy Smith, Attorney-at-Law

Four lawyers? Not one had a Punkerton address. Dana motioned for the waitress.

"Needin' a refill?" she asked, ready to pour another cup.

"No, just an answer. How far's it to Lubbock?"

"'Bout two hours on a good day. Thinkin' of headin' that way today?"

"Not today."

"With the mighty storm comin' our way, the roads probably be floodin'. You might want to add another hour or two. But if I wuz you, I'd skip the trip, honey."

Wonderful was all Dana could think to say. Not only were there no attorneys in town, but the few there were, were hours away. She wondered how much interest they might have in a case, which had its roots in Punkerton. She pulled a pad and pencil from her bag and jotted down the names and numbers. She left a quarter on the table and headed to the police station. The least the sergeant could do was to let her use his phone.

* * *

The woman who answered the phone at Baylor Fennings' office informed Dana the attorney was in the process of moving his office to Austin.

Michael Gates was no longer in practice.

Two down and two to go, she thought.

The receptionist at Howard Rhodes' office, located in Lubbock, put Dana through to the man. She identified herself and explained why she needed a way to bypass Brother Victor at the St. Aloysius Gonzaga Youth Home. She had to conduct interviews and to find a way to access the boys' files.

The man's voice, deep and husky said, "You might just as well consider yourself to be a lost cause, lady."

Dana was surprised at the man's flippant response. "That can't be!" Then, Dana realized how arrogant she sounded, yet she felt her frustration was more than justified.

"It's a well-known fact the brothers who operate the facility are as closed mouthed as a cloistered monastery. At least ninety percent of the boys when they reach the age of eighteen are transferred to state penitentiaries, where most are given life and some the death penalty. From what I know about Gonzaga, the boys are nothing more than a herd of cattle, waiting for slaughter, and the boys are treated as such."

"But you're in Lubbock. How would you know?"

"I'm not that far away, and I've had a few encounters with the place."

"That's so difficult to believe. I mean, the way the boys are treated, the attitude of the monks."

"Maybe so, but I'm telling you to lose an inmate is no skin off the brother's noses. It's one less to deal with. Did you ever look at the cemetery out back? It speaks for itself. Those who weren't gunned down for trying to escape the hell hole were diagnosed with some ailment the brothers claimed resulted in death."

Dana covered her mouth with her hand and gasped, "Mother of God, I had no idea things were that horrific! But their files. . .can't the court subpoena them?"

"Ma'am, that's been tried before and failed," Rhodes said.

"What do you mean?" Dana's patience was waning.

"There was a case about six years ago—a Ranier versus Gonzaga—involving one of the boys who pleaded innocent to the crime he was convicted of. An attorney by the name of James Huffaker tried to come to the boy's defense, but no matter how hard he tried, the brothers found a way to block his efforts. I don't know what kind of connections the brothers have, but they might as well run the United States Mint. It would be easier to rob the vault than to get information out of Gonzaga."

This was not what Dana was hoping to hear. "Is there anything else you know about the youth home?" she asked. "Know anything about the death of Ellie Banks' husband? I got a strange feeling someone is keeping his passing hushed up."

"As for the home, the monks aren't ones to play pool with. . .at least, Brothers Calvin and Donald. They've got a real mean streak, those two. If I were you, I'd keep clear of the place. They got their own way of handling things."

"But that's not possible. I've come here, specifically, to solve the murder of a young inmate."

"All I'm saying is don't count on getting any help from those guys. You're barking up the wrong tree."

"And Gary Banks' death. . .what's the real scoop? Sounds as if you're agreeing the brothers aren't ones to tell me the truth about his passing."

"Gotta run. I'm late for an appointment. Let's discuss this later." The man hung up the phone.

Dana stared into space.

* * *

Dana found Ellie sitting at the kitchen table, reading the Bible. Patches was asleep in a small leopard-print bed in the corner, and Ellie had already covered Maize's cage for the night.

"The Lord doth provide," she said. "Thank him for this rain; it's a true blessing." She closed the large, black-covered book and invited Dana to join her for some chocolate chip cookies and tea. "You look a might bit discouraged, Dana. Are the brothers giving you a hard time?" she asked.

Coincidental, she should ask. "You might say that. I had hoped to speak with Brother Donald but never got further than Brothers Victor and Calvin."

The woman placed a lemon into her cup, submerging it with a silver spoon. "I might have an idea for you."

"Really?"

"My husband, Gary, he kept a notebook. He'd come home from work most nights worn out and discouraged by what he dealt with at the home. His only outlet, I suppose, was writing in that little book of his. He never did show me what he wrote. Occasionally, he'd tell me some things that happened at the place but told me never to tell." She put the spoon down and sipped on her tea. She wiped the corners of her mouth with her fingertips and swallowed hard. "I promised Gary I never would, tell that is, but he didn't make me promise I wouldn't look at his notebook. I waited until now."

"Ellie, are you saying you might share what your husband wrote?" Dana felt an inner burst of enthusiasm much as she had when she'd first began to make headway with the Bernadette Godfrey case on Cape Peril. Dana reassured herself these crimes were called mysteries for a reason.

"Why not if it means you can learn more about Douglas Clifford." Her forehead filled with creases. She looked at Dana and said, "We need to be clear on one thing."

"Of course," Dana said.

"You must never tell anyone I *told* you a thing about the home. You must never say you heard it from me." Ellie finished her tea, and as Dana reached for a cookie, Ellie excused herself to find Gary's notebook.

Intuitively, Dana assumed Gary must have known too much. Better him dead than to squeal. The question arose again? Did Gary die of a heart attack? She needed to get to the bottom of this. Dana was convinced Ellie was honoring her husband's request not to repeat what he had told her about the youth home, but the woman also feared anyone knowing that it was she who might be the informant. Dana wondered if the woman's fright stemmed from some pact or contract she had made with the brothers. And, if so, what was it they didn't want her revealing?

Moments later, Ellie came back into the kitchen. She carried a burgundy-covered book about the size of a small address book, so tiny it could easily be hidden in one's pocket. "Gary made sure he never took his notebook with him anywhere. It was only at home, late at night, that he would write. I can still see him sitting by the kitchen table, his heavy brows curled low over his glasses. His pencil firm against the page. When the lead became dull, he'd take a knife out of the kitchen drawer and start whittling away at it until he, once again, had a sharp point. He always seemed much more relaxed when he finished an entry. Funny," she said, "he kept this thing in his medicine cabinet with his shaving supplies of all things. Suppose he thought that would be the safest of places if anyone came looking for it."

"Didn't you ever ask him what he was writing or why?"

Ellie scratched at the side of her lip. "No. From what Gary told me, I think, my husband knew there were only so many things I could handle. No, Gary wouldn't want to upset me. Must have been why he chose to write things down in his journal. He used to tell me I had enough to worry about running the household and all."

"After Gary's death, were you ever curious to see what he wrote?"

The woman set the book on the table and covering her lips with her hands in a prayerful pose, she shook her head. "Never," she said. "Sounds silly, maybe, but it's like I can hear Gary speaking to me. He'd say, 'You keep your darn nose out of things, lamb chop. You don't need to go worrying your pretty little head over things don't concern you.'"

The room filled with a bright, white light and a clap of thunder roared overhead like a bunch of train cars banging into each other.

Within minutes, a downpour began to pound against the roof as if someone were pouring it from overhead buckets.

Ellie turned on the Motorola radio, atop which sat her *Betty Crocker Cookbook*. An announcer in a scratchy voice, speaking above the static, said,

"Flood warnings are in effect for all of Lubbock County, including the outskirts of Punkerton. Wind gusts of up to seventy miles an hour expected later tonight."

"The last time we had a storm like this, it blew a hole right through the shingles. By morning, the place was under several inches of water. Had to get Barney Windell to clean up the place."

"Let's hope that won't happen this time," Dana said.

Ellie turned a page in her Bible. "Let's pray to Jesus, it won't," she said, as she flipped through the gold-edged pages of the book.

"If you don't mind, I think, I'll get to bed early and begin reading Gary's notebook in the morning."

"No dinner?"

"No, thanks," Dana said. "Storms put me to sleep." Tomorrow, she would begin to read Gary's journal. She would stay inside and see what she might learn from Gary's notes. For now, it was a start.

Chapter Ten

The alarm on the night table buzzed at seven a.m. Dana couldn't wait to open the pages to Gary's notebook. She was glad she had gotten a good night's sleep before contemplating the content of the journal. It would be a perfect day for just that. The rain slapped against the pane and the fields were quickly filling up with puddles of mud. She hurriedly got dressed, poured herself a cup of coffee, and curled up under the covers as she opened the maroon book to the first page.

August 8, 1952

Tried to settle down the little Clifford boy... a little guy who got admitted today. He huddled in his cell, crying like a baby.

When I asked what was bothering him, he got up and stood behind the rusted bars. I couldn't believe my eyes. The boy was only wearing a pair of underwear and a T-shirt, both of which were sopping wet. A puddle followed him from the corner to where he stood. His bare arms shivered, and his blond hair dripped into his face. He was barefooted.

"They hosed me, Mister Banks."

"Who did it to you?"

"Brother Calvin. Took me to the shower room. Let the nozzle splash cold water over me. . .again and again."

I went to the supply room and found some towels. I shoved them through the bars. "Dry yourself off, son, before you catch pneumonia."

The cellblocks, no matter the conditions outside, always remained damp—more like a moist swamp in the middle of a rain forest, the catacombs under the city of Rome.

"Why? Why did the brother do this to you?"

"Don't know. Guess, he plain don't like me much."

There ain't no damn reason to treat a kid like this! Calvin is a monster. Yeah, that's what he is.

So, Brother Calvin was abusing the boy? Dana had heard of such things in orphanages in Ireland and Germany but not in the States. She read on.

That night about ten to midnight as I was leaving my shift, I heard footsteps behind me. I stopped, the noise of rubber-soled sandals stopped. I turned around, face to face with Brother Calvin.

"Not so fast, buddy."

The brother took his fist and punched it in my face; my body edged backward against the wall, and I could feel my eye swelling.

"Try that nonsense again and you won't be walking out of here on two legs."

"Try what?"

"Don't give me that shit! You know exactly what I'm taking about."

His slender body had more strength in his little finger than I had in my whole body. I had seen him at work before. No doubt, he planned to speak to Brother Donald about me. He planned to write me up.

Just as Ellie had said. There was tension between the men, but it sounded like it had nothing to do with a personality clash. Gary was concerned over the welfare of Douglas Clifford; that could not be said for the brother.

Fiona Wharton, Dana's mentor who taught Dana the tricks of the trade ever since she had gotten into the crime business, had told her there was one mistake a true detective never wants to make. "Don't let your imagination get ahead of the facts." Dana paused for a moment. But isn't that what she was doing? If she were to believe Gary Banks' death was a homicide, then quite possibly whoever killed him might very well also be the murderer of the Clifford child. Once again, Dana heard Fiona's warning, "Be careful of speculating." Dana turned to the next page of the journal at the same moment she heard a knock on her bedroom door.

"Phone call, Dana," Ellie said.

Dana went to the kitchen and picked up the receiver set on an unstable wooden stand.

"Miss Greer, Rhodes here."

"How'd you know where to find me?"

"The sergeant. Told me you're staying with Eleanor Banks. Got me to thinking. Listen I may not be able to help you get a private audience with Brother Donald—."

The two laughed.

"But Mrs. Banks' husband. . .Gary—."

"Yes?" Dana pressed the receiver closer to her ear.

"One of the journalists at the 'Punkerton Press' did some investigating at the time of Mr. Banks' death."

Finally, Dana thought, Could I be getting somewhere?

"She seemed to question the cause of Mr. Banks' death. Didn't care to buy Brother Donald's explanation the man died of a coronary arrest."

In an effort not to be overheard by Ellie, Dana whispered, "Did she speak to the coroner? What did he say?"

"Max Freda? Never mind him, Dana." There was a long pause. "There's some people in Punkerton you're better off not messing with; he's one of them."

Not another one, Dana thought, but instead, she asked, "What about the reporter? What's the reporter's name?"

"Oh, that won't do you any good."

"But I could at least talk—."

In a somber tone, Howard said, "Greta Canfield's dead."

Before Rhodes could say anymore, goosebumps raced up and down Dana's arms.

"The folks in Punkerton say her death was a suicide. Need I say more?"

"You don't mean—?"

"Knew too much? You're on the right track, Dana."

Dana put the receiver down. She stood staring at a bowl of apples on the kitchen table.

"Dana, everything all right?" Ellie came into the room, holding Patches in her arms. "Dana?"

Dana shook her head from side to side. "All right?"

Ellie tried to lighten the mood. "Why yes. You look like the comic character Casper the Ghost."

Dana ignored Ellie's attempt at humor. "By chance, does the name Greta Canfield mean anything to you?"

Ellie set the cat down and looked away. She took a knife from the kitchen drawer and sliced into one of the apples as she held it over the sink. "Tragic story," she said, and walked into the living room.

Chapter Eleven

Ellie was right about her assessment of storms in the Panhandle. Although no sign of water inside, oozing mud blanketed the fields for as far as Dana could see. The black clouds darkened the early morning, and the rain continued to pour incessantly.

"Don't tell me you're going out in this?" Ellie asked Dana, as she shoved the living room curtain aside. Dana wore a short, khaki jacket with brass epaulets and matching buttons.

"I've got no choice. Happen to have any galoshes?"

Ellie dug around in the front closet, pulling out a pair of black rubber boots from the floor. "Try these if you like."

Dana slipped the boots on over her shoes with a good size to spare. "These'll do," she said.

Ellie reached into the closet and pulled down a hanger. "Here put this on. It'll keep you dryer than that little coat you're wearing."

Dana slipped her arms out of her jacket and into Ellie's raincoat. She glanced at herself in the hall mirror. She looked like something out of one of the alien movies the children were all going to see these days at the drive-in movie theater.

Ellie warned her to be careful as Dana ran out to the old truck. She started up the Chevy not once or twice but three times before the engine finally kicked over. The piece of cardboard she and Ellie had stuck in the open window the other night had stayed in place although it looked more like a sponge. She turned on the wipers until they swished back and forth, trying to keep pace with the heavy downfall. The tires slushed through at least six inches of mud, splattering it on the running boards.

As Dana got closer to the station, she saw a group of colored children dipping plastic boats in a deep puddle near the curb. The cuffs of the childrens' tiny overalls were soaked with the muck of the storm. They wore no coats and did not seem bothered by the splashing rain.

"What brings ya out in this hell of a mess?" Sergeant McKnight asked, as the wind slammed the door behind Dana. "Hear the Red River is near crestin'."

"Let's hope not. I'd rather not have to fight Mother Nature if I can help it. My hands are full enough with the war I'm raging with the brothers at the home. But I'm not about to give up until I get to the bottom of all this."

The young man picked a piece of crust from his eye and flicked it. "Well, butter my butt and call me a biscuit. You're one stubborn lady, butter cup."

Dana appreciated being complimented on her tenacity, rather than her looks as was usually the case.

"Take it the brothers ain't being too cooperative. Don't surprise me none."

"And let me guess. There's nothing the people of Punkerton can do to help?"

Sure enough but as for y'all, pretty lady, you're goin' at it like killin' snakes."

"Excuse me."

"Oh, it's an ol' Southern sayin'. It means you're sure goin' at this case with more vigor and enthusiasm than can be expected."

Dana liked the man's positive comment, though, she didn't agree. As far as she was concerned, she was spinning her wheels and getting nowhere fast. She didn't bother to respond to one cliché with another. Instead, Dana gave the sergeant a rundown of what she had come up with so far in the case including Gary's untimely death.

"I like the way you're goin' at this, Dana. There's been way too much scuttlebutt around these parts over Gary Banks' passin'. If it was an inside job, why hell, you might have the man who did in the Clifford kid." Sergeant McKnight grabbed a wad of tobacco from his top desk drawer and shoved it into the side of his mouth. "Too bad Greta Canfield ain't around. Seems she was on the same track as you."

"Let's hope things turn out differently for me."

"Yer meaning y'all don't believe she done died by her own hand?"

"At this point, I'm not sure who is telling me the truth, sergeant."

Dana got back into the truck and pulled out her collection of holy cards from her bag. "Saint Eustace, I need some help," she said.

* * *

Before she entered the youth home, Dana jotted down the last of the questions she hoped to ask Timothy Laughton. If she had to play by the rules, she would try. . .at least for now. It didn't sound like Shirley Mitford, the board member for the home, had any intentions of changing the ordinance anytime soon.

She knocked on Brother Victor's office door. He remembered her and immediately escorted her to the office of Brother Donald.

Dana could not believe she was finally getting to meet the head master. The room embellished in maroon furnishings with matching drapery reminded Dana of something she might find in a Papal office in the Vatican. On the wall, above a large mahogany desk, hung a painting of St. Paul in a gold carved frame. Brother Donald, a plump man, bore a bald head covered in freckles and a small mole on the side of his nose. Brother Victor introduced Dana and quickly left. Dana could have sworn the two men winked at each other.

"Miss Greer, so I've been told all about you. Sit down. Sit down, please."

"Good, I hope," Dana said, hearing the anxiety in her own voice.

The brother toyed with his mole. "Curious might be a better adjective. What is it you hope to achieve by your visit?" He slid a yellow card under the glass, covering the top of his desk. He cleared his throat. "Reminder about the board meeting tomorrow at eight a.m. on the dot. . .can't forget."

"I had the opportunity to meet Shirley Mitford. As a matter of fact, it's part of the reason why I'm here right now."

The brother's eyebrows shot up. "You did. . .met Miss Mitford? She's one of the best things that have happened around this place in years. She may be a woman, but she's got one strong voice behind that pretty face of hers."

Oh, geez, was all Dana could think. She chose to ignore the brother's comment. "Yes, I understand she instituted a new policy pertaining to visitors, so I've made a list of questions I'd like for you to approve. For Timothy Laughton—."

"Hmm. So, that's what you hope to achieve. To interrogate one of our inmates."

"No, only to ask him a few questions. He is the first one to find Douglas Clifford's body."

"And the first one to tell Stevie Ames what he claims to have seen." Brother Donald picked up a pencil and pointed it at Dana. "You see, Miss Greer, the brothers would prefer to keep private what happens within these holy walls. Our main source of income is derived from charitable efforts, and we don't need a soiled record. We pride ourselves on how things are run here." He tapped the pencil into the palm of his hand. Then, he began to bang it against the glass-topped desk.

"I can understand that, Brother; however, we are talking about extenuating circumstances, aren't we? I mean, a murder? That is why I was brought here. . .to solve the case."

He tapped his knuckle against his front teeth. "If indeed, it was a murder." He left his mouth hang open a moment before he continued. "Some of these kids come from the streets, Miss Greer, and bring with them all kinds of diseases, you name it. We've had to bury a number of them." He rubbed his mole again as if it was a diversion from what he planned to say next. "Now, let me see what you planned to ask the boy." He took the slip of paper from Dana's hands. He put on a pair of bifocals lying on his desk.

What is your favorite meal here?

What are some things you've made in workshop?

What part do you play in the gardening out back?"

His eyes scanned to the bottom of the sheet. "Sounds innocuous enough. Let me ring a guard for you."

Soon a man in a dark green uniform entered the room. He shook Dana's hand. "Walter Robinski."

Why did the name sound so familiar, she wondered, and then it came to her. Robinski was one of the guards on the G Wing. "Name's Dana Greer. I'm investigating the Douglas Clifford case. By chance, were you and Gary Banks friends?"

"He was a quiet man, kept to himself. I'm doin' a double shift now that Banks is gone," he said.

"Yes. Yes, we appreciate Walter's efforts," Brother Donald said. "Show Miss Greer to 458-39-2061's cell, won't you?" Brother Donald frowned, stood, and shoved the paper into the guard's face. Then, he grabbed Walter's sleeve. "And, by the way, let's be sure you're on time for the meeting tomorrow morning. . .eight sharp."

Walter nodded.

Dana followed Robinski through the halls just as she had the first time with Brother Calvin. Metal doors banged, locks clicked, keys rattled, boys shouted obscenities, and the smells. . .the terrible smells.

Robinski stopped in front of Timothy Laughton's cell. "I'll need to go in with you," he said. "But there's something you should know, Ma'am." The man glimpsed over his shoulder. "I may work here, but between you and me. . .well, let's just say, I don't abide by all the rules."

Dana was unsure exactly what the guard meant.

Robinski gently folded the sheet of questions and slid it into Dana's hand.

For the first time in dealing with the brothers, Dana felt things might be turning in her favor.

A tall boy with sandy yellow hair stood up from his cot as they entered. He wore Navy blue pants and a matching shirt, the typical prisoner uniform.

Robinski shoved him back down and took a seat on a small wooden stool.

"Hello, my name is Dana," she said to the Laughton boy. "Your name is Timothy, correct?"

The boy nodded.

"Do you mind if I sit down on your cot? I'd like to get to know you."

The boy, lanky and stiff, nodded once again. A tuft of his hair fell and covered one eye.

The guard stood with his back to them.

Dana put the paper with her questions back in her bag, rubbing her hand over the grainy cover of her miniature Bible. She took a deep breath. "Timothy, what is your favorite meal here?" The question sounded as stupid as Dana felt in asking it.

The boy looked to be analyzing the simple question when finally, his shoulders rose under his ears and then back down.

"Okay, I get it. You're not all that crazy about any of the meals, huh?"

He attempted a weak smile.

"I understand when not in school, the boys here are busy making things in the workshop. What kinds of things have you made?"

Timothy made the same movement with his shoulders.

Was he deliberately told not to answer Dana's questions? Or, was he trying to play difficult. . .a behavior found in adolescents when questioned by an authority? She went on to her next question. "As I drove up to the Gonzaga Home, I noticed a garden off to the side? Have you ever done any of the planting?"

This time the boy pretended to scribble into the palm of his hand with the other one.

He wants to write the answers. Dana got it. She found a pen in her bag and a piece of paper and gave it to him.

Timothy's eyes shot nervously from the guard to Dana and back to the guard again. Then, he began to scratch something onto the paper and slyly handed it to her.

I can't speak.

The brothers must have directed the boy to keep his mouth shut. That was all she could think.

The boy motioned for the paper and pen. Again, he began to scrawl something down.

Doctor Hansen. . .he cut out my !

My God, no. That's why Timothy was in the infirmary! He didn't; he couldn't have. The bile rose in Dana's throat. This place is nothing more than a snake pit! She could barely contain her disgust and anger.

The boy covered his mouth with his fingers and shook his head. Tears streamed down his cheeks. With his head bowed low, he began to make guttural sounds.

Dana had seen enough for today, nor could she expect anything more from the boy. She put her arm around his shoulders, and in a quiet whisper said, "I won't forget you. I promise. I will be back. . .soon, very soon."

Timothy looked up at her. His eyes red, blood shot. He hung his head, bent his shoulders, slumped toward the cold concrete wall.

Dana tapped the guard on the back. "I'm finished," she said. As a second thought while the two walked away from the cell, she asked, "Mind telling me why you don't abide by all of the rules around here?"

He scowled. "Take it from me, lady, I've been around here long enough to know this place is nothing more than a damn circus of horrors." He reached into his shirt pocket and handed her a card:

> Walter Robinski
> Knights of Columbus
> St. Rita's Catholic Church
> MA3 - 8780

Dana smiled and thanked the man. Walter became her first willing source to help in putting the pieces of this grueling puzzle together.

Chapter Twelve

Dana arose early the next morning before Ellie had awoken. She made a pot of coffee and took a cup back to her room. She thought about what Brother Donald had said. The brothers preferred to keep private what happened at the home. Their main source of income was from charitable organizations. She had been assigned to this case by Archbishop Boretti. She couldn't see herself stepping out of line, going above the archbishop to disclose the atrocities she had already been witness to. Once she solved the Douglas Clifford case, had accomplished what she was brought to the home to do, she planned to make public what she had learned no matter what it took. And, God willing, by that time, the truth might speak for itself. She opened Gary's journal to where she had left off:

August 9, 1952

Got a new kid admitted today. . .a boy named Timothy Laughton. Seems like a nice enough kid. Been told he stabbed a classmate in cold blood. Never can tell what you get here. If I were to see the guy on the street, I'd think he looked naïve, almost saintly. From what I've heard from one of the cooks, the boy got into a squabble with another boy and pulled a knife on him. Had something to do with the boy calling the Laughton kid a Jesus freak. A boy came to visit him today...a kid with a bowl haircut and acne.

Stevie, Dana thought. Timothy had confided everything that had happened that night to him. She read on:

I could have sworn I saw the two boys embrace. I ain't reporting nothing. I chose to stay out of it.

It more than likely confirmed the two boys were more than just friends. What Timothy did to his schoolmate was by no means condoned, but she could understand how the boy might have responded without thinking when someone tore into his religious identity. Dana wondered why someone didn't investigate these matters more. It seemed the penal system was so quick to transfer the boys to the home and to throw away the key, treating them like cold-blooded monsters. How incredulous that children who committed crimes were seen no differently than adults. Were they even given a trial? Did they have a chance to explain? Did one foul act earn them a lifelong sentence? What if it had all been a horrible mistake? Dana found Timothy a frightened soul who might well have thought he was doing good by reporting the death of Douglas Clifford. Now, he was in even worse shape being mutilated and being refused visits by Stevie. There had to be something done for these juvenile offenders and locking them in the home like a pack of howling wolves until they reached adulthood did not seem to be the answer.

Dana brought her empty cup to the kitchen.

"Where you off to so early this morning?" Ellie asked, a piece of Melba toast in her hand.

"I've invited myself to a board meeting at the youth home."

"You mean the brothers don't know you're coming?"

"Thought it might be more fun that way," Dana smiled. "Plus, I'm curious about learning more about Shirley Mitford."

"Good luck. What can I say after the way she treated us during our little visit?"

* * *

Dana had a little time before the board meeting began, so she decided to stroll over to the cemetery, a short walk away. She opened the rusted gate, squeaky like a rusted oil can. The grounds were muddy, and she could feel her heels sink into the wet soil. Row after row of concrete tombstones lined up like uniformed soldiers, similar to the boys in life, wearing the blue trousers and shirts. She was amazed at how many burial sites there were. What logical explanation could be offered for the number of deaths in such a short few years of life? Were these the boys who tried to escape and never made it? Were these boys whose lives were cut short as an easy and permanent form of punishment? Or, did some of these boys take their own lives when they realized it would be the only way out of the home? All three possibilities were too heinous to consider. Towering over the graves stood a large statue of St. Michael the Archangel, a spear in his chipped hand, and a dead serpent at his feet. About ready to leave, Dana noticed a small bouquet of plastic tulips and daffodils tucked neatly at the base of one of the graves. She stooped down to read the engraving in the stone:

Douglas Clifford
January 4, 1943 - February 28, 1953

The marking made her shiver. Nothing about who his parents were; nothing about him being a son to someone; just a nobody buried among others of like kind. Yet, strangely, his headstone was the only one someone cared enough about to leave a token. But who? Dana quickly got up and closed the gate behind her. As she meandered back to the home, she noticed a black car parked at the curb; its hubcaps missing. She had a weird feeling someone might have been watching her. She could have sworn someone was in the front seat, but when she quickly glanced over, she saw no one. She cautioned herself not to be silly. The visit to the cemetery, probably, had just unnerved her.

Dana arrived promptly at eight a.m. to a room already filled. Seated at the front of the meeting room adjacent to Brother Donald's office sat the brother along with Brothers Victor and Calvin, Walter Robinski, and Shirley Mitford. On the other side of the table sat the remainder of the board members and some Franciscan monks Dana had not yet met.

Shirley's lips were stained a deep purple and her rosy cheeks complimented them. In front of her was a notebook and pen. She looked about the room with impatience, focusing on the clock on the rear wall. "Let us bring this meeting to order. I will read the minutes from our last meeting."

Dana took a seat near the back of the room.

Shirley read from a list of passed and approved motions, reciting the one pertaining to visitors of the home as the last one read.

Dana raised her hand.

"I'm afraid these motions have already been approved and seconded," Shirley said. She scowled, her lips drawn like an upside-down *U*. When she spoke, her words were staccato-like. "I'm afraid, Miss Greer, you are not on the voting committee of this home."

Just then, the door opened, and Carl Fenton entered. He silently mouthed the word, "sorry," and took a seat next to one of the monks.

Dana stood up, her hands firm against the table in front of her. "Excuse me. Wait one moment. I happen to have a question regarding the minutes."

Silence fell upon the room, a graveyard at midnight. Facial expressions of those in the audience could be read as question marks, as eyebrows rose, and jaws dropped.

"I'm afraid—," Shirley began to say.

"Now, here, here, let the woman speak," Walter said. "If she is not voting, she has a right to speak according to the First Amendment."

Quiet grumbling sounds scattered until Brother Donald called for attention. "Go ahead, Miss Greer, but make it short, please. We've many important matters to discuss here this morning!"

Dana made sure she looked at each person in the room before she began to speak. "I will. I have come to Punkerton to investigate the death of one of the boys at your youth home. I have been here for almost two weeks now, and I believe, I have not come close to having any support from the staff in allowing me to further my fact finding. If anything, I have been queried as if *I am* a criminal, as are the boys here."

Almost everyone in the room glared with icy stares. Dana could sense the temperature of the room as if icicles were hanging from the ceiling. She knew those in attendance shunned her for her outspokenness, something the home did not relish, but she made up her mind she would speak nonetheless.

Like an arrow shot from a bow, Shirley Mitford stood up. "Excuse me, Miss Greer, but I find your accusations meaningless. The staff of Gonzaga prides itself on the work we do here, not on becoming involved in trivial accusations! Our job is not to accommodate your needs. Sorry!"

The cacophony in the room rose. People began to shout at one another. Some pointed at Dana and smirked. Brother Donald tried to call the room to order, but by this time, everyone was speaking at once. He pounded his fist on the table. "Please! I demand you stop. . .order, order!"

After moments of unrest, quiet was restored to the room; harmony returned.

Without seeking further permission, Dana continued. "I find your decision with regard to inmate visitation rules absurd, particularly, in the way it affects me and prevents me from going forth with my investigation into the Douglas Clifford murder case."

"I'm afraid, Miss Greer, we run a private institution here and make policies we believe are in the best interest and, I might add, safety of our boys. Now, please, may we move forward with our meeting?" Brother Donald asked.

Brother Calvin tapped Shirley Mitford's hand until the woman sat back down. She swiped her forehead with her palm. Brother Calvin sneered at Dana and shook his head.

Dana sat down. The reaction she received was just what she expected, but she felt it imperative to let those at the Board meeting hear her voice.

At the end of the meeting, Carl Fenton exited with Dana. He said, "Impressive, Miss Greer, some of us are pleased you are here and are interested in solving the Clifford case."

"Until this institution recognizes my role in investigating the murder of Douglas Clifford, I will not be able to get to the bottom of the case, I'm afraid." Dana thought, Why, didn't you have the gumption to support me at the meeting? What is everyone running away from? Why is everyone afraid to speak up?

Walter came through the door next with his thumb raised high—a true supporter.

Dana made her way out of the building. She opened the door to her truck and was about to step inside when she felt someone touch her forcefully on the shoulder. She turned and found herself face to face with Shirley Mitford.

The woman's dark eyes shone like miniature beads and the hair in her tightly wound bun stuck out in all directions. "Off the record, Miss Greer, may I suggest you keep your nose out of the business of the youth home? You saw what happened to Timothy Laughton. I'd hate to see similar action taken against you."

"Would you? I'm not so sure. From what I've seen around this place, I'd have to say revenge is not something new." Dana stepped up into the truck, when Shirley grabbed at the back of Dana's blue sweater, pulling hard on the threads.

"Do me a favor, Dana. Keep your sweet little ass away from me. I surely wouldn't want to see it buried in the cemetery out back." The woman released her hold.

With Dana's heart thumping in her chest, she slammed the truck door shut, locked it, and started the engine. As she backed away, she saw Shirley get into a green Ford truck parked next to her. In the passenger seat sat Brother Calvin. Dana blinked hard and squinted her eyes. She could have sworn she saw a pile of what looked to be white sheets on the back seat.

* * *

Dana managed to make the ten a.m. Mass at St Rita's Church. She shivered. She wasn't sure if her chilled feeling was the result of her encounter with Shirley Mitford or if it was due to finding herself in a Catholic Church once again since leaving it after her marriage to Nate.

While the choir sang the last verse of "Holy God We Praise Your Name," Dana followed a small group of people into the basement hall of St. Rita's Church. A large urn of coffee and a tray of doughnuts, resembling a mosaic of colors, covered a card table.

Pouring himself a cup, Robinski stood chomping on a chocolate sprinkled cake. Next to him stood the pastor, who had presided at the Mass.

Dana meandered over to them. "Hello, Mr. Robinski, Father."

The tall, broad-shouldered priest with wavy black hair and piercing green eyes looked questioningly at Dana. "Ah, you found me here of all places," Robinski said. He had a small twinkle in his blue eyes Dana had not noticed before. "Let me introduce you two."

"Who have we here?" the priest asked.

"Father, this is Dana."

"Dana Greer," she completed.

"She's from Punkerton. At least, she is living in Punkerton presently."

"Well, well, you sure won't find a Catholic Church there. Welcome to St. Rita's. Name's Neil."

She shook the priest's hand and tried to smile. "I must say a beautiful place," Dana said, as she stood admiring the stained-glass windows which depicted St. Rita as a young mother of two sons, another pane depicted Rita with her abusive husband as a soldier, and a third with her in the habit of St. Augustine of Hippo.

"I see you're intrigued with the glass panes. Did you know St. Rita is the patron saint of hopeless cases?" the priest asked. "The woman sure went through her trials but came out victorious."

"St. Eustace held the same title, so I've learned."

Robinski looked surprised yet impressed.

"I have a hobby of collecting holy cards. Have ever since I was a young child."

"Ah, so you're Catholic, I take it?" Father Neil asked.

Dana could feel her cheeks warm. "Was. . .er. . . am. . .but—." Dana fiddled with the blond curls resting on her shoulder. Something about being in church filled her with anxiety, let alone speaking face-to-face with a priest. Ever since she was sexually abused as a young child by her uncle, she had felt dirty, used, unworthy. She married in the Church but never returned afterwards. Her intentions were to come back; she missed the rich traditions and rituals. But, the time never seemed quite right.

"No business of mine. Sorry," Father Neil said. "I hear you're here on business. . .investigator, huh?"

"Yes, I go where I'm best needed."

"Well, you may be here longer than you expect. Breaking the Douglas Clifford case won't be easy," Father said, a scowl covering his face.

Dana knew the answer to the question she was about to ask but asked it anyway. "What makes you say that?"

"The brothers, the politics, the people. . .need I say more?"

Dana nodded as the priest excused himself.

Robinski motioned Dana to a quiet corner of the room. "How might I help?"

"What makes you so willing? I mean, I'm delighted to finally find someone in Punkerton who is not afraid to speak up."

"Don't get me wrong, Dana. Got a wife and nine kids to support. They attend Grace Presbyterian," he mumbled. "So, let's put it this way. I need my job. No question about it. But I've seen enough to know a man's gotta have a conscience, too. I've got to be able to look myself in the mirror."

"Know anything about Gary Banks' death?" Dana asked.

"Sure as hell, I do. Nice guy. Got written up once too many times for trying to protect the Clifford kid. That's one thing the brothers won't stand for. Called fraternizing with the boys."

"And?"

"Have you met Doctor Hansen yet?"

Dana shook her head and finished her doughnut. The comment Shirley Mitford made about revenge and what had happened to Timothy Laughton crossed her mind.

"Word has it the doctor spiked Banks' coffee to make it look like a heart attack. Stopped his heart in a beat. Story had it Banks' died of a cardiac arrest on the job. Nothing further from the truth."

"And his wife, Ellie—?"

Robinski shook his head, "Eleanor. Poor thing."

"She knows the truth?"

Robinski nodded. "Sworn to silence by the brothers. She knows better than to open her mouth. Don't know what they might have told the woman, but it had to be pretty frightening for her not to discuss her own husband's death."

"How awful! Whose idea prompted this?"

"Who else? Brother Calvin, I'm convinced. Donald runs the place in name only, but Calvin? He's one nasty man who sails that ship. And the doctor sure ain't one hell of a lot better. Those two are like bread and butter, but your guess is as good as mine."

"The Clifford boy. . .do you think—?"

"That I don't know. The poor kid was beat up so many times, I'm surprised he lived as long as he did."

"By the boys?" Dana asked.

"The boys and Brother Calvin."

"What about the Laughton boy. . .do you think he knows more about that night than he told Stevie?"

"Calvin sure thought so. That's why he convinced Hansen to remove the kid's tongue."

Just as Dana was about to broach another question, the pastor returned.

"Let's not forget about the usher meeting," Father said to Robinski.

"Sure thing, Father. I'll be right there."

Robinski walked over to the porcelain sink in the corner of the room. He rinsed out his coffee cup and said, "Sorry to rush off like this, Dana."

"I understand."

"Hey, should you have any more questions, just give me a call."

Dana was sure she would have more questions for the man. For one thing, she needed to find a way to get Douglas Clifford's records. By the time she had arrived on the scene, the boy's body had been buried in the cemetery out back of the home. She wondered who, if anyone, had attended the boy's burial. Were there relatives or friends? Did he have any enemies? Why had Brother Calvin taken such a dislike to the child?

The list went on; the multitude of questions made her jittery. She reached for the Bible in her handbag, and her jangled nerves subsided like they did whenever she sipped a hot cup of tea. On her way out of the church, Dana found a rack of holy cards bearing the image of St. Rita. She took one, picturing the saint standing with a man near the edge of a cliff. The picture resonated with where Dana presently found herself. So far, Robinski presented her with the only ray of hope she had in solving the case. She would make up another list of questions to ask the Laughton boy and return to the youth home. Perhaps, in time, the boy would come clean with what he learned about the murder scene.

* * *

When Dana returned to Ellie's place, she found her in the living room crocheting a lavender spread. Patches played with the ball of yarn at Ellie's feet. "Oh, didn't expect you this soon," the woman said, as she quickly attempted to stuff the piece into the bag at her side.

"Hope I didn't interrupt anything," Dana said.

"Oh, I might as well confess. I'm making the spread for you. . .a kind of going away gift. Hope you like purple."

"My favorite color but not sure I'm anywhere near close enough to leaving as of yet."

"That's good. Looks like we both have work to do," Ellie said. The woman laughed. "Nowhere near done with the project." As an afterthought, the woman set down her crochet hook and looked over at Dana. "How'd things go with the board meeting. . .Shirley Mitford?"

"Afraid the woman is much worse than we saw the other night. First, she tried to prevent me from speaking at the meeting. Then, while I was getting in the truck, she physically accosted me and threatened my life! Said if I didn't stay out of the matter, she would see to it I landed, like the Clifford child, in the cemetery out back of the home."

"My heavens, I'm so sorry, dear. I can't believe she said this to you. May I get you a cup of tea, something to eat?"

"No thank you. Plan to do some more reading right now." For a brief moment, Dana thought about confronting Ellie about the real cause of her husband's death, but she reconsidered. No sense making the woman anxious. For now, at least, she lived in fear of what the brothers might do to her if she was to reveal the truth. If the brothers were as ruthless as Dana was quickly learning, she could understand Ellie's reluctance to expose what she knew.

Dana slipped into some lounging pajamas and sat in the flowered stuffed chair by the window. The storm subsided, the room had an eerie silence to it. She opened Gary's diary.

September 19, 1952

Robinski told me I'd better stay away from the kid. He said if I got three strikes I'd be out. Not sure what he meant by "out." Can't believe the brothers could afford to fire me. I know too much. I've seen the way Calvin manhandles the Clifford kid. No kid should have to deal with that. If it means I'm the only one showing the boy any mercy, then so be it! The poor kid don't got any family or friends on his side. The only visitor is that seminarian, but he visits all of the inmates.

Dana glanced at her list of to-dos and began to check off those she had completed.

- *Gather more information on Timothy Laughton from the sergeant √*
- *Visit with Brother Donald, Head Master of the youth home √*

She realized, more than likely, she had exhausted her second source. Brother Donald offered little in the way of help, either out of ignorance or downright refusal. As for Timothy, Dana told herself no matter how long it took for her to solve the Clifford case, she would make sure someone helped the Laughton boy.

- *Arrange to speak again with Timothy Laughton*
- *Prompt Ellie to tell me more of what she knows*

Then, she added:

- *Arrange to meet Howard Rhodes to find out more about the coroner*
- *Arrange a meeting with Doctor Hansen*

Chapter Thirteen

After Dana's experience at the boys' home and her frightening encounter with Shirley Mitford, she would have preferred to stay in bed to continue reading Gary's journal. But last night before she retired, she called Robinski to thank him for his support at the board meeting and to arrange to meet him at the home. She planned to tour J Wing, which consisted of the boys' classrooms, the kitchen, the dining hall, and the infirmary. She hoped to get a better feel of what life was like for the boys when they were not in their cells.

* * *

They entered J Wing from the central rotunda. "Here are all of the boys' classrooms on level one."

"Why so many? This floor looks as if it could be a school!"

"One for elementary and one for high school students," Robinski said.

"Care if I take a peek inside?" Without waiting for Walter to respond, Dana opened the door to a classroom that obviously was one where students were taught history. The bulletin board pictured an airplane with the heading:

The First Trans-Atlantic Flight is Completed by Charles Lindbergh in the "Spirit of St. Louis" on May 21, 1927

Next to the announcement was a picture of three women holding a sign:

Women Are Given the Right to Vote

August 18, 1920

The last picture was a cover of a book. Beneath, it read:

F. Scott Fitzgerald Publishes the Great Gatsby - 1925

The blackboards were covered in mix and match facts and years. Dana felt a pang of sadness, realizing these boys were like any other children in terms of their education, yet their futures were already destined to live behind bars.

In a classroom with bright fluorescent lights stood one of the brothers and three young boys, working on a math problem on the board.

There were at least ten other rooms with locked doors on the floor.

"Shall we go upstairs to the kitchen and dining room on level two?" Walter asked.

When they got to the second level the scents of meatloaf and mashed potatoes greeted them. Dana immediately recognized the smell, as this was the only meal her mother cooked for her father and her. When her mother had her bad bouts of depression, this provided one recipe her mother could do from rote memory. "Seems the boys are provided some good meals around here."

Walter concurred. "Certain monks do all the cooking, but most of the food comes from the farm on the property."

As they passed the large, yellow tiled kitchen, monks could be seen stirring, chopping, and measuring ingredients. Dana had never seen such a large range, one with fifteen burners. Huge silver bowls lined the Formica counter top with what appeared to be some type of greens. Several glass milk bottles lined up on the opposing counter.

"The brothers prepare everything here in the kitchen, and others take the food and serving pieces to the cafeteria line in the dining room."

"The brother at the door of the dining room?"

"Making sure no boy leaves with any silverware. He does a pat-down with each child."

No sooner had Dana and Robinski turned the corner toward the dining hall then a rumpus could be heard.

"I didn't do it. Bobby Sullivan started it!" The boy's face was bright red.

"You, idiot! Kevin Wood shot it!" another boy screamed.

Now, a guard who Dana did not recognize stepped out from behind the serving line. "All of you in your seats!" The man swung his baton around. "Okay, who's first for a beating?"

"What the hell," Bobby Sullivan said. "Why don't cha agitate the gravel?"

"What'd ya say?" the guard asked, standing over the Sullivan boy—his baton directly over the child's head. "Who in the hell do you think you are, you little ankle-biter?"

The boy began to shake. "I ain't meant no trouble. I'm just sayin', it wasn't me who shot the spitball."

"Then, who did?" the guard asked.

The third boy repeated his accusation. "It was Kevin...Kevin Wood."

The guard walked over to the other table. "Did you? Are you the guilty one?"

The boy, who looked to be about ten years old, nodded.

"Get your ass up!"

The boy did as he was told while everyone in the dining hall began to clap and cheer.

The guard dragged the boy away by his shirt collar.

"What will happen to him?" Dana asked, Robinski. "I mean, it was only a spitball."

"Doesn't matter. The guards need to keep order and to do whatever it takes to do so."

"So, what does that mean?"

"More than likely a whack over the boy's knuckles with the baton."

Dana could not believe such a typical boy's game could result in such a severe punishment. "No warning?"

"Nope. They don't believe in that here. What do you say, we go up to the infirmary?"

"I guess. Maybe, we'll find Kevin Wood up there."

Robinski offered no comment.

The third level smelled like a typical hospital...scents of medicinal odors and cleaning products. She was amazed to see a couple of women in white nurses' uniforms. "Ah, so there are other staff besides the monks, I see."

"Yes. Four nurses work on a part-time basis with Doctor Hansen, who works two days a week. There are twenty beds up here. Sometimes, they are all filled, and other times, only a bed or two."

From what Dana had learned about Doctor Hansen's unethical practices, she questioned what nurse would be willing to work alongside such a man. She decided not to inquire, though.

Unlike a typical two-bed hospital room, here the white cots were lined next to each other, all in the same long room. Above each bed, there hung a wooden crucifix, and in the far corner of the room stood a marble statue of the Virgin Mary and a statue of St. Luke, the patron saint of physicians. The layout provided no privacy, but then again, the boys' home was a prison, not a state-of-the-art institution.

"Seen enough?" Robinski asked.

"Well, it sure isn't home, but I guess, it's not supposed to be."

Robinski smiled as the two made their way to the rotunda.

Chapter Fourteen

Although the rain had let up and the predicted cresting of the Red River never occurred, the day was still dark for mid-morning. Dana placed a quick call to Howard Rhodes and was pleased when he accepted her last minute invitation to meet at the Bean Grinder that morning.

She exited her truck at the coffee shop. Howard Rhodes had told her to look for a middle-aged man with a Donald Duck tie. She told him she had long blond hair and would be wearing red spiked heels.

Howard Rhodes flagged her down as she entered. He sat waiting in a corner booth, stood, and shook her hand before she sat down. "Can I order you anything, Dana? A roll? Coffee or tea? I see you found me. Must have been my bright yellow tie."

The two laughed.

"I'll have a coffee, black, please."

"I wouldn't have picked you out of a crowd to be a private investigator," Howard said.

"Neither would I have picked you out as being an attorney."

"See. It's gotta be the tie. I knew it."

"Must be my red heels," Dana retorted.

The two laughed again.

Howard motioned for a server. "So, you're fascinated with Max Freda, I see."

"Seems I've become quite proficient at striking out at getting to know people."

Howard winked. "Well, I hope you won't with me."

That uncomfortable feeling came over Dana yet again. She had a difficult time dealing with the commonplace bantering, which went on between members of the opposite sex. Although separated from her husband, Nate, she still saw herself as married. Her conscience kept a close eye on her behavior. Plus, she had to admit, being cheated on, and by a prostitute no less, did not instill in her much trust in men.

Howard continued, "If I can help, I'd like to get you to first base, at least."

Dana smiled. She had to admit the man's demeanor was doing something to calm her already frayed nerves. Up to now, Robinski offered to help, but he had been the only one.

"What would you like to know about the coroner?" Howard asked.

"I'd like to meet with him, but you had reservations." Dana knew what Robinski had already told her about Doctor Hansen's part in killing Gary Banks and the brothers covering it up as a coronary arrest. She wondered what else Howard might know about Max Freda. "Why do you suggest I not question the man?"

"Punkerton is an evil place. It explains why I chose to get a small place in Lubbock and conduct most of my work from there."

Dana tapped her finger over her lips. "Can't say I'm a fan of Punkerton myself, but it is where the crime occurred."

"I can tell you with certainty that other than the youth home, Catholics aren't welcome in these parts."

"So, I gathered, but what's that got to do with Max Freda?"

"It's more than that; Freda is the Imperial Wizard for the Texas area."

Dana sunk lower into the booth, taking her coffee from the server. "What? The KKK?"

"Correct."

"So, speaking to him about the home and the goings on there—."

"Not a good idea. Freda would as soon see the place go up in smoke. Talk has it he and his boys tried to do just that some years back, but one of the brothers got wind of it and stopped them before they carried out their plan."

"My gosh!"

"Small town, big problems; you see why I choose not to call Punkerton home," Howard repeated.

Dana sipped on her coffee. "First, I'm told there's no way I can subpoena the boy's records, and now I'm told to eliminate the coroner from questioning." Dana hated to be such a negative Nellie, but her investigation kept leading to dead ends.

Howard studied Dana's face. "Sounds as if I'm the prophet of doom, Dana. Don't mean to be." He finished his tea and rolled his thumb under his index finger. "Listen, I've heard *Giant* came out at the cinema. Elizabeth Taylor, Rock Hudson . .can I get you to join me?"

Dana could feel herself blush. She kept ruminating on her past: Nate, the ongoing affair, the separation. But maybe, Howard was right. She needed some time away from the investigation.

"I. . .I—."

"Know you're busy but taking a break from the case might just clear your mind some."

"Well, maybe—."

"Tomorrow night. Say I pick you up at six at Ellie's place. We'll do dinner and then the show."

Could it hurt any? Dana thought. Certainly, it sounded innocent enough. She'd make it a point to tell him about her husband then.

* * *

Dana drove over to the police station to place a call to the youth home. If only her luck could change, she hoped to speak with the doctor at the infirmary.

The sergeant was cleaning some dirt from his nails when Dana entered. "Y'all know, Dana, we might be as different as whiskey and tea, but I've been thinkin'. Y'all one ace-high lady."

"Why thank you. I appreciate the comment." Dana did not think too highly of the man as far as sergeants went, but she could tell the man meant well. She glanced at the black phone on his desk. "Might I—?"

"Bobtail 'er and fill 'er with meat, Dana, what y'all after?"

Dana figured the jargon meant to get to the point. "Your phone. . .could I use it to call the youth home?"

"Con sarn it, how them their brothers been treatin' y'all?"

Dana considered the sergeant must be feeling a bit more comfortable with her in town as he was beginning to let his Texas slang appear now and then. When she first met him, she could tell he tried his best not to reveal his accent for whatever reason. "I'm interested in speaking with the doctor there. . .Doctor Hansen." She paused for a moment expecting the sergeant to come up with some excuse as to why she should stay away from the man.

"Hansen, huh? When he's not at the prison, he runs his shop over on Baylor Street."

"Do you have his office number by chance?"

"I wuz fixin'to see the man myself. Gotta itch that just won't quit." He pointed over his left shoulder. He began fumbling through some papers on his desk. "Here," he said, handing a business card to Dana. "Like I said over on Baylor Street."

Dana reached for the phone and tried the number on the card.

"Doctor Hansen's office," a pleasant-sounding woman answered.

"My name's Dana Greer. I was wondering if I might speak with the doctor?"

"Are you one of his patients?"

"Oh, it's nothing medical. I just wanted to speak with him."

"Wait a moment." The woman put the receiver down. When she returned several minutes later, she said, "I'm sorry but the doctor only schedules time with patients."

"Could you give him a message then?"

"Surely."

"When will the doctor be at the youth home?"

"Tomorrow afternoon. He spends most Thursdays with the boys."

"Tell him he'll be spending some time with me tomorrow. Dana Greer," she reiterated. "Say around one?"

The receptionist started to reply.

Dana hung up the phone.

* * *

Maize kept repeating, "Pollie, want a cracker; I want a cracker" as Dana entered Ellie's house. "Pretty bird," Dana said, and to her surprise, the parakeet whistled.

A note was taped to the icebox:

> Not feeling well. Have a headache. Went to bed early. Leftovers on second shelf.

A perfect opportunity to grab some food and to return to Gary's journal.

October 15, 1952

Getting sick of the shit I see around this place. Brother Donald thinks he's so coy, but I've had the misfortune to see him with Brother Victor. I wonder how far back the two go. Spoke with Seminarian Carl. He's been coming to this place for months now for a practicum. He told me Brother Donald tried to pay him off, the first time he'd seen the two men together. Carl refused the money. Said he didn't want to get involved in any blackmail deals. The kid seems to have a good head on his shoulders.

"The seminarian. . ." Dana whispered. She needed to speak with him further. He seemed like a nice enough young man. He might be the one who could help her. After all, he didn't have anything to lose as far as Dana could tell. Once his practicum was complete, he'd return to the seminary to complete his studies. Gary ended his journal entry with:

The two-faced fools. Speak out against queers when, God damn it, that's what they are. Their special handshakes in the halls, their secret code words, their walks on the grounds together. Must think I'm some kind of idiot not to have put two and two together.

Dana began to wonder if any of the boys might have been privy to the brothers' behavior. Could there be more to why Doctor Hansen had removed Timothy's Laughton's tongue? Gary's words lingered in her mind. The abuse, the hypocrisy, and even murder. . .yet under the roof of a Catholic institution. The brothers wanted nothing but a lily-white demeanor. Dana would find a way to make the truth known, and when she did, who knew what the status of the home would be.

Chapter Fifteen

That night Brother Donald and Brother Victor climbed up the wooden stairs to level three of J Wing but not before looking over their shoulders. It was more habit than anything else. Brother Donald unlocked Room 39.

A stream of sweat ran down Brother Victor's temple. "You think the young guy is going to spill the beans? Saw him watching us the other night. What if he's a two-timing snoop?"

"So, what if he is? Do you think anyone would believe him? Two Catholic brothers in prestigious positions reported to be love partners on the side. No, I hardly think that'd be a headline anyone would believe."

Brother Victor's face covered in worry lines. "But, you tried to pay him off once before if you recall."

"And, did he accept? No. I don't think he gives a damn about us."

"I'm still concerned," Brother Victor said, a quivering in his voice. "The guy seems to show up at all the wrong times."

"Furthermore, he plans to be ordained soon. I doubt he'd want to cause a fuss with Rome and be seen as some sort of squealer. It wouldn't look good for the man." Brother Donald put his arm around Brother Victor's shoulders. "What'd you say we forget all of this nonsense?"

"What about the investigator? Think she might be suspicious?"

"My, my, aren't we the worry wart tonight! What makes you say that?"

"She's friends with Robinski, isn't she? And there's no secret that guy doesn't know."

"I agree I'm not the biggest fan of his, but let's face it. He also has nine kids to support. He wouldn't risk his job. Now, calm down, why don't you?"

"The other day in the rotunda—."

"Vic, stop! You're getting too carried away with this nonsense. Relax, why don't you?"

Brother Donald led Brother Victor over to the bed and pulled down the flannel sheets.

The two men undressed, carefully placing their brown robes over a chair in the corner.

The two climbed into bed for their usual hour of pleasure when someone banged on the door to the room.

"Holy Cow!" Brother Victor yelled.

Brother Donald placed the palm of his hand over Victor's mouth. "Shh."

The two waited in silence when they heard another bang.

Victor trembled. In a whisper, he said, "Don, who could be out there?"

"Hell if I know, but we're not about to open it. Give it a few seconds. Whoever it is will leave."

"This has never happened before," Victor said. "I knew it. I knew it. That seminarian or maybe the Greer woman—."

"Victor, get a grip. Your imagination is getting carried away."

They waited and when they heard no further disturbances, they returned to their illicit rendezvous.

Chapter Sixteen

The smell of iodine, Mercurochrome, urine, and the chemicals of cleaning products lingered in the air. Two men, dressed in white uniforms, scrubbed the marble floor outside of the infirmary. They excused themselves at least six times as they mopped around Dana and a guard who monitored two inmates on chairs outside the entrance. One of the boys bit down on his lips while the other pretended to play piano keys with his cuffed hands. What amazed Dana was the guard had no real control of the boys. Other than their cuffs, and the guard's wooden baton at his side, all three could easily move about if so desired.

The first boy turned toward Dana and said, "Hear you've come to find out what happened to Douglas, huh?"

The guard tried to quiet him by hitting him on the side of his temple with his knuckles.

The boy shoved his body aside.

"Let him talk," Dana said. "That's correct; I'm here to find out who did this horrible thing to Douglas."

The boy started to chew on the inside of his cheek. "Listen, don't believe that bull shit about the kid beating his old man and old lady."

The guard elbowed the boy and jerked him sideways.

The boy tried to push away from the guard once again.

"Please, leave him alone!" Dana turned back to the boy, "Who do you think is responsible?"

"Hell, if I know but not the kid." The boy rolled his tongue around on the inside of his cheek. "He told me so. Said he didn't have nothing to do with the murder."

"Is that right?" Dana said.

"The kid was a candy ass. Can you believe he came into this place—a joint with cold-blooded killers—and brought a stuffed rabbit?" The boy broke into boisterous laughter, his teeth bucked like a beaver.

"Shut your ass up. Y'all hear me?" the guard reprimanded.

The second boy spoke up lifting his chin toward the ceiling, rolling his eyes. "A little shit that didn't know his ass from a hole in the ground; that's what he was."

This time, the guard took the wooden baton by his side and lifted it into the sight of the boys. "You two gonna shut-up your God damn mouths or else."

The first boy gave the guard a dirty look.

The second boy grumbled something under his breath.

"Listen, the name's Dana Greer. I'm investigating the death of Douglas Clifford. Please let the boys speak."

The guard scowled at Dana. "The damn kids don't know what they're talkin' about."

The inmates ignored the guard. "The kid was a fink but not a murderer," the first boy said.

The second boy obediently nodded his head.

"He was a thief then; is that what you're saying?" Dana based her question on what she had learned so far about Douglas Clifford.

"Petty shit. He never did belong in this hellhole. Everybody around here knew that."

"How do you think he ended up at St. Gonzaga then?"

The second boy said, "Someone else must have done it; that's all I know."

"You think someone may have set him up?" Dana remembered Ellie's words. She had instructed Dana to keep an open mind and to be willing to learn from others at the youth home. Although Dana hadn't considered learning something directly from some random prisoners, she was quickly beginning to see that wisdom laid in the mouths of babes. . .these boys being not much older than Douglas Clifford.

Eager to hear more, the conversation came to an abrupt halt when a nurse opened the door to the waiting room and in a confused voice asked, "Did you check in, Miss? Do you have an appointment?"

"No, name's Dana Greer. I'm willing to wait until Doctor Hansen has a free moment."

The nurse started to close the door when she turned and said, "Doctor is taking a small break. Come with me, Denise, and I'll tell him he has a visitor."

"Dana. . .the name's Dana."

"Of course, Donna."

The nurse guided Dana to the doctor's office adjacent to the infirmary marked by an overhead light with a green, metal shade. The space resembled more of an interrogation room than a patient's exam room. Dana took a seat and waited for what seemed like twenty minutes or more. When the door opened, Dana jumped and blinked hard. A heavy-set man with his leather belt high on his waist and wearing a long, white lab coat entered. His voice raspy as if he had a pack-a-day habit said, "Doctor Hansen. You're Donna?"

"Dana. . .Dana Greer." Dana was getting tired of her own name at this point. But she found it often did her good to become frustrated as it tended to bring out the more forthright part of her personality. "You surely must have heard by now I am the private investigator on the Douglas Clifford case?"

The doctor wiped the corners of his mouth with his hand. "Yes, heard some rumblings about you."

"Let me not waste your time, Doctor, with meaningless introductions. I'm interested in learning what it is you know about the murdered boy."

He raised his eyebrows, his face pudgy and clay-like. He resembled one of the rubbery "Snap, Crackle, and Pop" rings she had found in a box of cereal as a child. His voice matter-of-fact like, he asked, "What's there to say? Found in his cell on the way back from mandatory lavatory with a knife wound in his jugular. Bled to death. One of the boys on his cellblock saw blood pooling from under the bars. Plain and simple."

His words cold, stark, callous. His attitude might explain how he gave no thought to obeying orders from Brother Calvin to remove Timothy's Laughton's tongue. An obedient follower who exhibited indifference. Might he have been instructed to carry out orders without thought to the consequences? Was he a man of no conscience, no regret, no remorse? A cold-blooded killer?

"Have I answered your questions?"

"Oh, yes. There is one more, though. Do you have any idea who might have wanted Douglas Clifford murdered?"

The man rubbed at his left eyebrow, swallowed, and in a quiet whisper said, "You're the investigator, aren't you?" He laughed like the Porky Pig cartoon character and walked out of the room.

* * *

Dana worried about how she would explain her movie dinner date with Howard Rhodes. Dating was not part of her job description. When Dana told Ellie she would not be having dinner with her, Ellie made an O face. "Remember the attorney I spoke with. . .Howard Rhodes?"

Ellie shook her head.

Dana couldn't remember if she had told the woman about meeting him at the Bean Grinder or not. "Well, I had sought him out to see if there was any way I might subpoena Brother Donald for the Douglas Clifford's records."

"I'm sure the answer was a no."

"It was. But he's been trying to help me, all to no avail. He thought it might be nice if I got out socially to clear my mind up a bit."

"Lovely, dear." Ellie proceeded to put the extra place setting back in the cabinet. "You just go and have yourself a good time. Lord knows you've worked for it."

"I don't know about that."

"I do. I've seen how tired you look when you get back here. Wish there was some way I could help."

"But you do. You've welcomed me into your home."

The two women hugged.

Dana went to her room to take a short nap before she proceeded to get ready. She refused to allow herself to call it a date. Rather, she told herself it was all in a day's work.

Shortly after six, the doorbell rang.

After Dana introduced Ellie to Howard, Ellie gave her a nod and a wink. Obviously, the woman approved.

* * *

While feasting on Chicken Parmesan and pasta in Ma Ma Mia's Italian Restaurant, Howard said, "We've talked about the boys' home, the brothers, and Punkerton. Why don't you tell me some about yourself."

Dana had difficulty swallowing the last bit of chicken. She had feared this question ever since Howard had suggested they go out. She gulped a drink of water from the fine-stemmed crystal glass before her. "Tell me what you'd like to know."

"Now, that sure is an investigative way out of things." He smiled. "From Bay View, Maine; solved the Bernadette Godfrey case on Cape Peril; came to Punkerton with high accolades; let's see, did I leave anything out?"

"Wow! You know quite a bit already."

"How'd you get into this line of work?"

"My father. , . He was chief of police for years. When I graduated high school, he seemed to think it natural I follow in his footsteps. He set me up in my own office. A woman named Fiona Wharton mentored me. . .was one of the best investigators in the business. When she passed away only a year ago and my father retired to Florida is when I decided to consult on murder investigations involving the Catholic Church."

"What about your mother?"

Dana fiddled with the tablecloth. "My mother died a long time ago." She did not think it was any of Howard's business finding out her mother had committed suicide in their old Dodge. Dana had graduated from elementary school only a week before. Her mother had not been able to attend the event as, once again, she was in one of her depressive stupors. Her mother did not drive, so Dana was doubly shocked to find her sitting in the driver's seat in their shingled garage. . .the door sealed shut, the engine running. Dana reacted to the scene immediately by taking the key out of the ignition and opening the garage door, but it was too late. The carbon monoxide had done its deadly deed. A few relatives were invited to her wake, and her body was taken to Bay View Cemetery, where she was buried beneath a tall maple tree. The church would have no part in Dana's pleading to have her mother's remains buried in the Catholic cemetery behind their parish church. A Father Chester made it quite clear suicide victims were not graced with eternal reward but, instead, were sent to the fires of hell. To this day, the thought made Dana shudder.

Howard swung his finger back and forth in front of Dana's face. "I lost you there for a minute. Are you okay? Sorry if I pried."

"Oh, my mind just wandered. I'm the one who should be sorry."

Howard sat smiling over the white glowing candles on the table. He moved restlessly in his seat. He cupped his hands under his chin. "No men in your life?"

Dana laughed. "Life wouldn't be that simple." She fumbled with the white linen napkin in her lap.

"So, tell me."

This was the moment Dana wished she could erase from her past, but the church would not agree. The church had declared once married, always married. Dana stalled with her answer hoping the man would move on to a more pleasant conversation. She sipped on her water glass and pretended to watch those around her.

Howard continued to wait, making the idle moments even more uncomfortable for Dana.

Finally, Dana blurted out, "I was married to a man named Nate; separated now."

Howard blushed. "Sorry, maybe I'm prying. Didn't mean to." He straightened the knot on his tie.

"No, no, I'd feel better telling you, actually. My husband was in the police force, and I was an investigator, working on a case that went cold. . .a prostitute, a Myra Pembroke, was found murdered in an abandoned motel." Dana could feel her voice cracking and worked at fighting back tears.

"Listen, you can stop there." Howard reached across the table and took Dana's hand into his own. "My fault. I invited you out to relax. I didn't intend to make you feel uncomfortable."

The kindness in Howard's grip encouraged Dana to continue. "No, I want to explain. As it turned out, my husband and the woman had been seeing each other ever since we married. I had no idea."

Howard squeezed Dana's hand. "Oh, my God. I am so sorry."

"I've moved on, yet sometimes feel as if I carry more baggage than I need to."

"Understood. Ever thought of lightning it a bit?"

Dana thought for a moment. "You mean divorce?"

Howard nodded.

"I'm Catholic. . .er in name only. The church doesn't approve of divorce."

"Well, let's just say I wish it did."

Dana only nodded. For some reason, she couldn't bring herself to smile.

The couple finished dinner and hurried to the picture show.

Chapter Seventeen

Dana arose early, unable to sleep. She wasn't sure if it had anything to do with the conversation she had had last night with Howard Rhodes. She questioned whether she might have told too much, whether she had been too honest too soon. Fiona Wharton had reprimanded her more than once calling her an "open book" better left closed.

On the night table, Dana had left Gary's journal opened to where she had left off reading.

November 1, 1952

What good does solitary confinement do to these kids? They come out after days of being locked in the darkened six-foot by six-foot clinker swearing their asses off, their hands balled in fists, their bodies stiffened from enduring days in the non-heated cell. Last night, I had the pleasure of releasing one—an Arthur Russell. The boy was animal like, kicking, biting. The boy had been sentenced to seventy-two hours for having spit at another inmate. I mean, Brother Calvin gets carried away with his orders, and Brother Donald only nods his god damn head in acceptance!

Dana set Gary's journal aside. How could anyone, even the wardens, work in such a place, she pondered. But from what she learned about Gary, he was not like the others; he had compassion…something frowned upon in the home. And what kind of men were Brother Calvin and Donald to be so heartless, so noncaring?

Just then, Ellie knocked on her door. "Breakfast is ready if you'd care to join me?"

Dana's stomach felt tied in a knot. The sooner she could untie what happened in the walls of the youth home, the happier she would be. Something about the place sent negative energy through her and left her feeling as hopeless as the boys.

Ellie had prepared a breakfast of eggs over easy along with grape marmalade toast.

Dana usually found the woman to be quite chirper. She had to be mourning the recent death of her husband, yet she went out of her way to accommodate Dana's visit. This morning, though, Ellie had a serious face, not the usually jovial one that greeted Dana.

Ellie said she had a confession to make.

The two women sat down at the table, already served portions for each of them on their plates.

"Last night, I couldn't sleep. My mind raced, and I felt so restless. Even a glass of warm milk didn't calm me down any."

"Sorry to hear that, Ellie."

Ellie paused, put her fork down, and said, "There's something I need to tell you."

The way Ellie spoke, Dana could tell she must have given some time and thought to what she was about to say. Dana placed her hand on Ellie's wrist, encouraging her to continue.

"Gary told me about one of the boys in the youth home. Name's Arthur Russell."

"Arthur Russell. . .yes."

"You know him, then?"

"Gary mentioned him in one of his diary entries. I only completed reading it this morning."

Ellie moistened her lips. "Gary said the boy hated the Clifford child."

Dana recalled the two boys outside of the infirmary. Could one of the boys have been Arthur Russell? "Why the antagonism?"

"My husband seemed to think Russell believed Clifford didn't have the typical hardened look of a criminal. Plus, the little guy never swore or caused a fuss with the guards as so many of the other boys did."

Sounded to Dana like the same story she had heard from the boy. "Did the two boys ever have an encounter?"

Ellie's face hardened as if frozen for a moment. She rubbed at her cheeks with both hands before she spoke again. "Oh, yes. Gary had to break the two of them up more than once during free time when the boys were in a group."

"That's terrible. Did Arthur Russell ever pay the price for his actions?"

"Solitary confinement, which only made the boy more aggressive toward Douglas."

Dana nodded. "I read about the clinker."

"During woodshop class, Russell took a wooden mallet, pinned Douglas down, and kept bashing him in the head until he drew blood. That's only one of the stories Gary told me."

"How terrible! Do you think he would have gone so far as to have wanted the boy murdered?"

"Without a doubt. . .given the chance." Ellie cracked her knuckles.

"Ellie, I appreciate you sharing this with me, but is there something else? Are you afraid for some reason. . .you know, you telling me this and all?"

Gnawing on her thumbnail, the color of her face gone ashen, the woman nodded. "Russell told Gary if he ever told anyone about his hatred of the Clifford boy, he not only would kill Gary, but he'd come after me, as well."

Ah, that explained why Ellie had been so closed mouth. Dana thought there was even more Ellie had refused to speak about. "When was the last time a boy escaped St. Gonzaga's? Ever?" The scene from the cemetery flashed before Dana's eyes. So many grave stones, so close together. Were some of the graves a result of the boys who tried to escape?

As if reading Dana's mind, Ellie said, "The few who tried are now in the cemetery out back. The guards are expected to shoot first and ask questions later. That's another unknown secret. There's a lookout tower on the top of the building, where the guards rotate duty. Gary hated when his turn came up. Don't know if he ever would have been able to pull the trigger or not."

"Did the Russell boy ever try. . .to escape?"

Ellie's looked away from Dana. "Not that I know of, but he told Gary he had plans to, and when he did, he would succeed." Tears formed in Ellie's eyes as Dana stood and put her arms around the shaking woman's shoulders. How awful to live with such a threat on her own life.

"I'm so thankful for this information. It gives me another suspect with a motive."

Ellie set her coffee cup down and dabbed at the corners of her mouth with a linen napkin. "Another?"

"I find it's better to have more suspects than less." Dana could tell the woman was eager to learn who the other suspects might be, but that's where her discussion about the case stopped short. Like doctors at a party, the guests want to ask them about their aches and pains. As a private investigator, Dana found the same to be true. Fiona had warned her early on to keep most thoughts to herself and to ask more questions than to reply with answers.

As Dana proceeded to take her dishes to the sink, Ellie asked, "How was the date last night? He's an awfully handsome man. If only I were younger—."

"I appreciated getting my mind off the case for a while, but today's another day. I'm off to the youth home."

Ellie smiled. "Want to let you know how much I appreciate your company, Dana. My life was getting pretty lonely before you came."

Dana returned the smile and headed to the Chevy.

* * *

In the lobby of the boys' home, Dana jotted down some questions for Timothy Laughton. The Gregorian Chant playing softly throughout the rotunda relaxed her and helped her to think. As before, she would run the questions by Brother Donald and have Robinski take her to the boy's cell.

When she completed her list, Walter happened to be walking by. He informed her the entire cellblock was presently in the workshop room. She was welcome to come and see the boys at work. Peering through the barred window in the door, Dana found the room resembled an auto assembly line with each boy being responsible for a minute part of the project. There sat Timothy attaching a medal of Mary after the second Our Father bead. With a pair of finger-nose pliers, he carefully twisted the wire, attached the small icon, and passed the task onto the next boy. The inmates sat in total silence, listening to a recording of the Monks of the Benedictine Abbey chant. The last inmate to receive the completed rosary dropped it onto a cotton square and closed the lid of a blue, velvet box. Walter assembled the gift boxes into a large crate.

Brothers Victor and Calvin, along with the seminarian circled the room, supervising the boys at work. If one did not know otherwise, the tranquil scene resembled a typical school room, where students were being taught a trade.

Robinski took Dana to the side. "What are you up to today?"

Whispering, Dana said, "I'm hoping to ask Timothy a few more questions after I get approval from Brother Donald." She glanced around the room again, where the boys continued progressing with their projects. "You have quite a group working with the boys today. . .Brothers Victor and Calvin and the seminarian."

"Sure do but I've got to give it to Carl. Why, besides the workshop help, he's like a big brother to the kids. Visits with them, helps them write letters, reads to them, plays board games. . . stuff like that. He's a friendly enough guy, not stiff like the brothers around here. He actually takes the time to compliment the boys, gives them a pat on the back now and then."

"Mind if I speak to Carl for a moment? I mean, I've met the man but did not have the chance to speak to him at length."

"Sure thing. I've got more than enough supervision today." Robinski motioned to Carl.

Dana still felt the man bore a striking resemblance to someone she knew, but she couldn't put her finger on it. Was it a singer? she wondered. Elvis? Fabian? As she and the seminarian stepped out of the workshop area, she explained to the man what she hoped to achieve, wanting more answers than questions.

"My prayers go with you," Carl said, "that's a mighty heroic task you have before you." He motioned the sign of the cross in the air. "Any way I can help, please let me know."

A perfect segue for Dana. "Actually, you might be able to do just that."

A bell rang, and all the boys immediately put down their work and stood with their hands clasped behind them. The brothers checked each boy as he left to make sure no tools or supplies were taken out of the workshop.

"Let's head for the lobby, where life is a bit quieter," the seminarian said.

The two found a small sofa upholstered in a maroon velvet. The picture of Pope Pius XII hung above it, framed in ornate gold and silver.

The man put his arm on the back of the sofa. "So, what would you like to know?" The young man seemed totally at ease and gave Dana his undivided attention.

"The inmate, Douglas Clifford—any idea who might have murdered him?"

The man bit down on his lower lip. "Around here? Hard to say. Most have guarded secrets to keep. You've probably picked-up on that."

The words of Fiona Wharton whispered in Dana's ear, "Act as though you know less than you do." Taking Fiona's advice, Dana replied, "Hmm, what might that mean?"

"Take Brother Donald and Brother Victor." Carl glanced over his shoulder as if half expecting the brothers to magically appear in front of them. Carl arched closer to Dana and spoke softly. "Known fact those two are queers, yet everyone chooses to ignore the issue. But who's to say if the Clifford kid knew?"

"You're saying the brothers might have had a motive if the boy had learned of their relationship, saw something he shouldn't have seen, for example?"

"Easily enough. Not too many around here I'd trust. Guess that's why I enjoy dealing with the young prisoners. For the most part, they're honest and open. The skeletons in their closets have already been exposed."

"What about a boy named Arthur Russell? Ever had any encounters with him?"

The seminarian's face hardened, his shoulders stiffened. "That scum? He blew a hole in his brother's head and laughed about how it made him an only child. The kid's got major psychological issues, not saying most don't. But this kid is one you don't want to turn your back on."

Dana, at first, was surprised to hear the young man of the cloth refer to the boy in such a derogatory way, but then, she reminded herself the seminarian had been around these young criminals for some time, and it would be difficult not to become a bit jaded. Dana recalled the threat the boy had made to Gary. "Do you think Arthur Russell could be a suspect, as well, in the murder of the Clifford boy?"

"I'd say so. He hated the kid, picked on him any chance he got. Brother Donald insisted Russell be put in solitary but let me tell you something. The kid came out with his fists slugging, drool running down his chin. Solitary's not the answer."

Dana's next question got interrupted with the blaring sound of a buzzer overhead, sounding much like the school fire drills she remembered as a child. The horn blew three sharp sounds, paused, and then two more shrill screams.

Everyone passing by in the rotunda froze in their spots, not a soul moving. The subtle breathing of those present was the only sound. Even the Gregorian Chanting had ceased.

Dana edged close to the end of the sofa. "The alarm. . .what's going on? What does it mean?"

Carl waited until the alarm subsided. The people in the lobby resumed their routine. "That was the sound coming from G Wing where the most hardened of the criminals are…probably someone snuck out with a cutting implement. Not the first time. It's actually pretty common around here. The boys will do whatever necessary if they've got a bug up their butt." The man immediately apologized for his use of slang in front of Dana. "It's easy to pick-up the lingo around here," he said, and smiled.

"Do you think they're planning for a fight, maybe an uprising?"

"More than likely, someone is preparing a stockpile."

The comment startled Dana.

"The closest thing ever happened to an uprising was about five years ago. A group of about six or eight boys fully equipped with workshop tools managed to take down one of the guards, grab his keys, and snuck out the back door."

"I'm sure that landed them in solitary confinement."

"Hardly. The guard in the tower saw it all, aimed his rifle, and within seconds, all of the kids lie dead on the sidewalk."

Dana felt her jaw drop. "Oh, my gosh! How horrible. The cemetery out back—."

"Yep. It accounts for the number of gravesites. The majority of those boys didn't die from natural causes." The seminarian looked as if he were about to say more but took one long look at Dana and decided otherwise.

"And the guard?"

"Was awarded some special honorary pin for the amount of kids he gunned down."

Dana's stretched out fingers covered the lower part of her face.

"The possibility of escape around here is plausible, you know. These guys may be cold-blooded murderers, but several of them have a higher IQ than average."

Ellie immediately came to Dana's mind. If Arthur Russell were to escape, his plan would be to come after her more than likely. Dana tried to quiet her worries. After the ruckus she had witnessed, she decided to postpone meeting with Timothy today.

* * *

Dana had no sooner walked in when Ellie told her the phone was for her.

"Hello, Dana Greer here."

"Walter Robinski. I take it you were still at the home when the alarm went off?"

Dana sensed fear in Robinski's question. "Why, yes, I was speaking to Carl Fenton in the rotunda."

"Best you know what happened back in cell block."

Dana could hear the anxiety in her quickened breathing. She prayed it wasn't as dreadful as the seminarian's story. "Please, go ahead."

"Kid by the name of Arthur Russell somehow managed to sneak a pair of wire clippers out of the craft room."

"I've been hearing quite a bit about this boy of late."

"He went after Timothy Laughton. This Russell kid hates him. Thinks Timothy's a goody two shoes."

Dana quickly put together two and two together. "So, you're saying if Arthur saw me questioning Timothy about Douglas, he might want to injure him?"

"Or, better yet kill him," Robinski said. "That Russell kid won't stand for a snitch."

"Doesn't sound like that's a very strong motive for murder."

"Maybe not, but these kids aren't necessarily into modus operandis. They're into revenge for whatever reason, no matter how slight."

"Or—."

"What were you going to say?"

"Or, more importantly, could it be Arthur Russell is trying to keep Timothy from telling me what he knows?"

"Arthur Russell murdering Douglas Clifford? Now, that would be a good motive. Russell despised Douglas."

* * *

Arthur sat in his solitary confinement cell, spinning a loose button on his shirt. He was used to these simplistic activities that kept him sane while waiting to be excused from his punishment. "Gotta find a way. Gotta find a way," he kept repeating as a mantra. There were none before him who found a successful way to escape the home, but he planned to be the first. Others had met their untimely deaths when the tower guard spotted them and riddled them with bullets. There had to be a way to escape without notice of the guard. From what Arthur had overhead from other inmates, the place had a basement. Once he had gotten a library book from Carl Fenton about underground passages in France and Italy. Apparently, they were quite common during religious persecutions of the Christians. He thought maybe there was an underground tunnel somewhere. The elementary school he attended before he murdered his brother had a passageway that led from the school to the nun's convent. There had to be a way out of this place, he thought. Perhaps the seminarian might find him a book about the history of the home. He could make up a lame excuse as to why he was interested in the subject. If lucky, he might find a blueprint of the building during its construction phase. Arthur rubbed his hands together. Maybe being in silence, in a dark confined spot, wasn't so bad after all. It helped him to think more clearly, to plan, and to scheme.

Chapter Eighteen

The next morning when Dana arose, the temperature was already in the high nineties, typical she supposed for this time of year. The air was still, and even though she had left her window open during the night, even the curtain refused to move. Out her window, it looked like a still life painting, a blazing sun overhead. The recent storm had not done much for the previous six years of drought.

She couldn't help thinking besides Robinski and possibly the seminarian, she had no idea how she was going to get to the bottom of the case. Then, her eyes glanced over at Gary's journal, resting atop her desk. So far, the only things she learned from it were Gary and Brother Calvin were at odds over Douglas Clifford. Gary had been warned to stay away from the child or risk the loss of his job. In addition, Brothers Donald and Victor were secretly lovers. Neither of these issues pointed to who the murderer might have been. She opened the small, burgundy book and read from an entry.

November 30, 1952

> *I always had a funny feeling about Shirley Mitford ever since she arrived here. She never has much to say to me at board meetings, but she seems to get along with the seminarian, seen chatting with him on more than one occasion. He's a likeable enough guy. Never heard him say a bad word about anyone. Shirley on the other hand...she's got two faces. She treats all of the guards as if we were a step beneath janitors or garbage pickers, even though, the place couldn't*

run without us guys. Yet, she seems devoted to the brothers, especially, Brother Calvin. I don't know what it is about those two, but they sure appear awfully chummy. Last week, I saw Shirley get into Brother Calvin's truck. I asked Robinski if he noticed anything going on between those two. He said he'd seen more than he cared to admit. I was about to ask what that meant, when I was called into Brother Donald's office. Another demerit, I guess. Arthur Russell said I hit him in the back with my baton while he was involved in a fist fight with one of the boys. I've seen that kid at work before. He's got a swing and a kick that can break bones. He don't need no weapon. I denied touching the kid. Why shouldn't I? To admit it would mean my job. Brother Donald wrote me up again.

Dana put the diary down. While lost in her thoughts, she didn't hear Ellie knock on the door.

"Dana," Ellie called. "Breakfast is ready if you care to join me."

Dana sat down with Ellie. Banana pancakes saturated with butter and maple syrup were the morning meal. "You sure have me spoiled, Ellie. I'm not used to eating this well when I'm on my own."

"My mother used to say, 'Start your day off right with a decent meal, and your day is bound to go better.'"

"Don't know about that. The food's been plenty good, but my days. . .well, let's just say, they could go better."

"Oh, honey, I knew it before you arrived when Sergeant McKnight asked if I'd open my place to you and show you some Southern hospitality."

"What's that?"

"Punkerton isn't a welcoming place, and the prison isn't much better. Everyone prefers to look the other way and to keep their mouths shut. It's been this way ever since Gary and I moved here. Think that's why Gary had the journal. He plain had to unload what was on his mind."

"Makes sense." Dana continued to eat her pancakes, picking up a chunk of banana with her fork.

"The notes. . .the ones Gary took. . .have they been of much help so far?"

Dana took a sip of coffee. "Yes. Your husband sure saw enough."

"How so if I might ask?" Ellie got up and poured herself and Dana another cup of coffee.

"Shirley Mitford. . .he wrote about her."

Ellie added some Ovaltine to her coffee. "Such as?"

"Your husband was under the impression she and one of the brothers might be involved?"

"Romantically?" She spun her spoon around in her cup.

"Implied but not stated, I guess, is the best way of saying it."

"I suppose that's why Gary preferred to keep things from me. Adultery isn't exactly something I care to discuss. I'm under the impression the Gonzaga Home is nothing more than a cesspool of Satan's doings."

"Wish I knew more about that woman. . .Shirley."

"All I know is she moved here from somewhere in the West. She never mentioned a husband or a family for that matter."

If Shirley Mitford and Brother Calvin were involved in an affair, it might offer another plausible reason for the murder of Douglas Clifford. What if Douglas saw something and planned to tell? Brother Calvin already had a deep-seated dislike of the boy for some reason and add to the fact the boy might squeal, the brother would have a good motive for murder. Dana decided it best she keep these thoughts to herself until she knew more. No sense making accusations without the necessary evidence.

* * *

Without making her plans known, Dana got in the Chevy and headed to Shirley's place, hoping to catch Shirley and Brother Calvin in the act. She parked her truck about a quarter mile from the Airstream. As she neared, she saw the trailer glowing in the light of the sun. Closer, a dog barked in the distance, growling nonstop as if she had put foot on the animal's property. Dana turned her head at the sound of a slight rustling. What she had at first thought was a dog turned out to be a large, golden coyote camouflaged with its surroundings. In its jaws, the carnivore carried a bleeding, headless robin. Dana turned away in disgust. She snuck over to the side of the trailer, not noticing a metal can that she tripped over. The container hit the side of the trailer, clanking loudly. Dana peeked around front.

The hinge creaked, the door opened a bit, and bare toes held the door in place. "Who's out there?" a male voice yelled out. Dana held her breath, hoping he would not investigate the sound. After a minute, the door slammed shut.

She crept around to the back of the trailer. That's when she noticed, hidden from view, the bumper of an old beat-up green, Ford truck. More than likely, the vehicle belonged to Brother Calvin. Gary Banks spoke the truth. Brother Calvin was having an affair with Shirley. Dana pushed to know more. She tiptoed over to the vehicle. Peeking inside, she saw the upholstered seats stained and torn. An opened box of religious metals lay on the floor of the passenger side, several scattered on the grey carpeting. She shielded her eyes against the glass of the back seat and confirmed what she had seen before. Neatly folded, lay the garb of the KKK. She pulled back suddenly, frightened at her findings. Brother Calvin, too. . .a part of the Klan. While making her way back to the side of the AirStream, she listened for a moment by a side window left open a slight crack.

"Sugar plum, I told you not to worry about what anyone thinks. Nobody's got a right to barge into your life. What you and me do in our private time is none of anyone's damn business."

"What about that hot-shot detective? What if she goes to Donald, tells him her suspicions? Christ, it could mean your position at the home."

Dana could hear some body movements as if the two were edging closer to one another.

"You really think Don would be crazy enough to believe the broad? No way! He knows what a devout man I am."

Shirley snickered. "Devout, my ass."

Dana could hear the two kissing.

"On the other hand, though, you've sure got one cute, little ass," Shirley said.

Dana could hear the springs on the mattress squeak along with some low, drawn out moans. She had confirmed enough for one day.

Chapter Nineteen

Dana had trouble sleeping. She hated it when her racing thoughts prevented her from getting a good night's rest. She turned on the light on her night table and opened the burgundy cover of Gary's journal.

December 6, 1952

Spoke with Timothy Laughton today. Told me how scared he is for his own life. That's saying quite a bit as the boy is tall and lanky and towers over many of the inmates here. The boy was on his way to mandatory night lavatory when I pulled him aside and took him into a dark hallway. The kid started bawling, telling me how he never meant to stab that kid in his school. Said he loved the Lord so much. Claimed he snapped when the boy called him a "Jesus freak." Timothy told me he goes on his knees every night in his cell, hoping and praying God will forgive him. I tried to console the kid as best I could and was about to ask him what he thought about Arthur Russell's behavior toward him when Brother Calvin spotted us in the empty corridor. He yanked Timothy by the back of his head and threw him onto the floor. A small tuft of blond hair lay next to the boy. "Don't let me ever find you fraternizing with any of the guards," he said. I tried to intervene and told him it was my fault, not Timothy's. He spat at me, pinned me against the wall, and said, "If I ever find you playing favorites with any of the inmates here, I'll see to it Doctor Hansen looks after you."

Hmm, Dana thought. There's that name again. . .Doctor Hansen. Dana imagined the man, Brother Calvin, in a hooded garment, his face a mere blacked out skeleton, a sharp sickle in his hands. She opened her notebook and began to draw. In the center, she drew a circle with Douglas Clifford's name in it. Like spokes on a bicycle wheel, she drew lines leading from the center to other circles. In one, she put the name Arthur Russell; in another, she put Doctor Hansen; in a third, she wrote Brother Donald/Brother Victor; in a sixth, she scribbled Shirley Mitford/Brother Calvin.

She stopped to read what she had written so far. She remembered when she had first arrived, she learned Brother Calvin had a morbid dislike for the Clifford child. Why she did not know, but she added another circle with his name alone. She tapped her pencil on her desk. Who else might want the boy killed? Who else would have a motive? She remembered while she was trying to solve the Bernadette Godfrey case on Cape Peril, it was helpful to go into the sergeant's office most mornings and run her ideas past him. Trying to do the same with Sergeant McKnight made no sense. For one thing, he had made it quite clear neither he nor the people of Punkerton cared to get involved in the case, and for another thing, he didn't seem like the sharpest tool in the shed. His role as sergeant appeared to be more of a family lineage thing than it did finding someone qualified for the position. Dana didn't know how well McKnight's grandfather or father did in the same role, but she sure was not impressed with Sam's performance. Dana made up her mind she would make up her erroneous questions to run past Brother Donald for his approval and then would arrange to have Robinski bring Timothy Laughton to meet her somewhere other than in his cell.

* * *

When Dana entered the chapel in the youth home, Robinski was already waiting there with Timothy. His left arm was bandaged from the wrist to the elbow, his encounter with Arthur Russell, she assumed. Timothy grimaced in pain.

"Figured this might be the safest place for you two to meet. And, you can forget Brother Donald's approval. Let's just say, we'll keep this confidential as long as no one sees us here."

Timothy sat in the first pew in the shadow of a large St. Michael the Archangel statue, much like the one she had found in the cemetery. Something about the sculpture comforted Dana. The angel spoke out about doing battle against evil. In some strange way, that was exactly what Dana believed she was doing ever since she had come to the boys' home.

"What better situation to be in," Dana said, but not before scouring the chapel for any unwanted visitors. The place appeared empty, not a soul around.

Robinski had given the boy a pad of paper and a pencil.

Dana asked, "Did Arthur Russell do this to your arm?"

The boy wrote,

Yeah.

Dana tried to keep her emotions from showing, blinking away the tears forming in the corner of her eyes. Although the boy had every reason to be in prison for what he had done to his fellow classmate, she still harbored sympathy for Timothy. He had paid his price, ten times over, for his sin, Dana thought. She hoped whoever murdered Douglas Clifford was not about to go after the Laughton boy next. "But, why would Arthur Russell do this to you?"

Timothy responded with,

He thinks I liked Douglas because he was so little and looked so innocent. Think he was just trying to get back at me.

Dana wondered if Arthur Russell might have another motive. If Timothy and Stevie were homosexuals, might the Russell kid think, perhaps, the same might be true of Timothy and Douglas? Dana asked her next question, "Do you think Arthur Russell might have had something to do with Douglas Clifford's death?"

The boy scribbled,

Don't know.

It was not the answer Dana had hoped for, yet on the other hand, she had to keep herself from jumping to conclusions. "You mentioned last time we met Brother Calvin had been mean to Douglas in the shower room, the night the boy was killed. Why do you think Brother Calvin singled out Douglas and was so abusive to him?"

Timothy did not write. He stared into the distance for a few moments. Then, his pencil skidded across the pad.

I heard Brother Calvin was beaten by his father. He ran away and entered the order.

Dana asked, "Interesting. Anything else you know about the man?"

The lead point pressed intently on the page as Timothy proceeded to answer.

Heard he wanted to become a priest, but he was not accepted. Maybe, why he became a brother, instead. I don't know.

Dana wondered if it might have had something to do with his abusive childhood and his anger management issues as an adult. As if reading Dana's mind, the boy wrote,

Maybe, Douglas reminded Brother Calvin of himself when he was a kid. I dunno.

Dana was impressed with the boy's assessment of the brother. Quite possibly never having had a child of his own, he may well have seen himself in Douglas. Dana continued with her questioning. "Was Brother Calvin mean to any of the other inmates besides Douglas?" She remembered what she had read in Gary's diary about Brother Calvin yanking Timothy by the hair and throwing him to the floor.

The boy began to write; then, he stopped and shook his head. By the look on Timothy's strained face, it was evident he chose not to dwell on his own suffering.

Before Dana asked her next question, she once again looked about the chapel, making sure no one had entered. If Brother Donald were to find out she was questioning Timothy in the chapel and without his approval, who knew what might be the consequences? In a whispered voice, she asked, "Do you think Doctor Hansen might have had something to do with the boy's murder?"

Timothy's eyes narrowed. He sucked in his upper lip and pressed his pencil to the paper.

Not unless Brother Calvin told him to do so.

Dana could tell the boy wanted to write more, so she paused and waited.

The doctor is a frickin' coward!

Timothy threw himself onto the kneeler and sobbed into the cold wood of the pew.

Dana put her arm around the boy. "Thank you, you have been a big help."

As Robinski was about to escort the boy back to his cell, Timothy stopped the man and motioned that he wanted to write something else.

You told me you'd come back for me. Help me!
Find a way to get me out of here!

Dana reread the boy's note. She reached out and hugged the boy. "I'll try. I really will," Dana said. "I won't forget you!" She had no idea how she would be able to accomplish such a task, but she knew she would do all she could. "I do have one more question for you, Walter, before you leave. By chance, do you happen to know where Brother Calvin went to the seminary?"

"By chance, I do."

Dana lowered her chin with a slight nod, encouraging Robinski to go on.

"Assisi on the Hill. . .it's in Lubbock. There's a young guy from St. Rita's going there now. Name's Luke O'Brien. I could ask him to give you a call."

* * *

That night Dana went to her room right after dinner. She began to read *Lift Up Your Heart* by Bishop Fulton J. Sheen. Sometimes spiritual readings relaxed her and restored her outlook on life. A private detective's job challenged her curiosity and tenacity, but it also confronted the darkness in humankind. No matter the means or the motives, murderers possessed a quotient of evil that had the capacity to rip at the soul of everyone involved.

Ellie cut short Chapter Six. "Telephone call from someone named O'Brien."

Dana glanced at the alarm clock on the table next to her bed. Eight-ten. Surprised the man from the Assisi Seminary would call her back that quickly, she hurried to the phone.

"Miss Greer?"

"Speaking."

"I had a message from Walter Robinski, asking me to contact you."

Dana explained she was an investigator attempting to solve the murder of a young boy from the St. Gonzaga Home for Troubled Youth. "I'm interested in learning some more about Brother Calvin. Mr. Robinski tells me the brother attended the seminary." Dana immediately realized the young man might assume she considered Brother Calvin to be a suspect and added, "Of course, he has no motive, you understand."

Luke O'Brien laughed. "Listen, my uncle is a private detective in Colorado, and I totally understand the whole thing about being innocent until proven guilty. Gotta start somewhere."

Dana sighed with relief. "So, how do you know the brother?"

"He was completing his final vows when I entered Assisi. I try not to judge anyone, but there was something about the guy that struck me as odd."

"In what way?"

"To be a brother means to be part of a community. Brother Calvin kept to himself, didn't engage others, didn't try to socialize. He spent endless hours in his cell."

"Anything else that stuck out to you?"

"The man liked everything just so. . .his way. He insisted to the head chaplain that we always leave the ribbon of our songbooks in place for the hymn we were to sing the following morning. To be sure everybody did, he'd wait until everyone left the chapel and then would go through each hymnal. Things like that."

"Did you ever see an angry side to the man?"

"Sure enough."

"Could you give me an example?" Dana reached for a paper napkin on the counter. She found a ballpoint pen and jotted down Brother Luke's responses.

"One night, we were completing our Prayers of the Hour. Somehow, I stumbled on the words in one of the lines. Brother Calvin turned, tightening his fingers around the beads of his rosary, and glared at me. As we were leaving chapel, he pulled me over by the sleeve of my habit. Said if I ever messed up again, he would see to it I never took my temporary vows."

"I see."

"He had no tolerance for any irritations, either. Someone coughing during Mass, a sneeze at the wrong time, a ruffle of paper from the missal. . .I mean, the man couldn't handle it."

Dana thanked the man for his input. She looked at the cat clock on the kitchen wall. The small hands on its belly were pointed to the eight and the three. Not too late to call Robinski.

"Walter Robinski, here."

"Got a call from Brother Luke O'Brien."

"Helpful, I hope."

'Quite," Dana said. "I do have one question for you, though."

"Sure."

"Did Douglas Clifford have any idiosyncrasies. . .I mean like a tic, a twitch in his eye—."

"The kid was a stutterer, a pretty bad one—."

Before Robinski could say anymore, Dana put the receiver back on the hook.

Chapter Twenty

Shirley couldn't believe it. Ever since she and Calvin had been involved in their secret affair, life had been bliss. Every time he showed up at the trailer, the two made love, sometimes more than once. Shirley didn't mind the man had a high libido. Life behind the prison walls, she speculated, would make any man hungry for sexual pleasures.

But tonight, she saw a different side of Calvin, one she had never seen before. He barged in the door, demanding she make him a bowl of vegetable soup. When Shirley opened the cupboard, the only broth she could see were cans of chicken noodle, tomato, and mushroom.

"Sorry, Cal. I've got everything but vegetable. How about some chicken noodle?"

Calvin pushed her aside. "Let me look." He grabbed two and three cans at a time, banging them onto the counter. "No wonder you can't find anything. This cabinet's a mess." He proceeded to throw out a box of pancake mix, some crackers, a bottle of barbecue sauce, and some maple syrup. "How long have you had these around? Bet they're stale as hell."

Shirley stood with her hands on her hips. "What are you doing?"

"Here you go," he said, and like pitching a baseball, threw her a can of vegetable soup. "If you put all of the soup cans together in the same place, this wouldn't be a problem."

"So, who are you...Betty Furness to tell me how to organize a kitchen?" She proceeded to warm the soup on the stove while he meticulously put things back in the cabinet, arranging each item by size, the smallest in the front, the tallest in the back.

He didn't bother to say much over dinner but complained every time Shirley's spoon clanked against her glass bowl. The slurping of her swallowing the hot soup annoyed him. When she went to butter a cracker, he told her the scratching noise bothered him.

"My, my, we sure are touchy tonight. I've not seen you act like this before. What gives?"

"Perhaps not, but I like things just so. Better you understand that now. It's who I am."

Shirley cleaned up the table after the meal. The wind picked up velocity and the AirStream began to shake, more like tossing from side to side.

"What the hell, are we in a tin can? For Christ's sake it feels like this piece of shit is going to flip over. Don't know why you prefer to live in this cheap excuse for a home."

Shirley tried to tell him about the AirStream when he rudely interrupted, "You should have got a Vagabond. Then, you'd be living in style."

"Listen, Cal, I don't know what's going on with you tonight, but if you don't like the way I live, I suggest you take your ass out of here."

Without giving it a thought, Calvin slammed the door behind him.

Shirley's heart throbbed. It was one thing if she had the upper hand and told others what she thought but quite another for someone to intimidate her and to tell her how to live her life.

Chapter Twenty-One

Before Ellie arose, Dana headed for the Bean Grind Coffee Shop. Today was the first time her notes began to make some sense. Everything she learned about Brother Calvin last night provided him with a motive for killing Douglas Clifford or, at least, instructing someone else to do so for him. Doctor Hansen was the next potential suspect on her list.

Dana found a table by the window and ordered a cinnamon roll with cream cheese icing and a black coffee. She didn't normally like to feast on sweets, but ever since sharing in Ellie's homemade desserts, she began to develop a taste. While she waited for service, she focused on the passersby on the sidewalk outside of the shop. Most were dressed in the apparel of laborers, probably farm hands, with jean coveralls and paisley handkerchiefs wrapped around their necks. She noticed a Negro man come around the corner. Two white men took one look and crossed over to the other side of the street. Dana wondered if the races would ever tolerate each other here in the South. The black man tipped the wide brim of his straw hat at them and continued down the walk, whistling to himself. All normal behavior in a town such as Punkerton, Dana thought.

The waitress set Dana's order down and asked, "Will anyone be joining you this morning?"

Dana was about to say, "No," when the front door opened and despite the temperature already in the high nineties with heavy humidity, a man in a blue serge suit stepped in and asked for a table. It was Howard Rhodes, of all people. Dana motioned for him to join her.

He shielded his eyes with one hand, and noticing Dana, came toward her.

"Surprise, surprise," he said.

"In Punkerton, no less," Dana added.

"Checking in with a client from St. Rita's, so I was just down the road a few miles. What brings you out so early this morning?"

Dana explained her interest in learning more about Doctor Hansen.

"Might want to check with the sergeant, but I heard he still keeps a small practice in town. . .only works at the home a couple times a week," Howard said.

Dana sipped on her coffee and set the cup down. "I've been there already. What I mean is I did speak with the doctor at the infirmary, but I'm interested in learning more about him."

Howard shook his head. "Library should be able to help."

"Where I'm headed after here."

The waitress came to the table. "Nice company," she said, looking first at Howard, raising her eyebrows, and then looking at Dana. "Care for anything?" The woman in the short pink and white uniform rested her elbow on the table with her bottom up in the air. The waitress had no qualms about flirting with the man, but Howard did not seem to pick up on her cues.

"Coffee, please," he said.

The waitress walked off with a, "Humph."

Howard tapped his fingers on the blue Formica table. "Might want to check the guy's standing with the AMA, the medical licensing office in Texas, even the medical school he graduated from."

A thought breezed through Dana's mind that she might want Howard to join her at the library, but she quickly rejected the idea. Like the waitress, Dana found the man to be highly attractive with his thick brown hair and five o'clock shadow. Plus, she had to admit, it was a pleasure being able to talk to one of a few people she had met so far who were interested in helping her get to the bottom of the Douglas Clifford case.

As if reading Dana's mind, Howard said, "If you'll give me an hour, I could meet you back at the library and help you do some research."

Although Dana's first impulse was to say, "Sure," she refrained. She reminded herself, she had come to Punkerton to solve a murder, not to find romance.

* * *

There was something about the smell of books Dana liked. Add to that, the feel of paper filled with words, and Dana found herself at home in Edgar Allen Poe library.

A middle-aged woman with cat-eye glasses, trimmed with rhinestones, asked if she might help Dana find anything in particular. The librarian wore a red-checkered scarf to hold her salt and pepper hair behind her ears. She wore a rubber fingertip on her left thumb. Her body motions spoke of efficiency.

Dana squinted at the woman's nametag pinned to her white sweater: Louise Canfield. Where had she heard the name before? Then, she remembered. Could it be the woman was related to Greta Canfield, the journalist who supposedly committed suicide shortly after investigating Gary Banks' death? In a small town like Punkerton, maybe the odds were not that unlikely. "Don't mean to pry, but might you be related to the former Greta Canfield?"

The woman removed her glasses and ran her hand alongside her nose as if brushing off a piece of lint from her cheek. She breathed in heavily. "Greta was my daughter. . .my only child."

"Sorry for your loss."

"Here, have a seat. So, you've heard." Louise dabbed at her eyes. "Greta worked at the 'Punkerton Press.' She always was the curious type, wanting to get to the bottom of things. You know, find the truth." She stared at the pearl ring on her finger. "Then, again, isn't that what good journalists do?"

"I totally understand."

The librarian put her glasses back on and looked Dana directly in the eyes. "Let me tell you. Greta had her hunches, her beliefs, and that's what killed her." The woman blinked several times to stop the tears collecting in the corner of her eyes.

"Are you saying no one wanted to listen to her?"

The woman nodded. "People around here are afraid of the facts. Instead, they live in silent betrayal of what they suspect could be the truth."

"Sounds as if you're in agreement with your daughter that Gary Banks did not die of a heart attack as the brothers would have us believe." Dana recalled the words of Walter Robinski. He had told her the doctor had prepared some poisonous cocktail. "Banks thought he was drinking coffee. Stopped his heart in a beat. Story had it Banks died of a cardiac arrest on the job. Nothing further from the truth." When Louise confirmed exactly what Robinski had said, Dana used it as a perfect segue to her next thought. . .the reason she had come to the library in the first place. "I'm here to gather some research on Doctor Hansen, to find out exactly who this man is. Know where I might start?"

"Follow me," was all the woman said, as she made her way to the back of the library, her wide hips waddling from side to side. "The past issues of newspapers are right over here." She pointed to long rolls. "It's all public records, you know."

The first thought to cross Dana's mind was that Punkerton certainly didn't make much news. The rolls were thin like sheets on a clothesline.

Louise slid the pages off the metal hinges with much dexterity as if she had done this many times. "Here, September 1947. Read this headline."

Doctor Fritz Hansen Brought Before the AMA

"You'll see the man has a record of defending his position before the American Medical Association, stemming back at least six years. The news was splattered all across Texas."

Dana skimmed the paper:

The American Medical Association questions Dr. Fritz Hansen about his involvement with a surgery, which took place on August 29, 1946, in which a forty-nine-year-old woman convulsed on the operating table and was unable to be resuscitated. From the pathologist's autopsy report, the hospital learned the patient died of asphyxiation during a routine tonsillectomy, having swallowed gauze pads and surgical sponges.

Dana read to the bottom of the article:

It was determined by the Texas Board of the AMA that Dr. Fritz Hansen have his surgical privileges permanently removed.

"This is unbelieveable," Dana said, "and he's still got a practice?"

"Look here. It gets even worse." The librarian pointed to another issue of the "Punkerton Press."

On December 3, 1947, the American Medical Association revoked Dr. Fritz Hansen's medical license to practice medicine in the State of Texas. Not only did he not abide by the Board's earlier decision to refrain from all surgical procedures but also attempted to abort two fetuses, both at a gestational age of twenty-one weeks.

Two weeks after the Board's decision to revoke Doctor Hansen's medical license, the President of the Texas AMA had a bomb threat made against his premises. A week afterward, the KKK planted a burning cross in the front of Dr. Leonard Tomatelli's residence. On the night of

December 23, 1947, Dr. Tomatelli's sixteen-year old daughter's body was found in a wooded area about twelve miles outside of Punkerton. Although the doctor was not arrested for any of the above incidents, anonymous sources claim the KKK played a part in both.

Was this a man who would stop at nothing to seek vengeance? Dana pondered. Interesting, she thought, that he would still have his own part-time practice. Then, again, it was in Punkerton, and who would care enough to get involved in the politics of that mess? It might explain why the man was more than willing to oblige Brother Calvin, no matter his demand. If it meant it gave him job security, Dana questioned to what lengths the doctor would go.

"Isn't this quite something to grasp?" Louise asked. "It goes even further." The woman began to fling her hands in the air.

Dana couldn't believe what she was hearing.

"Brother Calvin and the doctor's relationship goes way back. They both went to Punkerton High at the same time."

Dana bit down on her thumbnail. "Really, is that so?"

Louise Canfield used every facial muscle to convey her news. "Calvin, from what I hear, had a difficult time fitting in. Seemed to be the one man out. Kinda an odd duck, if you know what I mean."

Fiona had taught Dana to, "Always push for more. There's another drop in the driest of cows," she'd say. Dana had heard plenty about Brother Calvin's "odd duckness" from Luke O'Brien, all about his excessive compulsiveness and his intolerances, but might Louise know more?

"If someone in the class coughed too much, he'd excuse himself and leave the room. If a student rattled a piece of loose leaf too loudly, he was known to grab the paper out of the kid's hands. If the teacher's chalk scratched on the blackboard, he'd walk out. The school counselor advised his parents to take him to a psychologist, but of course, his mother didn't want anything like that on his school record."

"What about Calvin's father?"

"Well known around Punkerton; the guy was a drunk. Used to beat the boy pretty badly, too, but that was supposed to be a secret in the community."

The picture sounded almost identical to what Luke O'Brien had told her. "This has been most helpful, Louise. I can't thank you enough."

"Oh, but you can," the woman said in a hopeful voice. "Make sure the truth becomes known. . .what goes on behind those walls. Then, Greta won't have died in vain."

Chapter Twenty-Two

This was the first day since arriving in Punkerton Dana felt like singing "Oh What a Beautiful Morning." Seemingly, things were finally starting to go her way.

Even Ellie had brought out the fine China from her hutch. "Let's celebrate this morning and bring out the good stuff." She reached to the third shelf and brought down two crystal glasses covered in a light coat of dust. "You seem to be in a happy mood."

"I agree. There might just be cause for celebrating." Almost instantly, Dana regretted speaking.

Ellie set the stack of dishes down on the table. "Don't tell me, honey. You found the murderer?"

"Nothing like that, but I sure am learning a lot."

"Praise be Jesus, then. It sure enough is about time. You've got the patience of a saint."

Dana smiled. "That's what it takes to do this job."

"Ever get a case where you're at your wit's end. . .can't solve it, I mean?" Ellie asked, while she positioned the white cups and bowls with finely painted pansies on the blue tablecloth.

The reason Dana chose to get away from Bay View revolved around such a case. Shivers covered Dana's arms. Did she dare get into this with Ellie?

But the woman pushed. "Cold cases. . .that's what they're called."

"Once, the truth never came out. There was a lot of suspicion, but suspicion is not evidence, so the case went cold."

"Knowing you, honey, I bet you were fit to be tied."

"I came to terms with it eventually." Dana hoped Ellie's prying would stop there. The last thing she cared to discuss was how she considered her husband to be a suspect in the Myra Pembroke case.

"Well, good for you, Dana. A pretty thing like you don't need to be worrying her head over senseless matters."

"Agreed," was all Dana said.

The two of them enjoyed their eggs over easy and sipped on the last of their coffee.

"Here, let me help clean-up. Then, I've got some work to do. Dana couldn't wait to make herself some notes about the case and see how the threads were tying together."

Ellie refused her help and insisted Dana go about her business.

Dana sat at the desk in her room and made a list of all the reasons why Brother Calvin might be involved in the murder of Douglas Clifford.

- *Had trouble getting along with Gary Banks because the man favored the child*
- *Wants everything his way or else*
- *Has numerous intolerances*
- *Has issues with handling his anger*
- *Came from an abusive father*
- *Had a past of being ostracized and seen as different*

Dana set her pencil down for a moment. She remembered seeing the white sheets in Calvin's Ford truck. As difficult and as incredulous as it seemed, she wondered whether he might be a part of the secret Klan. If true, it would explain why he and the doctor could be in cahoots.

Dana began to ponder. Without a doubt, Brother Calvin had reason to do away with the boy. Maybe he saw too much of himself in the child. There were those who thought of Douglas as too innocent to have committed a grisly act of murder and, therefore, despised him for it. A background of abuse might justify the actions he carried out against Douglas. Add to the fact the child was a known stutterer, and it could easily have put the brother's anger on overload.

Next, Dana began a list of reasons why Doctor Hansen might be involved in the murder of the boy.

- *Lost his medical license*
- *Performed illegal procedures, such as abortions*
- *Went to school with Brother Calvin*
- *Had some connection with the KKK based upon the incident with the Texas AMA President*

With a record such as this, it was no wonder the doctor had a limited private practice of his own. Even that was quite surprising. . .unless his possible connection with the KKK gave him some leverage. Not only did he lose his license to practice medicine, but he was willing to carry out criminal acts. The fact he knew Brother Calvin from high school days might explain why the brother overlooked the man's medical background and saw fit to have him work in the clinic in the youth home.

Dana let her mind wander. And then there's Arthur Russell. What about Brothers Donald and Victor who had motives, as well? Dana's list of possible suspects along with their motives made sense, but she still needed to get her hands on the private records of Douglas Clifford. Her only hope for doing so was Robinski, yet the last thing she wanted was to put his future in jeopardy. He had nine children and a wife to support. Somehow someone needed to sneak into Brother Donald's office and remove the boy's files. The only time she could be guaranteed the brother would not be there would be when he was attending a board meeting. Robinski was obliged to attend the meetings, as well, so that idea did not sound possible. She fixated on the dilemma running it over and over in her mind. There had to be a way she could get Brother Donald away from his desk. Then, she had an epiphany. What if he was forced to attend to a false alarm? Dana remembered the seminarian explaining last week's distress call. Three buzzes, a pause, then two more ear-piercing screeches indicated a boy from G Wing had managed to remove something from the workshop. If Robinski could set an alarm that alerted only the administrative wing, she might have enough time to get into Brother Donald's office and to remove the files before anyone knew.

* * *

Without wasting any time, Dana headed to the youth home to find Robinski. Brother Victor met her at the door and directed her to the workshop, where the boys from G Wing were once again working on their religious icons. Arthur Russell chipped away at a wooden stick, forming it into the likeness of Mary. His sculpting abilities amazed her as his small penknife whittled and chiseled, leaving a small pile of sawdust on the table. His strict attention to his work gave the impression of a professional sculptor, not a boy behind bars for a felony. Timothy continued assembling the last of the rosary beads as he had done before. Carl Fenton moved between the tables as he patted some of the boys on the shoulder. He mouthed the words, "Good work." Robinski sat at the front of the room, eyeing the boys with the glare of a hawk. Dana stood outside the door, hoping to get Robinski's attention through the small barred glass window. Carl Fenton took notice and motioned to Robinski. With one hand on the doorknob, Robinski said to the seminarian, "Keep your eyes on these guys. We don't want a repeat of last time." Carl nodded.

"What's up, Dana?" Robinski asked in a hushed voice, as the two of them proceeded to the seating area in the rotunda. The Benedictine Monks' Gregorian Chant played softly in the background. The strong scent of incense seemed to permeate the room, yet there was no visual evidence of its source.

Dana glanced around to make sure there was no one in hearing distance. She explained how before she went any further with her suspect list, she wanted to learn more about the victim, who up to this point, had been described as an innocent looking boy, who never swore or caused a fuss with the guards.

"His records, huh? Yes, of course. How might you get them without being caught?"

"Exactly," Dana said. "I have an idea that might work." Dana proceeded to ask about the alarm system in the building and its specific uses in the home.

"I hear where you're going with this, Dana. You're wondering if there's a separate source to alert the offices in Brother Donald's wing. Correct?" Robinski's voice sounded weak as if filled with an element of uncertainty and fear.

Dana could hear Robinski grinding his teeth. "Please note, Walter, I don't want to, in any way, jeopardize your job here. I know you have a family to care for."

"There has to be a way," he said. "The main panel is probably somewhere in the basement. If I can find the wires that set off the alarm in that hallway, you'll be cookin' on the front burner." Robinski rubbed his right thumb against his fingers.

"Is there anyone who might know. . .someone you can trust?"

Robinski looked back at the workshop room. "I think, I may, Dana."

"You mean the seminarian. . .Carl Fenton?"

"Him all right. I've spoken with the young lad at length. Seems he's got a mechanical head on his shoulders. And if I were to trust anyone around here, it would be him. Let me talk to Carl. Give me a call later if you don't mind."

"Mind, not at all. If you're sure, Carl won't spill the beans to anyone."

Robinski shook his head. "He's going to be a priest for God's sake. Who better to ask for help? Speaking of which, I'd better get back to the boys."

For the first time in a long time, Dana left the youth home feeling as if she were on cloud nine. She hoped to get some background information on Douglas Clifford. . .some that might point her to more leads. For now, all she knew for sure was the boy was not liked by some of his fellow inmates as he appeared too innocent to be guilty of the murder of his adoptive parents. And for some reason, Brother Calvin had it in for the boy, as well. When Dana first arrived in Punkerton, she had been told the staff at Gonzaga went so far as to believe the boy might even be possessed. Dana remembered Ellie telling her the boy had been adopted. Could it be he had something against the parents that would give him a motive for murder? Ellie had also told her she believed the boy was illegitimate. Why would the biological parents have chosen to give the child away? Before Dana could go any further with her list of suspects, she needed to know who the boy found stabbed to death in his cell really was.

* * *

When Dana finished the evening meal with Ellie, the phone rang. "I'll get it," Dana said.

"Hi, Dana, it's Walter, and I've got a plan. I'm meeting with Carl Fenton tomorrow night when there aren't many people around. Carl says he knows exactly what wires in the basement need to be tampered with to make the alarm go off in the administrative wing. Everyone down that hall will think it's a fire alarm and will quickly leave. I tell you the kid is a genius," Robinski said.

"Sounds perfect," Dana said, but heard the quivering in her voice. She hoped Walter was right in saying he could trust the seminarian.

She had no reason to think otherwise. She shoved her thumb against her lip and reprimanded herself for being so paranoid. It happened to be one of the downfalls of being an investigator.

"Day after tomorrow, right after lunch, the buzzing will alert all the people from Brother Donald's wing to evacuate the building. Once they do, you go to work and get the files."

"I'll do just that, Walter. I can't thank you enough."

"Remember, move quickly. The alarm will only be set for a few minutes so as not to cause any suspicion. No one will be the wiser. They'll, like Carl said, suspect there was some evidence of smoke or a short in a wire somewhere. Be safe and get the hell out of there as soon as you can!"

Dana hung up the phone and sighed loudly. It was about time things started to work in her favor. As she was about to leave the kitchen, Maize flew around in her cage, repeating in a squeaky voice, "Pretty smart. Pretty smart." A yellow feather landed on the red linoleum.

Dana looked at the canary. "I hope you're right, Maize."

Chapter Twenty-Three

Calvin sat down on the over-stuffed couch and pulled a kitchen chair over to rest his bare feet.

"Been a rough day, honey?" Shirley asked, as she massaged the man's shoulders.

"I thought the day Hansen and me got rid of Banks, my troubles would be over, but that Greer woman is even a bigger pain in the ass."

"Well, we knew that. Can you be more specific?" Shirley moved her hands up to the man's neck.

"She being all buddy-buddy with Robinski...something about it I don't like."

Shirley stopped and stood before Calvin. "Are you thinking the two are up to something? I didn't care for the woman ever since she paid me her first visit."

"That's my guess. They must have something up their sleeves."

Shirley moved down to Calvin's feet and began to knead and rub them.

"Robinski is an apple polisher. Nothing he won't do to make himself look good in the eyes of Donald and Victor."

"Why worry about him then? Do you really think that broad will be able to sway him from his goodie two shoes way?" Shirley climbed into Calvin's lap. She straddled her legs around his hips. She ran her fingers around his ring of hair.

"Okay, maybe the guy's not a Benedict Arnold, but why take any chances?"

"You're not thinking what I'm thinking, are you?" She ran her fingers over his lips.

"Getting Robinski out of the picture? You're right on the money. Let's just say the boys and I pay the Robinski home a little visit."

Shirley shoved Calvin at arm's length and stared at him in silence for a few seconds. "Calvin! You wouldn't."

The man didn't answer. His face looked distant as if formulating ideas.

"I still say the one to keep your eye out for is that hot-shot blond. If anyone is going to stir up the shit, it's her."

Calvin laughed. "With her looks, she can stir me up anytime."

"Calvin!" Shirley got down from Calvin's lap and walked off to slice some cucumbers for a salad. "I've already warned her once."

"What'd ya mean," Calvin asked.

"Remember the time in the parking lot? We had just left the board meeting. I told her if she opens her big mouth once too many times, she'd be sorry."

Calvin stood up and put his arms around Shirley's waist. "You did, didn't you? I love when you talk tough like Rosie the Riveter."

"Sure enough did. I also told her if she stepped out of line, she might just end up in the cemetery out back."

"Geez, you sure did let her have it." He tapped her on the butt.

"You bet I did. I can't stand that little hoochie."

Calvin twirled Shirley around and kissed her hard on the lips. "Well, there's one little hoochie around here I can stand, but I prefer lying with her. What'd ya say?"

"I'm making us dinner…hot dogs and a salad. Why don't you get two beers out of the ice box?"

"That can wait," Calvin said. He took Shirley's hand and led her to the bedroom at the back of the trailer.

Chapter Twenty-Four

Dana awoke the next day to a bright ray of sun shining through her bedroom curtain. The heavy rains that suggested flooding, even overflowing the banks of the river in the drought area, never came to pass. She reminded herself sometimes the worse predictions never come to pass. She hoped that would be the case with her investigation.

Ellie met Dana in the kitchen.

"Think I'll pass on breakfast this morning. Only need a cup of coffee to get me going," Dana said.

"You sure sound chipper."

"Let's say the sun has put me in an optimistic mood."

"Not for long," Ellie said. "Forecast is for temperatures in the high nineties with seventy-six percent humidity."

"Even better. I plan to stay inside today to get some work done. Still got some more reading to do in Gary's journal."

"Don't let me stop you, dear. I'm off to a church function today with the ladies' guild." She carried the red fabric with the white stitched lily that she had been working on.

Dana opened the window to her room. A heavy smell of cow dung blew in from the nearby fields as she quickly slammed the window down. She reminded herself city girls aren't meant to be down home on the farm. She dressed in a thin cotton, sleeveless blouse and a pair of pedal pushers and propped herself up on a stack of pillows.

Patches cracked open the door to her room and slinked his way in. Within seconds, he was lying by Dana's side, purring contentedly.

December 12, 1952

> *Arthur Russell kid is a thorn in my side. Tough, agitated. Killed his only brother. He watches me like an eagle. He'd like nothing better than to get me out of here. The kid swears like a drunkin' sailor. Don't know where he learned words like this. . .off the streets, I guess. Some say he came from Harlem. Can smell those Lucky Strikes on his breath a mile away. Brother Calvin slips him one now and then probably as payment for him to keep an eye on me. The kid's defensive as hell. He hates Douglas Clifford. Starts a fight with him and then puts the blame on him. How can I be so lucky to have cellblock one, where those who enter are guaranteed a ticket to hell for all eternity!*

Would Arthur Russell have the temperament to kill when he got the urge? Robinski had acknowledged the boy sure had a motive for doing away with Douglas Clifford since he wasn't the typical hardened criminal. That part seemed to be confirmed based on what the boys outside the infirmary had to say and the fact Douglas kept his stuffed rabbit as a security blanket. Dana needed to find out more about Douglas' home life. She turned to the next page of Gary's journal.

> *The brothers demanded we decorate this place in the spirit of the season. Sure, so how does one*

turn a damp, concrete block filled with iron bars into something festive? Seems the idea came from Shirley Mitford, the only woman on the board. Trying to play her usual two faces, caring for the inmates and damning them all in the same breath. I strung up some lights in the corridor and brought in a small pine tree. The usual sound of the Benedictine Monks ceased as Christmas carols came out of all the overhead speakers. That's when the Douglas kid called me over. "Will Santa find us here?" he asked. Hell, I didn't know what to tell the kid. Broke my heart.

Interesting, Dana thought. His first Christmas behind bars, and he's worried about Santa not finding him. And this is a boy who would bludgeon his adoptive parents to death? It didn't add up. Dana flipped over to the next page.

The brothers had seen to it each boy received an apple, an orange, and one candy cane in a small stocking. I secretly snuck in a small package. . .a Donald Duck Golden Book. Although I thought I was doing good, the other boys found it an opportunity to taunt Douglas that he was nothing more than a sissy for believing in Santa Claus and even used their fresh fruit to toss at the boy on his way to the lavatory. I never admitted I was the giver, but the brothers knew better and wrote me up yet again for playing partiality with an inmate.

From everything Dana learned about the brothers, she kept asking herself how they saw themselves as Christian men of the cloth. The thought chilling, she got up and slipped on a sweater. Like melting ice cubes sliding down her back, Dana grabbed her upper arms and shivered. She felt more determined than ever to get to the bottom of the case and to get as far away from Punkerton as she could. Perhaps one day, she would write the powers to be in the Vatican and let them know she had found hell on earth. The doorbell rang interrupting her thoughts. She hurried to the front door, where the mailman held a large box and asked for her signature. "Oh, I'm not Eleanor Banks," she said.

"Are you Dana Greer?" he asked.

"Why, yes."

"Sign here, Ma'am."

About to close the door, Dana had a strange feeling, a sixth sense, as if someone were watching her. The mail truck pulled away and at the curb sat a black Ford with missing hubcaps—the same car that was parked outside of the cemetery. The vehicle's engine raced. She craned her neck and tried to get a glimpse of the driver, but the auto skidded away, its tires smelling of burnt rubber. A shiver came over her. Could someone have been watching her? Was someone making sure the package arrived safely and that she got it? She locked the door but couldn't shake the impression she was left with. Dana had no idea who besides the sergeant and some of the staff at the youth home even knew where she was staying. The box had no return address, and her name was scribbled in a red pen. She grabbed a pair of scissors from the kitchen drawer and began to tear open the parcel, excited yet apprehensive at the same time. She tossed handfuls of shredded newspaper onto the floor and dug deeper into the box. She pulled out a blue covered book with patchwork letters reading

Baby's Steps

She sat down by the kitchen table, totally confused at what she had found. She opened the cover, and on the first page read,

Baby First Placed in My Arms

The book belonged to Douglas Clifford's adoptive parents. Page after page, she read about Douglas' first tooth, first haircut, first steps. Photos covered each page from a bundled baby born in January and wrapped in a woolen green blanket to a curly-headed, blond toddler with the biggest blue eyes.

Other than the boy's name, there was no reference to his parents or any other family or friends. The book basically accounted for the first three years of the boy's life. But who would have sent her the

boy's baby book? Dana shuffled through the box, hoping to find a card, a letter, something that might give her a clue as to the sender but nothing. The box was empty. Just then, Patches skidded around the corner, meowing in a high-pitched squeal as Dana jumped. "Patches, you scared me!" she scolded him as the calico cat plunged into the empty box. But the more she thought, it wasn't the cat at all that stirred her. It was the box from the unnamed sender. The picture of the boy with the curly locks and the big eyes lingered in her mind. She owed it to the child to find out who would have wanted him dead. For now, Brother Calvin's name kept coming to the top of her list. Remembering the white clothing of the KKK in the back seat of his beat-up Dodge left her wondering what, if any, part the Klan had in all of this. Was there a message here? Was the mysterious gift meant to scare her, scare her enough to stay away from the youth home? If that was the case, she thought, the sender didn't know her as well as he thought. Tomorrow with her hands on the boy's file, her search for his murderer would grow even more intense until the cold-hearted killer was the one behind bars.

Chapter Twenty-Five

D ana wrestled, tossing from side-to-side, in her sleep and when the alarm clock went off, she jumped thinking it was the buzzer that Robinski and Carl Fenton had tampered with. Something about her personality or maybe it was her strong Catholic upbringing taught her to confront things head on, not working behind the scenes. To be upfront and to tell the truth, and now she felt she wasn't doing anything close to this. A false alarm? Stealing records? Not the way she saw herself dealing with her affairs, yet as far as she was concerned, she knew no other way to get her hands on Douglas Clifford's file.

She dressed quickly, chomped on a piece of dry toast, and swallowed her coffee with a gulp. "Sorry, Ellie, for my haste, but I need to get over to the youth home." Dana hoped to speak with Robinski, once she arrived, to make sure their plans were still on. If possible, she also hoped to spend some time in the chapel; a few quick prayers couldn't hurt either. Dana had fallen away from the church years before but not from her faith. Sometimes, it seemed as if that was the only thing she had left to hold onto.

Having been in the boys' home so many times now, the brothers did not bother to ask for her ID or her reason for being there. When she stepped into the rotunda, she found Brothers Victor and Donald huddled on one of the love seats, deep in conversation. If she saw what she thought she did, the brother's fingertips were touching, a rosary used to conceal their intimacy.

"Excuse me Brothers, might you know where Walter Robinski is this morning?"

Brother Donald quickly began to scratch at the mole on his nose, turned to the other brother, and said, "Any idea where Robinski is, Vic?"

"Check the chapel, why don't you. He usually starts his day there."

Dana nodded and headed toward the double doors leading into the chapel. There she saw Robinski, kneeling, his fingers gripped tightly on his black rosary beads. His lips moved slowly as he mumbled the meditative prayers. Upon completion, he used the silver crucifix to make the sign of the cross over his chest.

"Good morning, Dana. See you find your peace of mind in the same place I do."

Ever since leaving the church, Dana guarded her beliefs as if storing them in a metal vault. Someday, she hoped to find the combination and free herself once and for all, but for now at least, she preferred to keep quiet about her personal convictions. Any time confronted with questions about her faith, as the time the pastor, Father Neil, of St. Rita's inquired, Dana could feel her face flush and her eyes cast downward. Without a doubt, Dana internalized her guilt as best she could.

Changing the subject, Dana asked, "How did everything go last night?" while at the same moment fingering her miniature Bible, deep in the bottom of her bag.

"Owe it to Fenton. Man, the guy's a whiz. Told me before he entered the seminary, he worked for a security company. He knows about every bell, horn, and whistle."

"How lucky for us."

A shuffling sound came from the back of the chapel. One of the retired brothers entered, genuflecting halfway on an obviously stiff knee, and slipped into a front pew.

"Don't worry about Brother Abraham. Lost his hearing about ten years ago." Robinski scoured the otherwise empty chapel. "Give the alarm a few seconds for the wing to clear, then make your move. There are two file cabinets arranged according to the alphabet. Get the boy's records, stash them into your bag, and go out the door at the end of the hall."

"Sure thing, Walter. How long do you think it'll be before Brother Donald realizes the file is missing?"

"Don't worry about that. Doubtful he'd find any reason to go into the boy's records. And, if he should, by then, we'll make sure everything is back in place. . .nice and tidy."

"Walter, I don't know what I'd do without you."

Robinski looked up at the large crucifix in the sanctuary. "Let's just say we owe that guy a round of applause."

Dana laughed.

* * *

At exactly, twelve o'clock, the screaming siren went off. After counting to ten, Dana left the chapel and found the administrative team rushing for the front doors of the youth home just as planned. Their faces looked flushed, frightened, and worried. Dana tried to put aside the thought that this had been all her idea. She counted to ten again and made her way down the corridor. Two doors down on the left, she slid into Brother Donald's office, opened the *C/D* drawer of the file cabinet, and pulled out Douglas Clifford's file. Fortunately, the file was thin compared to others in the drawer. She dropped it into her bag and did as Robinski instructed, running to the back exit. No sooner had she pulled the door open then she came face-to-face with Shirley Mitford.

"In a hurry, are we?" Shirley asked, her dark eyes squinting, her narrow nose appearing like the beak of a crow.

Puffing, in between short breaths, Dana said, "Just surprised to see you, Shirley."

"My, my. I'd say I have more of a right to be here than you."

Dana's throbbing heart pounded in her ears. "I'm leaving."

"Wait one minute! I can't recall ever seeing you use this exit. Anything wrong with the front doors?"

"The alarm…the alarm went off." Dana thought quickly. "I was hoping to speak with Brother Donald when the buzzer went off. I ran to the quickest exit out of the building."

"Seems all's quiet now, Dana."

"So, it is. Now, if you'll excuse me."

"Why, of course." Shirley reached for Dana's wrist. "Pretty bag you have there."

Dana did not bother to respond. She ran toward her parked truck. She noted the small gathering at the front doors moving inward. She sighed deeply. "Just in the nick of time!" She glanced at her image in the rearview mirror...her face flushed, perspiring. If only she had made it out without confronting Shirley. Dana pulled a tissue from her bag and blotted her face. I got Douglas's files. That's what's important. Forget running into Shirley, she thought, as she started the ignition. Still there was something about driving away from the home and into Punkerton with stolen goods that made her uneasy. Being an investigator, she didn't particularly like what life was like on the other side of the tracks. Her chest felt tight and her breathing shallow. She ran her fingers over her upper lip, covered again in perspiration. To get her mind off things, she turned on the truck's radio. Les Paul and Mary Ford sang out their latest hit "Vaya Con Dios," – "May God Be with You." All she could think was how appropriate. She needed someone on her side right now. The old Chevy's tires squealed as she pulled out of her parking spot but not before noticing a black car to her left. It appeared empty. Its hubcaps were missing.

* * *

"Dana, you look like a scared puppy. Is everything okay?"

Dana was amazed at Ellie's intuitiveness. "I hope so."

"What's that supposed to mean, if you don't mind me asking?"

"On my way out of the home, I ran into Shirley."

"Dear, forget that woman. I think, her bark is worse than her bite. You have as much right to be there as she."

"If only she felt the same way," Dana said. She lowered her shoulder bag onto the living room couch. She tapped it with the tips of her fingers.

"Don't tell me. You did it? You got the Clifford's boy's files?" Ellie folded her fingers upward as if in prayer.

Dana nodded. "Hopefully, this file will be crucial to my learning more about this boy, yet I feel guilty, I guess."

"I see what you mean. It must be what kleptomaniacs feel after they've come home with their loot."

"Sleazy?" The comparison only made Dana feel worse.

"Or, maybe, proud of their clever trick, especially, if they got away with it."

"I'm only hoping I can get away with it. Some way, I've got to get through this file and see to it, it's put back in place before anyone notices it's missing."

Ellie's posture said it all. She pulled tightly on the chenille belt of her robe, turned slowly, and left the room in silence—almost as if she did not want to be a partner in crime.

* * *

Retrieving the boy's files presented enough anxiety for one day. Dana would start afresh in the morning, going through the papers. Before she went to bed, she opened Gary's journal to the page dated:

January 12, 1953

A new year but still nothing ever changes around here. The monotony, the routine, gets old, gets tiring. Guess, I should be happy I still have a job after my write-ups and all. But, I worry about Ellie. I want to provide for her, so when I'm gone, she'll have a little nest egg to fall back upon. That's why I took this damn job when I did. Most people my age would have retired by now, but I got to make sure my little sweetie is comfortable when the good Lord comes for me.

The entry sent goosebumps down Dana's arms. It was, after all, Gary's last entry into his journal, and it was almost fortuitous, as if he might have known his time on earth would soon be over. There was no way of predicting, however, what Doctor Hansen had in mind for him. In only days from the time Gary Banks had written the journal entry, his fate would be sealed.

Chapter Twenty-Six

Another storm headed our way?" Dana asked Ellie. The sky looked to be smothered in black smoke, and the crops in the fields stood stiff and still as if waiting to be pounced at any moment by an unrelenting prey. The muggy air from the open kitchen window crept in leaving the room sweltering and so moist it laid a thin layer of perspiration on Dana's bare arms.

"Let me get the radio on. Something about those clouds scares me." The static reception brought Ellie's ear close to the speaker.

"And for parts of northwestern Texas, a storm warning is in effect until eleven p.m. tonight. Heavy winds are expected up to seventy miles per hour, bringing the possibility of a tornado in its wake."

"I remember growing up in Kansas. Seems we spent more time in the basement than anywhere else."

"Got a basement?" Dana asked.

Ellie shook her head. "This place is a casualty waiting to happen. Gary wasn't paid that well, and this," she said, spreading her arm out from side to side, "is the best we could do."

Dana smiled. "You've made it a cozy, welcoming place." A memory flashed before Dana's eyes of Jay and Loretta's Victorian home, the one she lived in on Cape Peril while solving her last case. A beautiful home to the naked eye but internally filled with depression, mistrust, and secrets. Ellie, on the other hand, did all she could to make Dana feel at home in her place. She provided a safe lodging, where Dana felt comfortable approaching Ellie as a confidant and friend.

Ellie poured them each a cup of coffee. "That's what Gary always used to say. 'You've made this house a home.'" She shut the radio off. "Guess, we'll just have to wait and see what Mother Nature has in store for us." She put a large red mitt on her hand and pulled out a tray of freshly baked chocolate chip cookies.

"Mind if I work by the table today?" Dana asked. "I'm going to need to spread some things out."

"Not at all."

The two women shared some cookies after which Ellie began to wipe down the wicker tabletop covered with a sheet of glass. "It's all yours," she said, "I'm going to get to my crocheting."

It did not take long before the calm before the storm ended, and the winds began to whirl, thrusting small particles of dust through the screened window. Dana lowered the wooden frame with a bang and retrieved her bag from the living room couch. She reached in her satchel for Douglas Clifford's file. The memory of the three-year old boy with the blond curls and large, blue eyes came to her. She hadn't bothered to tell Ellie about the strange package that bore the boy's baby book so as not to frighten the woman. Dana still had no explanation as to who might have sent it and, equally important, why. Nor did she have any explanation for the black car parked out front that sped away once the package was delivered. Dana tried to reassure herself it might have had no connection whatsoever with the delivery yet could not explain why this car, too, had its hubcaps missing. She made a mental note to be more aware of her surroundings.

When Dana opened the manila file, she felt her body stiffen. She threw her hand across her mouth. The first page revealed a large photo of the boy, older now, staring back at her with his large eyes.

Something about the boy's innocent look struck her. She could understand why Arthur Russell and the others mocked the boy as he certainly did not bear the hardened look of a criminal and, for sure, not the appearance of a murderer. Beneath the boy's photograph was his date of birth.

January 4, 1943

Dana kept her notebook close by to jot down important clues from the boy's file. The next sheet was a copy of the boy's birth certificate.

```
┌─────────────────────────────────────────────────────────┐
│                                                         │
│              Birth Certificate                          │
│                                                         │
│                 This Certifies That                     │
│              DOUGLAS CLIFFORD (male)                     │
│                                                         │
│                    was born to                          │
│         CHANTEL DEBOUR         ▬▬▬▬▬▬▬▬                 │
│                                                         │
│         ACTRESS      occupation      SERVER             │
│                                                         │
│      date   1-4-1943         11:12 PM   time           │
│                                                         │
│   weight   6 LB 7 OZ        21 INCHES  length          │
│                                                         │
│             Blessed Mary Hospital                       │
│                                                         │
│             Los Angeles, California                     │
│                                                         │
│         Dora May Kettle, RN    Gustaf E Pearson MD      │
│                                                         │
└─────────────────────────────────────────────────────────┘
```

"Name and surname of father blacked out," Dana repeated to herself. If the child were illegitimate as Ellie had said, it would make sense the father's name would not appear. Dana kept repeating the child's mother's name: Chantel DeBour. Why was the name so familiar? Where had she heard the name before? Looking at the place of birth as Hollywood, it began to make sense to her. Chantel DeBour, of course, didn't she play the lead in "Men Don't Call Twice" by Paramount? Suddenly, the woman's face became clear in Dana's mind. She was a blond woman, who always wore her hair parted to the side with some type of glamorous barrette. The hair pieces always boasted shiny, colorful jewels...probably the real thing, not some faux glass stones. She spoke in a subtle French accent. All the men found her provocative and carried on about wishing they could be with her. But, she was married to a producer; Dana could not recall his name. Ten years ago, Dana pondered, Chantel DeBour would have been a mere thirty years old. Obviously, the father of Douglas Clifford was not named but was given the occupation of server. But why would Miss DeBour stoop to having an affair with a waiter? As farfetched as it sounded, Dana knew she would have to find a way to travel to California, but before she did, she would meet with Louise Canfield to see what information she might be able to provide about the starlet. She paused for a moment to catch her breath. Her excitement caused her to breathe quickly.

She turned the birth certificate over and went on to the next page in the boy's file. This one referred to the day Douglas was admitted to the St. Aloyious Gonzaga Home for Troubled Youth. Her eyes scanned over the document, where nothing seemed of surprise. The boy had been admitted to the home on August 1, 1952. Under *parent's names* were listed Harold and Nina Clifford, deceased. According to their birthdates, the couple was both fifty-six years old at the time of their deaths. Just as Ellie had said, Douglas Clifford's parents were in their forties when they adopted the boy as a mere infant. No mention was made as to the boy being adopted. This gave Dana even more cause for going to California.

She continued to look through the pages in the boy's file; most, of which, were accounts of his solitary confinement at the home for minor infractions. His first offense had been pushing a fellow inmate who called Douglas a *baby*. Another time, he had lingered too long in a stall during evening, mandatory lavatory. These hardly seemed punishable crimes. His last violation, meriting him an isolated cell, for who knew how long, was based on the boy screaming uncontrollably when his stuffed toy was confiscated. Dana shook her head in disbelief.

Under possessions at time of admittance were the words:

- underwear (2 pieces)
- torn T-shirt
- pair of jeans
- pair of socks
- tattered tennis shoes
- a baseball cap of the LA Dodgers
- a soiled stuffed rabbit

About to close the file, Dana noticed someone had stapled a yellow slip of paper onto the back cover.

In case of emergency

Nearest Next of Kin

Donna Iverson
438 Ender Way
Hollywood 5, California

LAkewood 7-4864

* No Known
Relatives/Neighbor

Could the boy have an aunt, a cousin? That's when Dana noticed the asterisk. Donna Iverson must have been a neighbor of Harold and Nina. The newfound information excited her. She began humming a Les Paul and Mary Ford tune and tapping her fingers on the tabletop. She thanked God she was finally onto something concrete. Now, if she could only figure out a way to get to California.

* * *

"So, you're looking for something on Chantel DeBour?" Louise Canfield, the librarian asked. She shoved her hair under her plastic tortoise-shell headband. Her hips waddled as she led the way toward the periodical section of the library. "Let's get some magazines." In minutes, the woman had found:

"You're an angel," Dana said.

Louise Canfield pushed her rhinestone-edged glasses up her nose. "All in my day's work, honey." About to walk away, she turned. "Mind if I ask why the interest in Chantel DeBour?"

Dana sat down at one of the long tables under the window and got out her notebook. "All part of an investigation," she said. To avoid being asked anything else, Dana quickly began reading. Cover to cover, she flipped through the pages finding one story here and one story there on the starlet's life. The overhead tick-tock of the clock muted into the background of the library's silence until Dana looked up at its face. Five forty-six. She couldn't believe she had been reading the movie magazines for the last three hours. She read over the notes she had made:

- *Chantel DeBour born on July 31, 1913*
- *Married three times, her present husband: Andrew Ziebrewsky, Paramount Producer*
- *Known to have had multiple affairs with such leading men as William Holden, Cary Grant, and Humphrey Bogart*
- *In 1942 became romantically involved with someone fourteen years her junior*
- *Rumored to have born the young man's child but put it up for adoption*
- *Starred in romantic comedies for Paramount Studios*

Before Dana left the library, she decided to do the math. If Chantel DeBour was born in 1913 and had her affair that bore her illegitimate child, she would have been thirty years old at the time, but that meant the father of the child would only have been sixteen years old. Dana redid the math again. A mere child himself, Douglas Clifford's father, according to the child's birth certificate, had been a waiter in Hollywood. But how would someone as famous as Chantel DeBour have met an adolescent who, according to the magazine articles, she fell madly in love with? The article "Is Love Blind" described Chantel DeBour ignoring the fact her year-long affair with someone slightly more than half her age would be problematic. The journalist had chosen his words carefully, and few details were offered. The story went on to say Miss DeBour had actually talked marriage with the young man before she found out she was bearing his child. A Catholic, Miss DeBour, refused to abort the child and, instead, put the child up for adoption. The article went onto say her decision was not unusual as numerous other stars had followed the same route, giving their children up for adoption.

Dana gathered the magazines onto a pile when Louise Canfield came up to her. "Hope the magazines helped. You did hear the latest, though, didn't you?"

"The latest?"

"Poor Miss DeBour passed away suddenly about. . .well, it's been a little over a year now. The library's collection is a bit behind. I apologize for that."

"What happened?"

"Her Chauffeur was driving her sports car on Route One when he missed a turn and slid down an embankment." Louise Canfield sat down next to Dana, crossed her legs, and rested her chin in the cupped palm of her hand. "The police investigation ruled he was traveling at a high rate of speed on a wet roadway."

"That's terrible." Dana chewed down on her pencil, leaving teeth marks in the yellow paint, intent on hearing more.

"I'm embarrassed to admit this, but I'm a big fan of the 'Daily Star.'"

"The tabloid?"

The woman's neck covered in a red rash. "Who knows, though, how much of that trash is true?"

"Her death, you mean?"

"No, not that. . .her funeral. According to the 'Daily Star,' it was quite a hullabaloo. Well, maybe a three-ring circus would be a more apt description."

"How so?"

"Seems everyone who's got a star on the Hollywood Walk of Fame was there—Bogart, Stewart, Holden, Lancaster, well, you get the idea."

Dana could feel her forehead wrinkling. "Is that so?"

Louise Canfield's eyebrows rose like two pointed arrows over her cat-shaped eyeglasses. "Now mind you, gossip is gossip, and God knows how much is truth, but that's what the tabloid said. She was buried in the Hollywood Forever Cemetery." The woman carried on obviously excited in her own telling of the story. "I hear someone delivers a dozen red roses to her grave each week. . .on a Sunday, I think. Talk about love. I mean, who would do such a thing?"

Dana got the distinct impression Louise Canfield could get a bit swept up in the stories of the stars. She thanked the woman for all her help and left the library, noticing she was the last visitor to leave as the clock chimed six o'clock. Her mind raced from one thought to another. She hurried toward the old Chevy and sat for a moment behind the wheel, trying to contain the excitement she felt. In addition to her list of suspects, she was quickly coming to know the victim.

* * *

As Dana stepped inside Ellie's house, the woman said, "I thought you'd never come home. You had a caller," she said, with a child-like smile across her face.

"Who was that?"

"Three guesses," Ellie continued in a playful way.

Dana assumed Walter Robinski was wondering how soon she could return Douglas Clifford's file.

"No, not Mr. Robinski. Howard Rhodes," Ellie said, with a wink.

All Dana could think was she was much too tired to return the man's call tonight. "I'll give him a call in the morning," she said. She supposed the good-looking attorney had plans to take her out to dinner again, but she already knew what her answer would be. The sooner she could solve this case, the sooner she could get out of Punkerton, and that wouldn't be soon enough.

Chapter Twenty-Seven

Early the next morning while still dark outside, Dana awoke to endless pounding on her bedroom door. She wondered if a tornado had been spotted. She jumped from her bed, opened the door, and found a white-faced Ellie standing there with one hand clutched over her chest and the other covering her mouth. She was hyperventilating.

"What is it? What's wrong?" From the way the woman was breathing, Dana wondered if the woman might be having a heart attack.

"It's, W, W—." The woman stuttered, hardly making any sense.

Dana sat the woman on the side of her bed. "Take a deep breath." She put her arm around Ellie's shaking shoulders. "Take your time."

Ellie trembled. Patches entered the room and jumped on the woman's lap, trying to lick her face.

"Shoo, not now," Dana called.

In between Ellie's sobs, she mouthed some nonsense syllables.

"Take it easy, dear. Breathe deeply."

Again, Ellie began to speak, "I jus. . .just got. . .a call."

Dana nodded and repeated the woman's words. "You just got a call, from whom?"

"It's Walter. . .Walter Robinski. He's dead!" Ellie's head fell onto Dana's shoulder as she mumbled, "God, no!"

Dana could not believe what the woman had said. "That can't be. Walter Robinski... dead?""

Ellie lifted her face toward Dana's. With one hand, she attempted to catch the tears that rolled down her cheeks. "Sergeant McKnight called. Told me to tell you. He's on his way now to the Robinski house." Ellie continued to cry uncontrollably.

"What happened? Did he say what happened?"

In a shaking voice, Ellie slowly mouthed, "The KKK."

"Ku Klux Klan?" Dana felt her heart throbbing against her chest, tightening with each pulse. She felt short of breath, light headed.

"That's all the sergeant told me." Ellie pulled a handkerchief from her robe pocket and   dabbed at her nose. She could hardly keep her eyes open, swollen and red.

Dana felt incompetent consoling the poor woman when her own defenses broke down. The two women held each other tightly as Dana, with difficulty, whispered in Ellie's ear, "I must get ready. I need to head over there."

* * *

When Dana and Ellie arrived at the man's house, they found the chilling remains of the KKK's work in the front yard—a smoldering white wooden cross. Tiny, black embers floating in the early morning air. But why? Dana kept ruminating. Walter was a strong Catholic and a parishioner at St. Rita's, and as far as she recalled, he had been an usher at the church for some time. The only explanation had to do with Robinski's involvement with Douglas Clifford's files. The white garb in Brother Calvin's truck...it made sense if he was a member of the Klan and found out what Walter had been up to, it would be a perfect motive for murder.

"They gotta find a way to stop them," Ellie said, her voice hopeless.

Several cars were parked outside of the man's house. The sergeant and another gentleman in uniform were standing on the porch. The cruiser read Lubbock County Sheriff.

"Terrible time to meet y'all like this, Miss Greer," Sergeant McKnight said. "We," he said, pointing to the sheriff, "got all this under control."

"The cross? The KKK? When?" Dana's curiosity along with her exasperation at the sergeant's flippant remarks led her lashing out with questions.

The sergeant said, "Was last night, aroun' ten p.m. Walter done come home from a church meetin' and found this here cross. They shot him in cold blood."

That's when Dana noticed the fresh splattering of blood in the tall blades of grass, marking a path where Robinski had, obviously, tried to escape from his attackers. "How horrible! Is that all you know?"

"Welcome to talk with the Missus," he said, motioning the sheriff down the three cement stairs. "She's inside talkin' to her minister."

"I'll do that. Thanks for your help." Dana noticed the house appeared incredibly serene for a home that housed nine children. Mrs. Robinski sat on a couch near an upright piano. A minister sat alongside her on a floral loveseat. On a nearby chair sat Father Neil from St. Rita's. The remainder of the people Dana did not know and assumed they must have been neighbors or churchgoers from Grace Presbyterian Church or St. Rita's. At least thirty people filled the small living space. Some stared into oblivion, into disbelief, while others let their tears flow freely.

Dana introduced herself. "Mrs. Robinski, Dana Greer; I worked with your husband on the Douglas Clifford case."

The woman's eyes were swollen almost to the point of being shut. She kept a linen handkerchief under her nose. "Walter spoke of you many times. Please, please have a seat."

Dana smiled at the minister and shook hands with father before sitting down next to the woman.

"I am so sorry, Mrs. Robinski. Walter was a wonderful, caring man. Are you able to tell me what happened last night?"

In between sobs, Mrs. Robinski began to explain. "Walter came home from a meeting. I heard his car pull into the driveway. That's when I heard the shot. By the time I got to the door, three members of the KKK ran to an old car and drove away. My Walter…my Walter staggered over the lawn and collapsed."

"By chance, did you happen to notice the make or the color of the car?"

"Why, it was beat-up and green. . .yes, it was green."

"A Ford? A truck?" Dana felt convinced. Brother Calvin was behind the murder of Walter Robinski. Without positive identification of the vehicle, Dana could not say for sure, but her assumption told her she was on track.

"Couldn't say. Drove off so quickly." She paused to blow her nose. "That's when I saw the cross and found Walter. . .nearby. I called the sergeant. He came by with the coroner, and they took my Walter away." She sobbed, her body shaking. She mumbled into her handkerchief, "such a good man, such a good man."

"God has taken him to a better place," the minister added, in a consoling voice.

"Your children?"

"My neighbor next door has willingly taken them. . .until. . .until the funeral."

Father Neil inserted, "The Mass will be in two days with the burial following out back of St. Rita's cemetery. It was Walter's wish." He looked at Dana, who knew she must have looked questioningly at the priest. "It's what Walter wanted, and Helen has agreed."

Dana knew the man was the breadwinner of the household and immediately wondered how Helen and her nine children would carry on. As if reading her mind, the minister added, "Helen and the children will be going to Omaha to be with her sister and her husband. They have a large dairy farm and offered to take the family in. Such giving people, God bless."

Dana reached into her bag for a tissue and along with Helen and the others in the room began to cry. The reality of Walter being gunned down. . .the violent act against such an innocent individual. . .it was too much to bear.

Father sat next to Dana. "I know what you're thinking. Don't go blaming yourself for this."

"I never should have gotten him involved. If I hadn't—."

"No, Miss Greer. The KKK is a merciless group. Their hatred of Catholics is a well-known motive for their acts. Punkerton is their territory."

In between sniffles, Dana said, "Father, it had more to do with Walter just being Catholic. He was murdered for a reason. It's my fault. If Walter had not gotten involved with me, he would be alive."

Helen looked up and patted Dana's hand. "Father is right, Miss Greer. Don't go blaming yourself. Walter would never have wanted that."

"But, if only I hadn't—."

The woman gently pushed aside a blond curl blocking Dana's face. "You're speaking about the boy's file, aren't you? Walter told me."

Dana looked over at Helen. "He did?"

Mrs. Robinski nodded. "That's what's so odd."

Dana wiped her eyes and listened.

"Only yesterday, Walter told me, before he left for his meeting, 'I must tell the Greer woman to see Carl. Best she gets the file returned as soon as possible before someone realizes it's missing.' Why, it was almost as if he knew I would be the one who would have to relay the news to you."

"Quite fortuitous. I see what you mean." The thought sent chills over Dana's arms. She kept thinking she should never have involved Walter in the plot to retrieve Douglas Clifford's records. How could she have known it would come to this, yet from what little she knew about the KKK, they were an aggressive, heartless group who would stop at nothing to achieve their results. The Klan had members behind the walls of the youth home.

She offered her sympathy again and said she would be sure to follow Walter's advice; in fact, she would do it immediately.

* * *

The usual heavy scent of incense permeated the rotunda of the boys' home as she stepped inside along with the chants of the Benedictine monks overhead. What stood out as unusual was a large picture of Walter Robinski on an easel in the center of the room. The frame was draped in a black cloth. Under the picture were the words: *Rest in Peace*. There were numerous bouquets of fresh flowers in vases beneath and beside the picture. It was obvious the man's work and reputation had been appreciated. . .at least, by most. As she took her eyes off of the large photograph and the makeshift shrine the brothers had put together, she heard, "Tragic, isn't it. Only yesterday the man and I were in chapel together, praying the rosary." In his hands, he held a manila file.

She turned to look over her shoulder. "Carl, I'm so happy to see you."

The seminarian hugged her tightly. "So sorry to lose such a good man, but the Lord must have better plans for Walter. If there is anything, Dana, anything at all I can do to help you, please let me know."

"Is there any way I can ask you to return this?" She opened her bag as Carl peered inside.

"Sure, why not? I was on my way to put this chart in the cabinet. . .a new entry." He lowered his voice, "It's the perfect time. No one will suspect a thing." He tapped Dana on the shoulder.

She handed him the file and noticed there was not a soul around. "Thank you, Walter," she whispered to herself. She stole into the chapel and prayed, "Eternal rest grant unto you and let perpetual light shine upon you." She may have left the church a long time ago, but she still remembered the beautiful prayers she had memorized by heart as a child.

Chapter Twenty-Eight

Shirley ran the vacuum across the bedroom carpet when she noticed Calvin's whites piled in a corner. "That man," she said to herself, "so sloppy." She bent and picked up the sheets, letting out a scream. The clothes were stained in dried blood. "What the hell has Calvin been up to?"

The Airstream door slammed shut, and Shirley ran to the front of the trailer. There stood Calvin in his brown monk's habit. "You know, we discussed you coming here in that garb. Do you want to be noticed?"

"Needed to get out of there in a hurry. Plus, if you recall, you do live in the middle of nowhere. I hardly think someone will be looking," Calvin responded.

"One never knows. That snoopy bitch might be crawling around here."

"And if she is, I'll tell her I've come to hear your confession." He laughed.

"A brother hearing confessions? I doubt she's that stupid. She knows you're not a priest."

"It was just a joke. Why the somber mood today?"

Shirley debated whether she should tell Calvin what she found on the floor to their room. She knew it would not have been his intention to leave the soiled garment out in the open. He must have forgotten to take it to the home's laundry.

Calvin grabbed Shirley around the waist. "What's for dinner? Don't see anything on the stove."

"Been busy cleaning. This place is a pigsty."

"What'd ya expect for a tin can?"

"Don't go there with me, Calvin. This happens to be my home."

"Just kidding. You sure are touchy."

Without thinking, Shirley blurted out. "And why shouldn't I be?"

Calvin sat on the couch and plopped Shirley on his lap. "My little, sugar plum, tell me what's troubling you?"

"Um…. Do you really want to know?"

"Why not? Can it be that awful?"

"The KKK…what have you been up to?"

"Why'd you ask?"

"Your whites…I found them."

Calvin stood up in such haste he almost shoved Shirley on the floor. "Give them to me!"

"Fine. Take your shit. All I'm asking is why are they covered in blood?"

"As if that's any business of yours." Calvin opened the icebox and found a blackened banana. He left the peels on the floor and chomped on the rotten piece of fruit.

"Afraid it is when your filth is left behind here. Now, tell me. Who did you kill?"

Calvin's forehead creased. "Kill? Who said anything about killing?"

Shirley could feel her chest tighten. "All that blood sure didn't come from a cut finger, Calvin. That's someone's blood, and I want to know who."

The man grabbed Shirley by her shoulders and pushed her onto the couch. "Okay, all right, if you must know...Robinski's gone. A few of my brothers targeted his house last night. When he pulled into his driveway and got out of his car, I pointed a gun at him and shot him at close range. It was a blood bath. What more can I say?"

Shirley ran her finger over her lips, smearing her red lipstick. "I don't give a shit about the man. But, why? Why not the dumb blond bombshell? She's the one we want to get rid of!"

Calvin sat next to Shirley. "I know. I know. Give me time. I'm working on it. Robinski wasn't as innocent as you might have thought, though."

"Really?"

"Got the so-called blond bombshell to get into the private files...heard it myself from a little bird."

"Ah, I wondered what she was doing the day I saw her leaving by the hall door. You're saying, *that's* what she was up to?"

"Uh huh."

"In that case, I guess, they both deserve to be scratched!"

"Like I said, baby, give me time."

"Speaking of time, how much do you have?"

Calvin kissed Shirley long and hard. "I got all the time in the world, baby."

Chapter Twenty-Nine

Dana entered the vestibule of St. Rita's Church. She scanned the pews in front of her. People, who were there to pay their last respects, filled the church from front to back. An usher came up to her and said, "Would you like for me to find you a seat?" On the lapel of his jacket, he had pinned a photo of Walter in his full Knights of Columbus regalia.

"Please," she said. Surprisingly, the man led her to a row near the altar, where one spot was still available. She thanked the man, genuflected, and sat down. Those seated in the first two pews were the monks from the boys' home along with a few guards dressed in their green uniforms. Sandwiched in between the habits of brown, she saw Carl in his usual black seminarian clothes. With Walter gone, Carl would be the only one to understand her desire to find the murderer of Douglas Clifford and the only one she felt she could trust.

Walter's casket, a mahogany box covered in dark blue roses surrounded by baby's breath, graced the center aisle. Although Dana believed she had an explanation for Walter's death, still it seemed so dream like, as far from reality as she could imagine. Across from her sat his wife and their nine children, taking up the entire pew. The sounds of sobbing, coughing, and clearing of throats could be heard from the front to the back of the church. As the Mass began and the choir sang, Dana let her mind wander. She kept coming back to the same conclusion; someone must have targeted Walter in retaliation for him having set the alarm. If Brother Calvin had wanted revenge, it would have been simpler to do away with the man in the same way

Doctor Hansen had done away with Ellie's husband. The KKK obviously wanted to make a scene…to prove a point.

When Father Neil began his sermon, he spoke about his personal friendship with Walter and all the man had done for the church. "Ever vigilant, that's what we must be," he said. "The KKK has never been our friend, and for that reason, every single Catholic in this church must be on guard."

In her heart, Dana appreciated the priest's advice, but she disagreed with his message. The KKK didn't pick Walter as a random Catholic to gun down. No, there was more to the story. Her theory held this act was intentional, an act of revenge. The only thing Walter did in the last week, which made him any different from the man he always had been, was to help her retrieve Douglas Clifford's file. But the questions kept badgering her: Was Shirley somehow aware of what she had done, and if so, how did she hear about the plan? And of the brothers, was Brother Calvin the only one in the home who was a KKK member? Dana let the thoughts swirl in her mind until she felt her head pounding. She would go to the reception after Mass but keep it quick. She needed to rest. One of her migraines was on its way.

* * *

One of the ushers from St. Rita's stood in the gathering space in the basement of the church and poured coffee for those waiting in line. Dana noticed a few of the boys from G Wing were in attendance and, as always, under the watchful eye of the two guards. One of the boys was Arthur Russell and the other a boy she had never seen before. Both of the boys chomped on chocolate donuts. Odd, she thought, that of all the boys chosen to attend Walter's funeral it would have been Arthur. It was common knowledge the boy was a troublemaker with a streak of violence.

Entering the room, Dana saw Carl along with Brother Donald. She made her way over to them.

"Sorry to hear this awful news," Brother Donald said, in a smug voice that spoke more out of obligation than empathy.

Carl motioned for Dana to step aside. "All is well that ends well," Carl said, giving her a wink. She knew he was referring to the file having been returned unnoticed, and she nodded with a smile.

"I keep going over and over what the KKK had against Mr. Robinski. I've gone over this so many times in my mind my head is splitting. I'm giving my condolences to Mrs. Robinski and heading back," Dana said to the seminarian

"It is odd," he said, "but I wouldn't try to read too much into this. Like Father said, random acts do occur and to the least deserving of people. Trust in the Lord."

"You're right, Carl. Maybe my mind has been working overtime."

At about the time Dana was about to pay her respects to Mrs. Robinski, Howard Rhodes came down the stairs.

"Dana, sorry to have to meet at such a time as this."

She nodded. "By the way, how did you know Walter?"

"Father Neil and I play golf on Saturday mornings. When he told me he was burying one of the guards from St. Aloysius, I knew I wanted to pay my respects. When I was involved with the case at the home, I met a number of the guards. Walter stood out to me. Seemed like such a great guy."

Dana wiped her eyes with a small, embroidered handkerchief.

Just then, Carl tapped her on the shoulder and said he was leaving. Dana introduced the man to Howard.

The two men shook hands and Carl left.

"Who's he?" Howard asked.

"Another one of those great guys," she said. "He a seminarian doing an internship at the home."

Dana was about ready to say good-bye to Howard when he touched her arm. "Know now's not the best time for this, but I've been trying to get in touch with you. Did Ellie tell you I called?"

Dana shoved a strand of her blond hair behind her ear. "Oh, yes, she did. I've been so busy, too busy, I'm afraid."

"I was hoping we might get together again before I left."

"Oh?"

"Yeah, I've got a case I'm working on in Southern California. Hoping it'll take me no more than a week, but I'm flying out tomorrow. Maybe, we could get—."

"California, tomorrow?" Dana could not believe her ears. She repeated her question.

"Are you okay, Dana? You look awfully pale."

"Oh, yes, yes, I'm fine. Well, actually, I get these migraines."

"Say, why don't you go home and get some rest. If it's okay with you, I'll give you a call later tonight."

"Sure, sure," was all she could say.

She offered her sympathy, once again, to Helen Robinski and headed toward her truck.

* * *

Once Dana got back to Ellie's, she hurried to get ready for bed. She pulled the blinds shut and slipped under her covers, but not before jotting a note to Ellie:

Sorry to have missed you at the funeral reception. Left suddenly. Have one of my migraines.

As was common whenever her stress got the worst of her and one of her unbearable headaches hit, the nightmares followed. Walter Robinski met her at his own funeral. "Come inside," he said, motioning her into the vacant church. "Inside, inside, inside," his voice echoed against the walls. She touched the side of her head and felt it throbbing. He lifted the lid of the casket, the blue roses scattering across the pink marble floor. "Come inside," he motioned to the empty coffin. Its ivory satin lining began to rise and fall like a heartbeat when she awoke screaming, clutching at her pillow. She gasped. Something stood out to her about the dream. . .the word *inside*. Could that be it? Was Robinski trying to tell her his death was the result of an inside job? Before she put all the blame on Brother Calvin, could there be others connected to the KKK? She remembered what

Howard Rhodes had told her. The coroner. . .that was it, wasn't it? He was the head of this area's Klan. The only one she could think of who might know the coroner personally was Doctor Hansen. Could it have been the doctor who feared that Walter and she were getting too close to solving the case? She slowly rose, massaging the sides of her temples with her hands.

She ventured into the kitchen and found Ellie sipping on a cup of cinnamon tea. "Ellie, did you happen to make a note of Howard Rhodes phone number?"

"Missy, shouldn't you be resting? I know all about migraines. My mother used to get them."

"Afraid there isn't time for that now. I need to speak with that attorney."

Ellie showed her a scrap of paper by the phone on which she had scribbled the man's number. As Dana dialed the phone, she could see Ellie's face, a look of uncertainty, unsure what Dana was up to.

"How's the migraine?" Howard asked, before even saying hello.

"Better," she said. "I got to thinking about what you said earlier. . .about going to California."

"Yeah, yeah, maybe we could get together when I come back."

Dana felt herself getting irritated. He was a nice man, but dating was the furthest from her mind at this point. "Maybe," she said.

"Hey, I won't take a maybe."

"Well then, okay, okay." She paused, changing the subject. "Your trip to California—. I actually have some investigative work to do. . .in regard to the Douglas Clifford murder."

"Want to come along?"

"What are you talking about? Are you serious?" Could he be joking, she wondered.

"Perhaps, if you call the airlines, you could get a last-minute ticket."

Dana repeated what she thought she had heard. "Last-minute ticket?"

"Sure, wouldn't mind the company. The flight's far from a puddle-jumper." He laughed.

What was the likelihood Dana could fly to California to investigate Douglas Clifford's past? It almost sounded too good to be true.

* * *

Shirley ran into Brother Calvin as he came from the J Wing. She pulled him to the side. "On your way to the chapel?"

"What'd ya mean?"

"Well, you've got plenty to be thankful for, I'd say."

Calvin whispered, "You mean Robinski?"

Shirley fingered a string of pearls around her neck. "Sure do. One down and one to go, I'd say."

Brother Victor passed the two of them, nodded his head, and smiled.

"Better be careful what you say around here. I'd hate for you to be taken seriously," Calvin said.

"But I am. You can't tell me your boys couldn't—."

"Shirley, please. Not here. Can we talk later?"

Shirley huffed. "I suppose, but you've got rosary tonight in the chapel. I won't be seeing you." She tried to reach for the sleeve of his brown habit, but he shirked away.

"Then, it'll have to be another time. I said not here!"

Shirley watched as Calvin walked away. Either he was too afraid of who might see them together, or else he was playing the part of a coward, too afraid of taking on the Greer woman. The more she thought about it, the more she doubted it was the latter. After all, if Calvin was capable of convincing Hansen to rip out Timothy's tongue, and if he was able to gather up his boys to do away with Robinski, she knew he would listen to her plan. He loves me too much not to do what I say, she thought.

Chapter Thirty

The PanAm stewardess came through the aisle clearing the trays of chicken gumbo with gravy and mashed potatoes. Tray tables rattled shut. The flight attendant announced that in another twenty minutes, the plane would be landing in Los Angeles.

Howard turned toward Dana, "So, you believe in miracles, do you?" He smiled revealing his perfectly aligned white teeth.

"If you're referring to me being here, I'd have to say yes."

He adjusted his maroon and blue striped tie. He ran his hand through his thick brown hair. "Let's say, I hope to see more miracles coming this way."

Dana could tell the young attorney had a habit for taking most of what she said as some type of romantic innuendo. There was no doubt she found the man handsome and a pleasure to be with, but she had no intention of giving him false hope. Dana turned the conversation back to the real reason why she had decided to accept Howard's offer. "I'm expecting to learn more about Douglas Clifford on this trip." The sound of the double propellers whirling made it difficult to speak or hear.

Howard nestled closer, "You were saying—?"

In a loud voice with a staccato sound to it, Dana repeated, "Douglas Clifford. . .need to learn more about the boy."

Howard nodded and settled back into his seat. "I wish you luck," he said.

Amen, Dana thought. Maybe, just maybe, Howard was getting the hint that her acceptance of his offer to fly to LA was strictly business.

* * *

The plane roared along the tarmac and came to settle at Gate G. The passengers hustled to exit the plane. "Could we plan dinner sometime tonight?" Howard asked, his voice sounding hurried, yet excited.

"I appreciate your offer, but my plans are to get to the bottom of this case as soon as I can."

Howard's eyebrows rested low over his dark, brown eyes.

Dana took out the return itinerary from her bag. "Let's plan on meeting at the airport on Thursday at seven p.m., shall we?"

"Our flight back to Texas?" He looked like a puppy that had been reprimanded.

Dana nodded. "I hope I'll have some good news by then to share with you."

"Sure, sure," was all he said. He stood and looked over his shoulder at Dana. "Good luck."

Dana could tell he had finally taken her hints. Under any other circumstance, she probably would have jumped at his offers for dinner. And who knew where she and the handsome man might end up, but for now, Howard Rhodes was not a person of interest in the case, and quite frankly, she did not have the time to invest in him.

She hailed a cab. "I'm going to be heading to the Department of Public Health. Might you know a decent hotel nearby?" she asked the driver.

"The Moulin Rouge is a decent place if you're only here on business."

She smiled to herself. Seemed even the cab driver picked up on her desires. "Great, that's what I'm here for." On her ride to the hotel, Dana made a list of the three places she hoped to visit over the course of her short trip:

- *Department of Public Health - Birth Registrations*
- *Paramount Studios*
- *Donna Iverson - 438 Enders Way*

Dana asked the cab driver to wait while she booked a room. She had every intention to use her time wisely. The hotel clerk handed her the key to Room 531. She told him she was in a hurry and asked if she might leave her small piece of luggage at the front desk until she returned.

She ran out to the cab, and told the driver, "Department of Health, please."

The brown ten-story brick building hovered at the corner of a busy intersection. Dana paid the driver and made her way up the concrete steps, losing count after twenty-seven wide stairs. She stood at the top to catch her breath and let the warm summer air brush across her face. A woman wearing a plaid jacket sat behind the information booth.

"Could you direct me to the records of birth?" Dana asked.

The woman chomped on a piece of pink bubble gum and pointed toward a long hallway behind her. "Elevator to the sixth floor," she managed to say.

The place reminded Dana of a train station with people bustling about in all directions. She rode the elevator with eight others, two of whom got off with her. She noticed they parted ways, obviously knowing where they were headed. Dana interrupted one of the secretaries typing from a stack of green sheets, looking back and forth at her keys.

"Birth records? Straight ahead, ninth desk down. . .a Mr. Myers can help you."

Dana assumed the woman must have been asked that very question many times.

A gentleman in a black and white tweed coat with a long white goatee looked up from the pile of folders on his metal desk. "May I help you, Ma'am?"

Dana explained the purpose of her visit and told the man what she had learned from Douglas Clifford's birth certificate.

He cleared his throat and from a Smith Brothers' tin popped a small red cough drop into his mouth. "Ah, yes, another movie star."

Dana bit down on her lower lip. "What's that supposed to mean?"

"We get a lot of them here. You didn't mention a name for the father of the child."

"Exactly. That's what I'm wondering."

"Wonder no further, Ma'am. The child was illegitimate and probably put up for adoption before the mother even laid eyes on him." He thought for a moment. "You say the mother's name is Chantel DeBour? A looker, that's for sure."

Dana found his comment a bit non-professional, but then again, this was the booming metropolis of LA. He'd probably seen it all.

The man continued, "Hollywood's sure going to miss her. Tragic, isn't it the way she died? Well, I've heard her chauffeur was driving the sports car at the time of the accident. Guess Miss DeBour never applied for a driver's license."

Dana didn't intend to be rude, but she could tell the man did not plan on ending his story anytime soon. She interrupted with, "Any idea how I might go about—."

"Finding the young man? No, no. Once a name is scratched out like this one, the record stays as is. As I was saying, more than likely, the child was put up for adoption; at least, that's what I've seen happen in the past. Those sisters down at the City of Angels. . .did you know that's what Los Angeles means. . .the City of Angels?"

"No, I guess I didn't."

"The City of Angels is the place most of the kids go when they're illegite."

Dana could tell the man must have been in the department for years and had many stories he longed to tell.

"Like I was saying those sisters down there must have hearts of gold. Sometimes a kid don't get adopted for years and is left for the sisters to deal with. The movie stars could care less; you know, their money grows on trees now, don't cha know?"

Dana attempted a smile. "Where might I find the adoption center?"

"Conveniently enough, right across the street, then two blocks up. Place has a tall black wrought iron fence around it. Looks non-too inviting, but those sisters, like I said—."

"Heart of gold," Dana said. She thanked the man for his time and ventured off to find the City of Angels before he had a chance to complete his thought.

The smell of city buses, the honking of traffic, and the sound of a siren in the not too far off distance completed the picture of downtown Los Angeles, so unlike anywhere she had ever been. A street car came bellowing down the side street, and Dana luckily jumped back from the tracks onto the curb just in time. When she saw two sisters, dressed in the habits of the Little Sisters of the Poor, coming toward her, she knew she couldn't be too far from the adoption home. The two nuns nodded, and one said, "Bless you."

Dana entered through the tall wrought-iron gates and buzzed the bell at the front door of the orphanage.

A young nun, who appeared to be in her teens, opened the door. "Yes?"

"My name's Dana Greer. I've come to speak with one of the sisters about a child who, I believe, was adopted from this agency."

"Why, of course. Please follow me."

The nun hummed a song from the recent movie "Roman Holiday." She paused and tapped at the closed door on her left. She peeked inside. "Sister Raphael, a guest is here to see you." Then, the nun turned and faced Dana. "You can go in now."

Sister Raphael reminded Dana of the Mother Superiors she'd had when an elementary student. A kind, yet aged face, one that had earned every wrinkle. The nun stood and introduced herself.

Dana and she shook hands. The nun asked her to have a seat. The office walls were covered in painting replicas of the Sistine Chapel, leaving hardly any bare space.

Dana explained the purpose of her visit.

"How dreadful," the elderly nun said. "One never knows what path lies ahead for us, does one? You come with the same question, though, that so many do. I sadly turn hundreds of people just like you away each month. Afraid our records are sealed, and there is no way I am at liberty to release any information to you."

"I understand, Sister, and I do know of the boy's adoptive parents. That's the reason why Douglas Clifford was sent to the St. Aloysius Gonzaga Home for Troubled Youth. He was accused of killing his adoptive parents."

The nun immediately bowed her head, "Jesus, Mary, Joseph, no. A troubled young man, you say?"

"It could be the boy was innocent; that's what I'm hoping to find out," Dana said.

"Praise be Jesus, let's hope so."

"As for the biological father of the child—."

"Oh, Miss Greer, we sisters have no way of knowing. When a child is sent to us, we receive the same birth certificate that you have. To protect the integrity of the father, names are blacked out."

"But what about Chantel DeBour, Sister? Is there anything you could tell me about her that might help?"

"Oh, dear, Miss, I've never had the good fortune to see Miss DeBour. Once the child is delivered at the hospital, the infant is brought to us. You see, there never is such a thing as a change of hands."

Dana thanked the nun, handed her one of her cards, and found her way to the front door. She remembered when she was a young child; it had been her wish to become a nun. There was something to be said for the quiet sanctuary of the soul only a convent could provide. Why, she even used to play dress-up and give herself various nun's names, acting out the part of a cloistered nun. . .the order she would have entered if she had—. She always paused at this point. Things had changed for her in second grade, and just like Sister Raphael had said, she had no idea before then what path lay ahead. She recalled again that night as if it was yesterday. Her uncle had given her the small Bible with the white grainy cover as her First Communion present. Hours later, he had taken her out on his rowboat for a small trip around the lake. A sudden storm seemed to erupt from nowhere, and she begged her uncle to take her back to shore. That's when he demanded she get down on her knees and service his sickening need. In the process, the boat rocked, waves gushed overboard, and she fell out of the boat. She remembered being pulled from the water by her long ponytail. She recalled, to this day, the pain she felt, how she had screamed. No words were ever spoken about that experience, and a few short years later, her uncle had gotten killed crossing a street. The secret they shared stayed with Dana. Not only had she feared water ever since that day, but she never quite saw herself the same since. She felt soiled, dirty, unholy. She knew God would never want her to wear the blessed garbs of a nun. Dana knew her life would have played out much differently if she had not agreed to go on her uncle's boat. The only concrete, positive memory of that night was the miniature Bible she still carried wherever she went. In some strange way, the little book brought her comfort and offered her security unlike what the giver of the gift had provided.

Dana reached for the small Bible in her bag while she hailed a cab. Tomorrow, she hoped, would be a more productive day.

Chapter Thirty-One

D
ana exited the cab and stood in awe in front of the tall metal gates leading into Paramount Studios. People paraded through the streets dressed in various costumes, ranging from ferocious looking tigers and lions, to women dressed in long, flouncy gowns from the cowboy days, to monsters in fur coats and strange masks. It reminded her of Halloween when she was a child. She remembered her mother working diligently at her Singer sewing machine with yards of satin and strings of lace and ruffles. Once she wore cardboard stars covered in foil; another year she was Mr. Peanut, complete with shells all over the burlap. Dana laughed to herself. When she went up to doors yelling, "Trick or Treat," the people knew exactly who she was dressed as. Dana always believed she was the best-dressed child on Halloween night, and it had usually earned her an extra handful of candy.

Dana squinted in the bright sunlight, could it be? There outside of Studio Six she spotted Humphrey Bogart and Fred MacMurray in their Naval officer uniforms. "The Caine Mutiny" due to come out next year, she thought. The sound of laughter and the chatter of bantering voices created a happy energy, an almost magical spirit. Dana wandered about until she came to a woman wearing dark rimmed glasses, her black hair cut in a bowl-shape, with short-cropped bangs. She looked friendly enough. Dana excused herself and said, "Might you know where I could find someone willing to speak with me about the late Chantel DeBour?"

The woman took a step back, removed her glasses, and readjusted them on the bridge of her nose. "You from a tabloid?" the woman asked, her voice almost manly and with a definite smirk on her face. If words could cut, hers would have sliced a brick.

The woman's reaction took Dana off guard. "No, actually, I'm a private investigator working on a murder case." Dana was not one to brag, but sometimes, she found it necessary to put people in their place by flaunting her credentials.

"Oh, really?"

"Yes, really," Dana said.

"Well, you know, Chantel was not run off the road if that's what you're thinking."

"Actually, I'm working on a murder case of someone Miss DeBour might have known, but I'd be interested in hearing your take on her death."

"Funny thing is Miss DeBour didn't drive, didn't even have a license. Actresses are like that. Confident on the screen but introverts behind the scenes, shy. I suppose you could say some even lack confidence. Low self-esteem, yes, that's what I'm driving at. Her chauffeur drove her wherever she needed to go. Drove her sports car for her. Some thought it ridiculous she didn't demand to be shuttled about in a limo like most of the stars, but Chantel preferred her little roadster."

"Interesting."

"Now, what were you saying about a murder? Should I get a reporter?"

"I'd wait until the case is solved. I'd like to speak to someone who could answer some questions for me about Miss DeBour."

"In that case, you see the stucco building with the green roof? I'd try there; ask for a Connie Litton. She's a costume designer, but she knows all the stars personally. Maybe, she might be able to help you."

Dana was about to say thank you when the woman put out her hand. "Anytime. The name's Edith. . .Edith Head."

The famous designer? Dana could not believe who she had been speaking with. She nodded and sheepishly headed for the building on her left.

The smell of strong clothing dyes filled the air and the song of Singer sewing machines whizzed loudly. Aisles and aisles were filled with various garments on satin-padded hangers and covered in clear plastic packaging. On the side wall were rows of spooled thread in every color.

"Needin' anything?" a man's voice called out to her.

"I'm here to see Connie Litton."

The man pointed to a woman who wore a felt hat with a bright pink feather. "She's the fifth machine down," he said. The woman at the machine looked like a character out of a movie, wearing a fuchsia jumpsuit and hot pink glasses to match. Around her neck, she wore a plastic nametag.

Dana interrupted her work with, "Excuse me, but I'm looking for a Connie Litton."

"That's me. Prefer to be called Candy." The woman blinked several times with obvious fake eyelashes, which appeared to be an inch long. Her cheeks matched the color of her outfit, and her lips were a shiny red.

Dana proceeded to introduce herself and in order to add some clout to the purpose of her visit, she mentioned that Edith Head had referred her. A white lie of sorts.

"Listen, I'm just about done here. What do you say we get some lunch? It'll be a lot quieter to talk over at the Paramount commissary."

Dana relished the idea. Not only was she hungry, but she also hoped to learn as much as she could about the starlet.

Candy checked out at the time clock next to the door, and the two of them walked a few hundred yards over to a small brick building, a sign over it saying "Commissary."

"Hope you don't mind bumping into a few stars. When not on the sound stage or in their trailers, many of them like to stop in for a quick beer and burger."

Candy made it sound like a normal day of work, but to Dana, the idea thrilled her. What fun it must be to rub shoulders with the people most only saw on the big screen.

The hostess, dressed as the comic book character Little Lulu, sat the two women in a green booth with a white Formica table. Her black, tightly wound curls bounced as she walked in front of them.

Posters from past and recent movies were splattered all over the walls. Framed, autographed photos of several movie stars covered any bare spots.

"Say," Dana whispered, "wasn't that Audrey Hepburn who just passed us? The one in the black pantsuit?'"

"Sure enough," the woman said. "She's playing the part of a daughter of a chauffeur in the movie 'Sabrina.' You must see it when it comes out; it's already getting great raves from the people at Paramount." Then, she gave Dana a long stare through her hot pink glasses. "A pretty woman like you must have a man in your life."

Dana pressed back in her seat, ready to speak but no words came. "I'm sorry. You caught me off guard with your comment." Yet, Dana used the remark as a natural segue to add, "Afraid I've not much time for that; men that is. You see, I'm in the middle of trying to solve a murder."

"You're with the LAPD, then? A cop? Not a model?"

Dana laughed. "Hardly. No, I'm a private investigator paid solely by the Catholic Church."

"Catholic Church, hmm? Not a churchgoer myself, but if I were, I'd choose to join the Catholics. Seem like an honest bunch of people." Candy positioned herself as if she were looking into a mirror. She shook her head and totally out of context said, "You look much too pretty, dear, to be getting your hands involved in such grisly matters; murder I mean." She paused for a moment. "And, the Catholic Church? Are you telling me they've got sinners, too?"

The woman's seriousness made Dana laugh. "I read in a 'Dear Abby' column, where Miss Van Buren said, 'The church is a hospital for sinners, not a museum for saints.'"

"Perhaps, perhaps, but you appear to. . .what is it. . .too sophisticated to be hanging around any lowlifes."

"Thank you," Dana felt the tips of her ears, warm to the touch. My job is actually quite rewarding when a case gets solved. As a matter of fact, that's why I hoped to speak with you, Candy." The seamstress was a talker, but Dana knew she only had so much time to get as much information from the woman as she could.

Dana went on to explain the story revolving around Chantel DeBour and her son Douglas Clifford.

"A shame, such a shame. A young boy set up like that. At least, that's what it sounds like to me, anyway," Candy said. "Far as I'm concerned, our society is too quick to put juveniles behind bars. I mean, most haven't even had a chance to be a kid yet."

"I agree and that's why I'm trying to find out who might have wanted the boy dead."

"Well, let me tell you one thing, dearie. You may or may not know this," she said, as the pink feather on her hat swayed forward and then backward, "but I've heard it all, working here the past thirty years. How can I help?"

Dana felt relieved the woman had finally gotten to the point of their meeting. Dana admitted, though, she liked the woman's forthrightness and spontaneity.

The server, a teenage boy dressed in a Superman outfit, brought frosted mugs of water to the table, and Candy did the ordering. "We'll have two Cokes and two of your Paramount burgers."

For a moment, Dana found herself distracted by the waiters and waitresses, all likenesses from the popular comic books. There was Ginger and Jughead, a couple of Donald Duck nephews, and even one boy padded out to look like the chubby Little King character.

"Quite the crowd, huh?" Candy interrupted.

"They're all so young, which reminds me. I've been told Miss DeBour had been dating a young man, several years younger than she. Might you know anything about him?"

"Him? Who didn't? It was the talk of the studio. Oh, I don't mean affairs don't go on around here; it's part of the business, I'd say, but Miss DeBour's interest in a mere adolescent shocked everyone, I think. I mean, a grown woman with a child. . .whoever heard of such a thing?"

"The boy—?"

"A server right here at the commissary. Like they say, it was love at first sight." Candy hovered over her water glass obviously interested in sharing her juicy news. "What surprised everyone was Miss DeBour was around thirty at the time, and the boy was a mere sixteen! I mean, that's the kind of stuff that starts gossip. Andrew Ziebrewsky, the producer—her husband, never got wind of it until it was too late. Some think he was too busy to take notice; others say he was hittin' the bottle; while still others believe he had his own romantic affair going on the side."

Andrew Ziebrewski. . .Dana remembered reading about him in one of the library magazines.

"Her husband didn't have a clue until Miss DeBour began to show. Must have been at least six or seven months along when he realized she was doing more than starring in movies. Either he paid a deaf ear to the Paramount gossip, or he chose not to believe it."

Dana was pleased the woman finally offered so much background information on the starlet without her having to ask too many questions.

Candy finished the last drop of water in her glass. "You know, Miss DeBour was Catholic. . .didn't believe in any back-alley abortion. No, she went ahead and had the child and gave it up for adoption. By then, Andrew was history."

"Do you know if she ever considered marrying the boy?"

The woman chuckled. "Her? Some talk has it she was more than ready to walk down the aisle with that mere child. As for him? Hardly, the only reason he got involved with her in the first place was he was nothing more than a wanna be actor on the side. Thought she might be his ticket to stardom."

"But, you're saying Miss DeBour was actually serious about the boy?"

"People around here couldn't believe she could be that naïve. She fell head, foot, and sinker for the boy. Think the two of them might have married, but the kid left her once he found out she was bearing his child. That's the way it always is, isn't it? My mother used to tell me, 'A man gets what he wants, and he's off to find another.'"

Dana nodded as the server brought their orders.

Candy squirted the mustard and ketchup on her hamburger until it dripped down the sides and pooled onto her plate. For the next several minutes, the woman went silent, shoving the burger into her mouth, completing it in about seven quick bites. "We learn to eat fast around here. Only get a half-hour lunch." She gulped her glass of Coke down her throat in three simple swallows.

Dana found herself more interested in what she was learning than in eating, and when the server asked her if she was through with her meal, Dana nodded.

"You eat like a bird," Candy said. "No wonder you have such a great shape. And, your hair? How do you get those perfect curls? Ever think of modeling? Like I told you, I thought you were one."

Dana smiled as her face felt warm to the touch. "No, not really."

"That's about all I know, Miss Greer, about the lovers, that is."

"The boy" Dana asked. "Do you remember anything about him?"

"Tall, dark, rather like a young Julius La Rosa. By the way, talk has it Julius may be coming out with a brand-new album. You know, ever since my husband walked out on me, I fall asleep listening to Julius La Rosa's records." Candy paused and toyed with the rim of her Coke glass. "Did you know the boy sang in the Navy choir. . .such a good-looking young man."

"Whatever happened to the boy who resembled him. . .Miss DeBour's lover?"

"God knows. He sure didn't stick around here none. He tended to be what some said was a mama's boy. . .a little bit too close to his mother, if you know what I mean. Might explain why he went after an older woman; he probably saw Miss DeBour as a mother figure."

"Interesting. His mother? Know anything about her?"

"Nope, other than the two skit and skedaddled out of here." Candy looked at the clock on the wall. "Afraid I'd better get back to work. I'm sewing a costume for Judy Garland."

"How exciting!"

"Not as exciting as your work," Candy said, as she paid the server and wished Dana luck with the case.

Dana had to agree with Candy. Her work did become exciting when the pieces of the puzzle were slowing coming together. Dana handed one of her cards to Candy and asked her to call if she thought of anything additional that might help solve the case.

Next, she would see if she could pay a spontaneous call on Donna Iverson, the woman listed in Douglas Clifford's file. She peeked in her bag and looked up the address. This would be her last stop, and she hoped it might be as successful as her visit to Paramount.

* * *

When the cab turned from the business section of LA and closer to the residential areas, the appearance took on a less glamorous and glitzy appearance. Other than an intermittent palm tree here and there, Dana thought it looked pretty much like any other city, USA. If anything, she found the streets to be a bit disgusting with scattered papers, cigarette butts, and decaying road kill. The homes, mostly stucco with red tile roofs, got smaller and smaller, most without garages. Rusted out old cars and dented trucks lined the dirt driveways. In between the houses, a storefront popped up or an abandoned building.

The cab came to a stop and pulled up in front of a small, pink stucco house, where a Radio Flyer wagon, a tricycle, and a large ball rested on what was left of the burnt grass out front.

"This is 438 Ender Way, Ma'am. You're lucky. It looks like someone's home. Some of the places around her aren't safe to even enter in the daylight."

"Yes, yes," Dana said, asking the driver if he might wait for her while she paid a short visit.

"Sure can," he said, "but the meter keeps running, Lady."

Dana scowled at the man and stepped out on onto the side of the curb.

A small boy with ruffled brown hair and blue Dennis the Menace overalls ran out the screen door at the same time a woman's voice yelled, "Be back by six before the street lights come on."

Dana's pumps tapped along the twisted stone walkway to the woman's front door. "Might you be Miss Iverson, Donna Iverson?"

The woman slammed the screen and peering through its grid said, "I'm afraid I don't know who you are."

At the moment Miss Iverson was about to close the storm door, Dana said, "Please, please, wait one minute." She briefly introduced herself and explained the purpose of her visit, focusing on the death in the cellblock at the St. Aloysius Gonzaga Home for Troubled Youth.

"Douglas is dead?" the woman said, more as a question than a statement. "How can that be?"

"Yes, murdered in his cell at the boys' home."

Donna Iverson opened the door, "Please come in." In the same breath, she told a toddler, "Jimmy, pick up those toys and go play in your room for mommy." The boy grabbed a pile of green plastic army men and headed down the hall. "Here, have a seat," she said, tossing a tinker toy onto the worn carpet. "Could I get you something to drink? Don't have too much. Water?" She looked at Dana with an incredulous look. "So, little Douglas…dead?"

Dana sat down on an armchair, the wood covered in scratches, the blue fabric frayed. "No, thanks. I promise I won't be long. I'm wondering how well you knew the Clifford family?"

"JJ, short for John Junior, my son, played with Douglas all the time. The boys were about the same age."

"What type of child was Douglas?"

"Sweet, a little honey. That is until he turned around eight or nine. Started to get into trouble with the law. Small things, you know. . .stealing, breaking a window, things like that. That's when I told JJ he was no longer allowed to play with Douglas. Didn't want no bad habits rubbing off on my kid, you know? Why you can understand. . .a bad influence and all." Miss Iverson thought for a moment. "Always felt sorry for the boy, though. The couple, Nina and Harold, were much too old to be taking in a newborn. They must have been at least forty at the time."

"What was the relationship like between Harold and Nina Clifford and the boy as he got older?"

"They loved the boy as if he was their own even after his run-ins with the police. Far as I know, the boy felt the same way about them."

"So, you don't know of any encounters where the boy was mean to his adoptive parents, called them names, anything like that?"

"No, Douglas acted like any other boy his age, and they seemed like any other family. I never got the feeling the boy was unhappy. . .curious maybe but not unhappy."

Quickly, Dana changed the subject. "The night Mr. and Mrs. Clifford were killed. . .June 1st of last year...were you at home; did you happen to see or hear anything out of the usual?"

"No, Nina and Harold went out for the night. . .their anniversary or some such thing. I remember the night as if it was yesterday. . .June 1st. Nina asked if I could look after Douglas until they got home. Like I said, by that time, I wasn't crazy about the boy, but I knew Nina and Harold never went out and felt they deserved a little time alone. I said 'yes.' The kids and me had dinner, and then the boys played a game of Parcheesi before I had them get ready for bed. That was around nine."

"About what time did the parents return?"

"Oh, I'd say around ten. By then, JJ, my boy Jimmy, and Douglas were sound asleep. I checked in on them with my own eyes. I told Nina to let the boy spend the night. No sense trying to wake the kids."

"Did she let him stay?"

Donna Iverson nodded. "Funny thing, though, about six in the morning, Douglas got up, came into my room, and said he wanted to go home. I didn't see a problem with that. I assumed Nina and Harold were home, and off he went but not before taking his ragged, little rabbit. Carried the thing around with him wherever he went."

"But, let me get this clear. Douglas stayed at your house the evening, spent the night, and then left early the next morning?"

"That's right." Donna Iverson nodded.

Dana remembered Sergeant McKnight telling her Douglas was found home alone, sitting in the living room. His face was a blank stare, humming some church song, oblivious of the turmoil surrounding him. That was around eight a.m. The Cliffords were bludgeoned to death with Douglas's baseball bat sometime before the boy returned from the Iverson house. Someone had called the police and reported the murder but who? And did Douglas even realize his parents were dead? Might he have thought when he got home that they were still asleep? Could the door to their bedroom have been closed, leading the boy to think so? Dana bit down on her lower lip. She looked at the woman. "Are you sure the boy spent the entire night here, the night the Cliffords were killed?"

"I'm sure, but I slept soundly until I was awakened by Douglas at six a.m."

Dana's thoughts whirled. Someone had gotten into the house during Douglas's absence, taken his baseball bat, and bludgeoned the parents to death, then left to make it look like the boy had committed the crime. But one thing didn't make sense. Whoever had murdered the parents must have thought Douglas was asleep in his room at the time, and that the blame would be put on the boy. Unfortunately, that's what the police must have assumed, as well.

The woman toyed with a small, tarnished locket around her neck. She looked puzzled. "I plain don't believe it. Douglas would never have killed his parents. A bit of a troublemaker yes, but a cold-blooded killer? I don't believe it. . .no way."

"Good question. That's what I want to verify."

"Maybe the killer is the one who called in the crime, making it sound as if he was the boy," Donna Iverson said.

"I was thinking along those lines also." Dana paused for a moment.

"Anything else I could help you with?"

"I did have another thought. Did Mrs. Clifford ever mention if the family had any enemies? Anyone who made threats against them?"

"No, not that I know of. Then again, Nina and I weren't all that close. Small talk over the backyard fence. Nothing personal, though. Seemed like a nice enough family. Can't imagine why someone would plot to murder them."

"I see." Dana thanked the woman for her time, handed her one of her cards, and asked if she thought of anything else to please give her a call.

* * *

Dana exited the cab at the airport and hurried to the terminal, where she was to meet Howard Rhodes. She found him sitting in the gate area, reading the "Los Angeles Times."

When he saw her, he stood. "Dana, so happy you made it. I was getting worried about you." He looked at his watch.

"So much has happened in the last two days."

He put his paper down. "Good or bad?" he asked.

"Let's just say, good with a question mark."

The PanAm stewardess announced the plane was boarding as the two made their way down the aisle to their seats. Dana squeezed next to a man, whose lap was covered with a stack of comic books. "I'm a collector. Have been for years. Did you know one of these books...take this *Felix the Cat*...someday, it will be worth a mint."

"Nice," Dana said.

Howard sat on the opposite side of Dana. "What's the question mark for?" he asked, his eyes sparkling with a hint of curiosity.

Dana explained what she had learned in the last several hours from her visit with Donna Iverson. "From my conversation with Donna, the timeline doesn't add up. If the boy left the Iverson's and went home Sunday morning, and the call about the murder came in before Douglas arrived, it doesn't make sense that he killed his parents." Dana thought for a minute. "Unless——."

"Yes?"

"Unless unbeknown to Donna while she was fast asleep, could Douglas have gone home and committed the crime?"

"Interesting! Suppose that's one theory."

"On the other hand, if he slept through the night and never went home, it means the boy could have been framed for murder. Someone else could have done away with the boy's parents and made it appear Douglas committed the crime. But who and why?"

"A true set-up," Howard nodded.

Dana pondered. What would be a possible reason to frame a nine-year-old for murdering his own parents? Dana remembered how her prior mentor Fiona Wharton had warned her so many times about getting ahead of herself, skipping steps, coming to conclusions too abruptly—all in an attempt to solve a case. She hoped she wasn't doing that, yet she wanted to share her ideas, to hear them spoken out loud to see if they seemed to make good sense to someone other than herself.

There was a long moment of silence before either of them spoke. "Sounds as if you've got more leads to check out."

Dana nodded. "Thanks for letting me tag along."

While Howard continued with, "My pleasure. Who wouldn't be happy to travel with a beautiful lady like yourself," Dana ignored his comment, deep in thought. For the first time since the case started, she felt she had more pieces of the puzzle to consider. For sure, she had more answers but, then again, even more questions.

Chapter Thirty-Two

The minute Dana stepped inside the doorway to Ellie's house, Ellie met her with a relieved look on her face. "Perfect timing. There's someone on the phone for you. Couldn't quite make out the name, but I think, she said her name was Sister something."

Dana ran into the kitchen and put the receiver to her ear. "This is Dana Greer."

"Miss Greer, how are you, dear? This is Sister Raphael at the City of Angels."

"I'm fine. Thank you, Sister."

"Happy I found you in, Miss Greer. I got to thinking some more after you left the agency yesterday. Glad you left me your card."

"Yes, yes?" Dana could not wait until the nun got to her point.

"There was a note. . .a small, handwritten one. . .scrawled onto Douglas Clifford's paperwork when he was signed over to us."

"But I thought the files were sealed?"

"This is our own internal admittance form that's stapled to the front of each child's file at the time they are brought to the home."

"What did it say? Who signed it?" As usual when Dana got excited, believed she was onto something, her questions often had a way of getting ahead of her.

"Signed by Miss DeBour herself. It gave the number of an attorney."

Dana was baffled with confusion.

"The note said in the event Miss DeBour was to die before her son, the attorney be called. Perhaps, you should be trying to make contact with Miss DeBour."

"I'm afraid that won't be possible, Sister. I heard the woman died in a tragic accident over a year ago."

"Jesus, Mary, Joseph, no."

"Yes, Sister, in an auto accident."

"Perpetual light shine upon her soul."

"Sister, might I have the name of the attorney?"

"Surely. I can't see it doing any harm. The man's name is Theodore Prussia. Do you have a pen? I'll give you his number."

Dana reached into her bag, still hanging from her shoulder. "Go ahead, please."

"Well, that's odd," the nun said.

"What's that?"

"The phone exchange isn't one I recognize."

"Could I have the number, please?"

"It's MA 7 - 2298. Do you recognize the *MA*?"

"Why, yes, yes, I do. It's Mayberry. That's an exchange from somewhere in the East, I believe," Dana said.

"That's odd. Do you think Miss DeBour might have been from the East?"

Dana found the nun's healthy curiosity a breath of fresh air. "I'm wondering that myself, or maybe he was a friend of Miss DeBours. No matter, I'll give the man a call."

"I'll pray for you, Miss Greer. May the Holy Ghost help you to get to the bottom of this."

Dana thanked the nun and began dialing the Mayberry number. The phone rang and rang. If the extension were out of the area, it might very well account for why no one was picking up, she reassured herself. She would try again in the morning.

Ellie entered the kitchen. "My, my, you look happier than, I think, I have ever seen you. Want to celebrate with a cup of tea? I happen to have some brewing."

Dana had been so excited she failed to smell the cinnamon and apple fragrance in the room. "I'd like that," she said.

As the two women sipped on their tea from China cups, Dana began to tell Ellie all that had happened in California, ending with her recent call from Sr. Raphael. Under normal circumstances, Dana would have been speaking with the police chief who assigned her the case, but she had given up hopes of dealing with Sergeant McKnight. True, he had contacted her about the investigation, but as far as she was concerned, he was worthless in terms of wanting to get involved. . .totally worthless. And, in a town the size of Punkerton, she learned there actually were no police, per se. Sergeant McKnight was all she had. No matter that the station was called the Punkerton Police Department, McKnight was it.

"Your trip proved helpful then?" Ellie asked.

"The people I met were more than willing to help, yes."

"But this Sister—?"

"Sister Raphael, yes?"

Ellie scratched the side of her cheek. "She must not have known about the boy's murder. Sounds as if his adoption had been completed ten years ago, and that was that."

"Right you are. I thought the same thing. The agency seems to be such a busy place I can see why things might not get acted upon or filed away without notice."

"Such as the whole thing with the attorney. Do you think the movie star left a Will?"

"Interesting you should ask because I was thinking the same. Was there money left for the boy in the event of Miss DeBour's death?" Dana sipped on her tea.

Ellie swallowed hard and stared across the room. She twirled a pearl button on her housedress. "I just thought of something strange."

Dana waited for the woman to continue.

"Isn't it odd Miss DeBour's death, Douglas Clifford's, and his adoptive parents all fall within less than a year of each other?"

"Right you are, Sherlock: March 3, 1952; June 1, 1952; and February 28, 1953. Dana, impressed with Ellie's thought process, asked, "You're thinking the same thing I am. Might someone have done away with Miss DeBour in order to gain access to the woman's Will? And was Douglas in some way included in that Will?"

"Yet from what I read—excuse me for saying so, but I read in the 'National Harpoon'—her death was a mere accident. Her sport's car swerved off the road and into a ditch. She was found dead at the scene along with her chauffeur." Ellie set her cup down with a clink on its tiny saucer.

"So, the newspaper account said. It makes me wonder if anyone did an autopsy on the woman or at a bare minimum, at least checked on the car," Dana said.

"Are you meaning someone may have tampered with the brakes or something on Miss DeBour's car?"

"Why not? It would make sense, making the whole incident appear like a mere accident when, in fact, it was all planned."

"There's another unanswered question, though?"

"What's that?" Dana asked, as she finished the last of her tea.

"If Miss DeBour's death was a deliberate act, why would someone wait that long to do away with the movie star?"

Dana ran her index finger over her lower lip. "I see where you're heading with this. If Douglas Clifford was to be part of the Will, why wait until the boy was almost ten years of age to do away with Miss DeBour? Why not sooner?"

Ellie's hands flew into the air. "I've got it! I've got it!" She jumped up from her seat. "What if the contents of the Will were only recently learned?" She clapped her hands together as if in an applause.

Dana tapped at her lips, nodding several times.

"What do you think?" Ellie asked, sounding proud of her potential assessment.

"That just might be the answer. You might be onto something. Could it be the movie star had only written up a Will prior to her death? Is it mere coincidence that shortly after she filed the Will she passed away?"

This time Ellie nodded.

Thinking out loud, Dana continued, "And if Theodore Prussia, the attorney, found out the Will's proceeds were to go to a deceased child—."

"Maybe there was a second beneficiary," Ellie said, completing Dana's thought.

Dana stood up and took her cup and saucer to the kitchen counter. "With Douglas Clifford out of the way, what if the proceeds of the Will were meant to go to his caregivers?"

In an exuberant voice, Ellie almost shouted, "The boys' home, of course."

"Which would explain why someone in the home wanted Douglas out of the picture," Dana stood up from the table and poised her hands in a prayerful mode.

"Oh dear! The plot thickens. How do you ever keep this all straight?"

"I love to draw."

Ellie squinted her eyes and crinkled her nose. "Draw?"

"Diagrams, actually. I need to draw this out and see, for myself, the connections and where to go from here. An old friend taught me the technique." Dana smiled to herself as she envisioned Fiona Wharton standing beside her. Then, she heard Fiona warn her, "Don't be so quick to jump to conclusions."

"You're right; you're right."

Ellie looked at Dana with a confused expression. "What was that? What were you saying?"

"Nothing. . .just thinking about what my old friend told me."

"About drawing? Good advice. I'd be so confused about now I'd just throw my hands up."

"Don't think I haven't done that," Dana said.

The two women laughed.

* * *

At the desk in her room, Dana pulled a sheet of paper and a pencil from her bag. She began to draw.

Dana began to think out loud. "All of the potential suspects would have had reason to kill Douglas Clifford in hopes of gaining access to Miss DeBour's Will. It appeared now, though, that Arthur Russell, the tough thug, or for that matter any other of the inmates would have to be ruled out.

Who did away with whom and why???

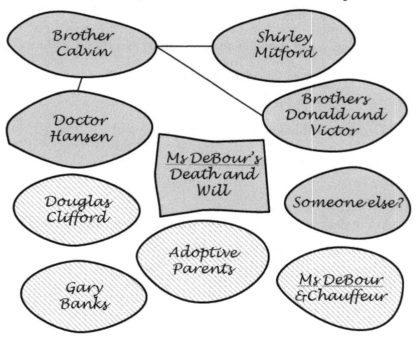

"Quite possibly Brother Calvin did away with the boy. He certainly had more than enough motives. He, himself, was abused as a child, and he was known to torment the Clifford child. If in any way, he found Douglas to be irritating, such as being the stutterer some said he was and the fact he appeared naive, in Calvin's way of thinking, he would have been more than intolerant of the child. Yet, if the proceeds of the Will were to go to the home, what part, if any, would Brother Calvin get?

"On the other hand, if Brother Calvin and Shirley Mitford were lovers on the side and Douglas Clifford had inadvertently seen the two together, murdering their eyewitness would have made sense. Maybe, Brother Calvin along with Shirley would find a way to confiscate the proceeds from the Will once the money was paid to the youth home. Dana would not put it past those two.

"Another possibility could be Doctor Hansen was the guilty one. He was known to have performed illegal procedures and even had his medical license terminated. Known to be more a follower than a leader, who was to say he didn't kill the boy in the same way he took orders from Brother Calvin to have Timothy Laughton's tongue severed and Gary Banks's heart stopped with the poisonous drink. But, the proceeds from the Will would have had nothing to do with him, Dana thought.

According to Carl Fenton, the seminarian, Brothers Donald and Victor were secretly known to be homosexual lovers. Here, again, if Douglas had seen the two men together, it could be that the affair would find its way, given the right channels, to Rome. That would, more than likely, be cause for grave concern for the brothers. Certainly, the two brothers could be thought to be caregivers of the boy."

As far as Dana knew, once a person was declared deceased, a Will became public domain. She set her hopes on Theodore Prussia as the person to confirm her belief. If she was correct and the boy's caregivers were the ones next in line to receive the monies from the Will, it would only be a matter of time until she could figure out who murdered Douglas Clifford.

After the last couple of busy days, Dana found herself exhausted and readied herself for bed. The sooner morning came, the sooner she could speak with Theodore Prussia and get to the bottom of the case.

Dana put her pencil down and rubbed her forehead. She could feel one of her migraines brewing. Yet, she forced herself to continue pondering who else might have stood to gain from Miss DeBour's Will. Someone had murdered Douglas Clifford to step into the beneficiary role and to claim the benefits of the Will. If the second recipient of the Will, after the boy's death, was to be his caregivers, as far as Dana could conclude so far, that put the blood of the boy on the hands of someone in the boys' home.

Chapter Thirty-Three

Morning could not have come sooner for Dana. She immediately placed her phone call to Theodore Prussia. Dana explained how she had gotten the man's name and phone number and why she thought he might be able to help. She explained Douglas Clifford was sentenced to the youth home, accused of murdering his adoptive parents.

"I recall the Will. Why, of course, I do. Miss DeBour's parents were long time clients of mine before they passed away. I used to live in LA myself but moved out here to avoid all of the congestion."

"Could you tell me who the beneficiary of Miss DeBour's estate was?"

"The Will states the estate of Miss DeBour is to go to her only blood relative, her son, Douglas Clifford, when the boy reaches the age of ten. Miss DeBour specifically requested the proceeds of her Will be left in trust until this time and then used to send the boy to the Academy of Mary Mother of God in San Diego, an exclusive boarding school. Any money left at the time of his graduation was to go to the young man for his own discretionary use."

"The age of ten?" According to what Dana and Ellie has discussed last night, that would totally explain why Miss DeBour's plight, her accident, happened at the time it did…right around his birthday. Is he the only beneficiary then?"

"Not exactly. Perhaps, I shouldn't get into this, but Miss DeBour and I had a long talk at the time of the preparation of her Will. A lovely woman, a good-hearted woman. Lived with guilt for years over having had an illicit love affair with a mere boy. When she could no longer bear the sin, she told me she confessed to a priest. The priest recommended for her penance, I guess, that she also leave a small amount of her estate to the boy's adoptive parents, and if they should be deceased, to whomever were the legal guardians of the child at the time of her death." The man paused, and Dana thought the connection had been broken.

"Are you still there?" she asked.

He continued his thought. "Why, the child was born out of wedlock. Who would want to leave any proceeds to such a child? That might explain why Miss DeBour had put the majority of her estate toward the boy's education. It's plain shameful; that's what it is. Of course, I wasn't at liberty to say that; plus, how could I speak against her confessor?"

Dana disagreed with the man but decided to keep her thoughts to herself. She could hear the man muttering to himself. She continued, "You know Douglas Clifford died on February twenty-eighth."

"So, I heard. The Will designated in that case, the monies go to the boy's caregivers, a Mr. Harold and Mrs. Nina Clifford."

"The parents are deceased, as well," she said, "murdered in their own home."

Theodore Prussia breathed heavily. "Wondered why I heard nothing from them once the boy died. Christ be told. And as you said murdered in their own home. What's become of today's society?"

Just as Dana figured. With the boy and his adoptive parents out of the way, who would the caregivers be other than the brothers? If a heart could sing, Dana knew hers would. This was exactly the news she had hoped to hear.

"Interesting job, you have there, Miss. For now, the only thing that can be concluded is the brothers at the home would legally be the boy's caregivers. That is—."

Dana let the man gather his thoughts.

"That is unless there's a biological father in the picture."

"Next of kin, for sure, but from what I've gathered, he has not been on the scene since the child was given up for adoption. At least, that's what Sister Raphael from the adoption agency in Los Angeles told me." She stopped for a moment. She could hear the man tapping a pencil as if to gather his thoughts.

"Hardly could the father of the child be seen as a caregiver. . .in that case."

"Thank you, Mr. Prussia, you've confirmed what I needed to know."

Dana was about to hang up when the man called out to her, "Wait one moment. You understand, as is often the case in Wills, however, a relative will show up to claim what he or she feels is justifiably his or hers."

"The father? You mean, the child's father might appear out of nowhere?"

"Can't say I haven't seen it happen, Miss. Wanted you to be aware of the possibility."

Dana gave Theodore Prussia Ellie's phone number. "Please call me immediately if such should be the case."

"I'm sure something like that could put a tangle in your web."

"What's that? Oh, yes, a complication in the investigation. Right, right." Dana thanked Mr. Prussia and hung up the receiver. After what the attorney had just told her about a relative having a claim to the Will, she began to wonder if Douglas Clifford's biological father might be considered a suspect?

Chapter Thirty-Four

Dana awoke with a start. Ellie stood outside her door calling, "Telephone, Dana, telephone."

Dana glanced at the clock on her night table. She could not believe she had slept until ten o'clock. Grateful for Ellie's wake-up call, Dana threw on a robe and went to the door.

"Mr. Rhodes is on the phone."

"Great," Dana mumbled to herself. "Good morning, Howard."

"How's my favorite detective?"

"Might I also add and the only one you know?"

Howard chuckled. "Anymore thought on how your trip to California went?"

"Got a few minutes?" she asked. "I'd like to fill you in on all of the details."

"Ready as you are."

Dana began at the beginning about Douglas Clifford's mother being the starlet Chantel DeBour and his father being a young lover.

"That story could be made into a movie. Let's see who the cast could be—."

Dana ignored the man's comment and continued. She told Howard about Douglas' adoption and the news of Miss DeBour's attorney. "His name's Theodore Prussia from somewhere back East."

"Did I hear you correctly. . .back East? Seems a bit odd considering Miss DeBour was from Hollywood."

"The attorney said he had been a friend of the DeBour family for some time. Mr. Prussia actually lived in Los Angeles once upon a time."

"Wait a minute," Howard said.

"What's that?"

"There may be more than one connection with this attorney. The young guy Miss DeBour was having the affair with. . .where was he from?"

Dana thought for a few seconds. "Good question. I assumed Hollywood." Then, she remembered Candy speaking about Miss De Bour's lover. She had said something about the boy skipping out of town as soon as he realized he had impregnated the star, but Candy didn't mention if she had any idea where the boy went. Dana made herself a mental note to call Candy the moment she got off the phone. "Let me do some more checking on Douglas Clifford's biological father. If he's originally from back East, I may be onto something."

"You're one sharp cookie," Howard said.

Dana hated those trivial expletives men liked to give women. She wondered how many men would appreciate being compared to a dessert.

"If you need my help, you know I'm only a phone call away."

She also knew the man cared much more about getting to know her personally than he cared about assisting her in solving the case.

"I'll keep that in mind, Howard," she said, as she gently put the receiver back on its hook.

Ellie poured some maple syrup on a stack of pancakes she had taken off the stove. "Here, dear, help yourself. Don't mean to eavesdrop, but how are things going between you and Mr. Rhodes?"

"That's the problem, Ellie. They never *were going*. I think, Mr. Rhodes would like to think otherwise, but it's not the case."

Ellie stuffed a bite of pancake into her mouth and offered no comment.

Dana appreciated Ellie's kindness. She enjoyed spending time with the woman who made her feel so welcome. Dana finished the last of her breakfast and rinsed her dish in the sink. Patches sat on the windowsill chasing a fly with his paw.

On her way to her room, the doorbell rang. "I'll get it Ellie." The postman seemed a bit surprised to see Dana at the door again. "Oh, I remember you. Brought you a parcel before. Say, do you have any idea who that idiot was out in front of your house?"

"What? I'm not sure I understand."

"Guy in a black car, missing hubcaps, who almost rode over me. He was parked right there," the man said, pointing to the curb, where Dana recalled seeing a car with the same description the last time a package was delivered.

"I was stepping out of my truck when he gunned his engine. Good thing I stepped back when I did. Excuse me but the jackass would have nailed me flat on the pavement if I didn't move as quickly as I did."

"No, I have no idea who that might have been. Sorry, though."

Goose bumps covered Dana's bare arms. How many times had it been now…two, three…that she had noticed the vehicle?

The postman shook his head and handed Dana the parcel. "Afraid this thing wouldn't fit in the box." With his eyes squinted, he added, "Seems light enough."

He attempted to shake the package when Dana said, "Thank you." She took the box from the man's hands and went into the kitchen.

In a scratchy print, the label bore her name: *Dana Greer*, but there was no return address.

"Who was at the door, Ellie?"

"The mailman. Seems someone sent me a package."

Ellie walked over to the kitchen table and, like a child on Christmas morning, excitedly peered over Dana's shoulder. "Sure is wrapped well."

Dana fumbled with the tape, slitting the box open with the edge of her fingernail. Shredded paper poured out of the box like popcorn overflowing a bowl. She reached down deeply into the package and brought forth a ragged-looking stuffed bunny with black buttons for eyes, stiff broomstick-like whiskers, and a missing ear. A tattered blue satin ribbon wound its way around the toy's neck.

"My, my, what have we here?" Ellie asked.

Dana's lips began to tremble involuntarily. She tried to speak, but no words came. She recalled what Donna Iverson, the Cliffords' neighbor, had told her the day she paid her a visit. Dana held the stuffed toy in both hands, trying to keep her hands from shaking.

"Dana, here have a seat. This rabbit. . .you know who it belongs to?" The wrinkles on Ellie's forehead deepened.

"Douglas. . .Douglas Clifford. . .it's his," was all Dana could say.

"How do you know this?"

Dana briefly explained what Donna Iverson had told her the night she watched the child for the Cliffords. "Mrs. Iverson had said that about six in the morning, he got up and said he wanted to go home. She didn't see a problem with that, and off he went. She made it a distinct point to tell me the boy did not leave her house that morning until he took the toy with him."

Ellie made an O face. "You're telling me this stuffed toy belonged to Douglas Clifford?"

Additionally, Dana remembered when studying the boy's file that a stuffed toy had been listed in his possessions when he had been admitted to the home. That might have explained why some of the prisoners, such as Arthur Russell, might have poked fun at Douglas, a nine-year-old boy with a tattered, stuffed toy as a security blanket. It also personified an innocence not likely found in a hardened criminal as he was described to her, hardly something one might expect from a child who bludgeoned his parents to death with his own baseball bat.

Dana told Ellie about the youth home records and the belongings with which Douglas entered the youth home.

"He had it with him in his cell?"

". . .the cause for much of his treatment at the home. Boys like Arthur Russell were poking fun of him. But, they may have been onto something. Would a cold-blooded killer require a stuffed toy for security?" It didn't add up. And, furthermore, it still did not provide an answer as to who would have sent the toy to her. Someone had possession of not only this but of the boy's baby book, as well. Dana felt now was the time to share this information with Ellie. "This isn't all I've received."

"You mean there was another package sent here?"

Dana ran to her bedroom and retrieved the baby book of Douglas Clifford. "Look at this."

Ellie took the book from Dana and began to page through it. "This obviously was meant to be a keepsake for the child when he grew up. It's beautiful. But, who would have gotten his hands on it?" Ellie, void of color, shook her head from one side to the other. "This is not good. Someone is obviously trying to give you a good scare, and I don't like the looks of it. How frightening to send you the dead boy's belongings. Who would be that sick?"

This time Dana shook her head. "And, why?" For a moment, the two women went silent. Dana remembered what the mailman had said about the black car. Was someone trying to make sure Dana was the one to get the boxes? Someone was watching her, had been for some time.

Ellie broke the quiet with, "Like I said, the only thing I can think is, it's meant to scare you."

"Perhaps, but I won't let myself go there. If it is some kind of morbid message, I refuse to back down now. I plan to find out who did this to that poor, little boy, and in turn, who killed his parents."

Ellie stood up and put her arm around Dana's shoulders. "You will. I know you will."

Dana nodded but she had to admit, the strange packages were enough to take her back a bit. She held the stuffed rabbit at arm's length and stared into its button eyes. She put the ragged toy back into its box. She glanced at the clock on the kitchen wall. Ten-thirty. That meant it was eight-thirty in the morning in LA. Dana explained to Ellie she needed to call the costume designer, Candy, at Paramount to see if she might get some further knowledge as to the whereabouts of Douglas Clifford's father.

"Sure thing, dear, you go right ahead. I'm going to clean up a few dishes and get to my crocheting. Got a feeling you're going to be out of Punkerton in no time, and I need to get working on that afghan of yours."

"You're so sweet, Ellie, but as for cracking this case anytime soon, I'm not quite as positive as you."

Dana looked through her bag for the telephone number of Paramount Studios and called the Costume Design Department.

"Costume Design Paramount Studios. Can I help you?"

Dana could hear the whizzing of the sewing machines.

Someone yelled out. "Find me the purple spool of thread."

"Could I speak with Candy?" Dana raised her voice to be heard over the commotion.

The man screamed, "Candy, phone for you."

"Candy, here."

"It's Dana."

"So good to hear from you again, Miss Greer. What can I help you with?"

"Douglas Clifford's father. . .the young man who impregnated Miss DeBour?"

"Ah, yes, the one who left as soon as he realized?" she asked.

"Any chance you might know where the boy was headed or where he was from originally?"

"Like I told you, in this kind of environment, people talk a lot. Not to say, they know the facts, or what they're saying, you hear?"

"I understand."

"Some said Miss DeBour's lover was from somewhere back East, but who knows?"

Bingo, Dana thought.

"He and his mother came out West, so he could make it in movies. It was a pipe dream, of course, like so many others who come here. That's why scuttlebutt has it the boy had one intention only in getting involved with Miss DeBour, and that was to make it big.

Needless to say, when Miss DeBour found herself pregnant and married, the kid skipped town like a scared rabbit."

"Back East?"

"Who knows?" she repeated.

Dana thanked Candy for her help and told her the supposed rumors were just what she wanted to hear.

"One last thing, Candy. Any word on what he did in the East?"

"Nobody was that specific."

Dana ran over to Ellie who was humming a Christian song intermittently saying, "Chain ten, crochet three."

"Great news, Ellie. Douglas Clifford's biological father is from the East. That gives me two good reasons why Miss DeBour's Will was prepared by Mr. Prussia…her family had been clients of his and the child's father was from there."

"I'm so happy for you. See, I told you in no time you'll be on your way to solve some other crime in some other place."

"I hope so. I hope you're right."

Three shrill rings came from the kitchen phone.

"Why don't you get it, dear?" Ellie said. "Slip stitch, crochet one."

Dana, a bit reluctant as she hoped it wouldn't be Howard Rhodes calling back, picked up the receiver.

"Dana Greer?"

"This is she," she said, recognizing the voice but not quite sure.

"This is Sergeant Logan from the Cape Peril Police Department."

"Oh, my gosh. How nice to hear your voice again. How are things on Cape Peril?" Dana hadn't spoken with the sergeant since leaving Cape Peril after solving the Bernadette Godfrey case. She had such fond memories of working with the man.

The man cleared his voice. "Actually, things aren't too bad on the Cape, but I'm afraid the news I have for you is not good."

"I'm sorry to hear that. Is something wrong at Holy Name School?" That was the school Bernadette Godfrey attended before she was murdered.

"Dana, I don't know how best to say this. It's difficult for me to have to tell, but your husband, Nate Greer. . .he passed away last evening at Bay View General Hospital."

"Nate? My husband? My God, no! What happened?" Dana pulled over a chair and sat down, her adrenalin pumping, her body feeling weak and almost faint.

"He was on a call. . .a domestic assault call when the guy pointed a forty-six at him and shot him through the head. Afraid he didn't stand a chance. Was DOA in the ER."

No words slipped through Dana's lips. Her mind whizzed through her past, her years of marriage to the officer and then her shock when she found out he had been having an affair with Myra Pembroke, a prostitute, for just as long. When the young call girl was found dead in a motel room, Nate and Dana were the ones assigned to the case, a case that went cold. In her heart, Dana believed all along her husband was the murderer, but she had no concrete evidence to go on. Dana could hear her heart throbbing at the tragic news as well as the whole backstory that plagued her mind. Living with the nightmarish thought had in many ways kept her entombed in a relationship that had died long before now. With no evidence and only a hunch, how could she tell anyone she believed she was married to a murderer?

"Dana, are you there? Dana?"

"Sorry, yes, I am." She took a deep breath and tears rolled down her cheeks. She cleared her throat. "Afraid I got lost in my thoughts. This is so unbelievable. . .so shocking. Nate was always so careful with a gun. I can't understand—."

"From the way it was described to me, I don't think Nate stood a chance. The guy who shot him was a sharp shooter and an ex-marine."

"I see," were the only words Dana could manage.

"Hearing about someone's loss, especially a mate, is never an easy thing to bear." He paused for a moment. "Do you plan to come for the wake?"

Without giving the question even a minute to register, Dana said, "No, no, I won't be there. I'm tied up with a case right now and won't be able to break free." In her mind, she knew. She had no obligation to a man who not only cheated on her but who, more than likely, murdered his lover. "Sorry, I won't be attending." Hearing herself say the words, Dana felt convinced of her decision.

Sergeant Logan breathed quietly into the receiver. "Sorry, Dana."

She replaced the receiver on the hook, her hand shaking uncontrollably. She dabbed with her free hand at the frozen tears on her face. Thirty-six years old. . .Nate only thirty-six years old, killed in the line of duty. His wake would be commemorated with the usual hoopla that went with any officer killed in the line of duty. Surely, as his wife, whether separated or not, Dana's place was at the side of his coffin. She knew this and so did everyone else concerned, but as far as Dana believed, her marriage, her relationship, had died years ago, long before anyone realized. Why would she want to attend a burial now? Her allegiance to Nate, her feelings, had been buried deep in her soul for the past years. In some way, it had enabled her to move on with her life. Of late, unless confronted with someone's question about her marital status, she hardly ever thought about Nate. It was better that way; it was healthier that way. Yet the shocking news immobilized Dana. Her legs could hardly move. She made it to the archway of the living room, holding onto the edge of the wall. "Think I'm going to lie down for a bit, Ellie."

The woman looked at Dana. "Is everything okay? I've never seen you look like this." Ellie got up and moved toward her.

Dana rubbed at the dried tears on her cheeks. "Just received some unsettling news, I'm afraid."

"As if you need bad news to add to what you're already dealing with. I'm sorry, dear. Is there anything I can do to help?"

Dana shook her head and headed toward her bedroom. She had a feeling she would not be getting much done today. It would take time for her to work through the news of Nate's death.

The word *widow* would be one she would be forced to embrace. The title seemed inappropriate for someone as young as she. She suddenly felt alone as if she were isolated on an island not of her own making.

* * *

Dana could not believe it was nine o'clock at night, or that she had slept for so many hours. Upon sitting up, her thoughts immediately took her back to her wedding day, and as if staring into a photograph, she could distinctly see the expression on their faces. A picture of contentment but also of commitment. As if looking into a mirror, Dana saw herself: the white roses braided through her hair, the string of fresh-water pearls her mother had given her, the Chantilly Lace veil. There, too, she saw Nate, glancing over her shoulder. His buzzed haircut, his crystal-blue eyes, the designer tux he had rented. They had had a short engagement, but it did not deter the two from making the decision to marry, and Dana never regretted her choice. She had only been a private investigator for a year, only nineteen years old when she met the man who was to become her husband. There were those who tried to discourage them from marrying, saying a relationship between a police officer and an investigator could never endure. The life was too demanding; the hours unpredictable. Others told her she was too young, too young to know what love was about. They had told her it was only puppy love. But, Nate and Dana chose to ignore the naysayers.

When Myra Pembroke's body was found years later, and Nate and Dana were put on the case, it was then the rumors began. Initially, Dana adamantly refused to believe the terrible tales that Nate and Myra were lovers. . .had become lovers shortly after Dana and Nate had married. It couldn't be, she told herself. People were jealous of their relationship. There were those who were looking for a motive in the prostitute's death. For months afterward, Dana ignored the comments and the harsh stares others gave her. Yet as time passed, and she continued to contemplate the case, she realized Nate had no alibi for the night Myra Pembroke was killed; he was not with her. More and more, she reflected on the many times she *was* left alone. Her husband had excuses that seemed to make sense and that were work-related, yet Dana began to have doubts. Even after the case went cold, Nate acted troubled going over the details of the crime. Well, it was as if he was trying to put it out of his mind, to move on, willing to put the file in the basement of the police station along with the other cold cases. Now, that Dana thought about it, he did not involve himself much in the case, preferring Dana do the bulk of the investigation.

He repeatedly had said, "Why waste time on this one? That Pembroke woman was nothing more than a skank."

Dana would protest saying, "She was still a human being and not deserving the death she endured."

Nate would ignore her remarks, and once the case was closed, unlike her, he seemed to be relieved. Was it the arguments they had about the case, their differences in opinions, or would their marriage have eventually fizzled until it was squelched of any life no matter what? The case cold, so too, their marriage, they parted ways, separated, but never officially divorced. Now, she would have no choice in the matter. Nate was dead, gone forever from her life, and she would move on just as she'd been doing all along.

Chapter Thirty-Five

Y ou still don't look so good," Ellie said, watching Dana pour
herself a cup of morning tea.

"I'm not feeling well, Ellie."

"Don't mean to pry, but does it have something to do with the
call you got yesterday?"

Dana thought for a moment. She had a choice to make. If she
responded positively, Ellie would inquire more adamantly. If she told
one of her white lies, she wouldn't have to get into the details of her
husband's sudden death. She could pretend the call from Sergeant
Logan had all been a nightmare. She shoved her blond curls behind
her ears and went over to the table with her tea, reconsidering how
she felt. "Maybe it's time I be honest with you, Ellie. You see, there's a
reason why I've chosen to do the traveling investigative work that I
do, working contracts with whomever calls me in to solve a case."

Ellie sat across from Dana and dabbed at her lips with a linen
napkin. Her eyebrows rose, forming deep creases in the bridge of her
nose.

Dana could tell the woman was more than ready for her story.
Dana explained why she had gone the private investigator route and
that her father, who was Chief of Police in Bay View, opened the
agency for her. She mentioned her father had retired, once her mother
had died, and that he had moved to Florida. Dana explained how she
had met her husband when he was a law enforcement officer, and for

a time, they had gone into a partnership, solving cases together; that is until the Myra Pembroke murder went cold.

"Dear, dear, I can understand now why you might have felt discouraged not being able to get to the bottom of the investigation. It was just too close to your heart, dear."

"There's more than that to be discouraged about, Ellie." Dana explained the rumors that had circulated about Nate's and Myra's affair and how she intuitively felt her husband was the killer but could never prove it and, for a time, chose not to believe it herself.

"Who in their right mind wouldn't go into a state of denial, dear? It's one thing to learn your spouse is cheating but quite another to realize he also might very well be a murderer! Land's End, and now the man goes to his grave without you being able to prove your theory. No wonder you're upset, dear."

Dana breathed in deeply. She could feel her eyes fill with tears. She pulled a handkerchief from the pocket of her capris. She sneezed, blew her nose, and coughed, tears rolling down her face as she blinked to regain her vision.

Ellie put her arm around Dana's shoulder. "My, my, you're one strong lady, Dana. To have all of that bottled up inside you and to still carry on with your work. I'd say, you ought to be mighty proud of yourself. I'm not a therapist, but I'd say your feelings sound pretty normal to me. After Gary's death, I felt as if my world wasn't worth living, there was no point in going forward. But, believe me, time does cure all. Take it day by day. That is all you can do, honey."

"You're right, Ellie."

"Do you think it would help to talk to someone? What about Father Neil over at St. Rita's?"

Dana stared at the scene in the kitchen wallpaper. The cows basking on the hillsides, a small goat by their side, a newly painted red silo standing tall in the sun. . .such a peaceful, pastoral landscape. She glanced from the serenity of it and looked at Ellie. "Such a sweet thought, Ellie, but I'm ready to go forward. I need to move ahead with the Douglas Clifford case. That's my focus. Furthermore, it's time I stop in to see Sergeant McKnight," Dana said.

Ellie cocked her head to the side. "But I thought you and the sergeant didn't quite see eye to eye. Sure doesn't sound like the man's been of any help to you so far."

"We don't, and he hasn't, but it's time he knows where the investigation is headed. So much has happened. He needs to be brought up to speed."

"Don't mean to be so pessimistic, but do you think McKnight'll actually care? I mean up to this point, the man has been so foot loose and fancy free."

Dana smiled. "He has but it's time he starts acting like a sergeant and not someone who got his badge in a Cracker Jack box."

The two women laughed.

* * *

When Dana entered the station, she took a step back, her jaw falling. "Brenda," she called out, and the woman rose from her secretary's desk, and the two women hugged.

"Long time, no see," Brenda said.

"Glad to see you're back. How's Stevie doing?"

The woman's relaxed, happy face quickly turned into one of sadness. "Afraid Stevie is no longer with me."

"Oh?"

"About a month ago, I found a mysterious note tacked to my front door. It said in dark black lettering:

WE HATE QUEERS!

I awoke in the middle of the night to a cross burning in our front yard."

"The KKK."

"I became so scared, Dana. I immediately called my sister in Ohio and put Stevie on a bus. I love the boy too much to see anything bad happen to him."

"Understandable."

"That's when I came back to work. Had to get my mind off things. I miss Stevie so much."

"I know you do, but you did the right thing. You had no choice."

Sergeant McKnight came out of his office. "What y'all gossipin' 'bout?"

"Brenda told me about the KKK warning she received."

"Yep, there's no sayin' when they'll all stop their shenanigans as long as they keep being able to git away with it."

"Well, I think, it's terrible a mother and son have to be pulled apart because of a corrupt organization such as the KKK."

"Try telling that to Max Freda," Brenda said.

"Pleased to have Brenda back, though," McKnight said, as he asked Dana what he could do for her. The two went into his office.

"I think it's important you know where I'm at in the Douglas Clifford case."

The man looked at her as if she were speaking in a foreign language. "My how time flies," Sergeant McKnight said, straightening two papers on his desk. "Where y'all been keepin' yourself, lady?"

"Much more has been happening than I'm sure you'd care to know," Dana said. She could feel the sharpness in her words. But, no matter what, Dana heard the truth in her words. The young sergeant fulfilled his role in name only, a position given him from his ancestors. Dana did not wait for the man to acknowledge her but went on to tell him everything she had learned so far. Dana quickly filled him in on what had transpired and brought him up to date with the findings from her California trip and her communication with the attorney Theodore Prussia.

The sergeant opened his desk drawer and stuck a toothpick into his mouth. "Sounds to me, y'all been a busy bee," he said. "But, I'd be careful if I wuz you."

"What's that supposed to mean?" she asked, not sure if she cared to hear his response anyway. By this point, she had more than lost respect for the man who wore the bright silver star on his uniform pocket and based his position of authority on those who had come before him.

"Max Freda. . .besides tearin' open bodies in his autopsy business, he's dun got friends."

"Friends?"

"Sure of it. Behind the walls of that ol' youth home."

"What makes you say that?"

"That Canfield woman over at the library. . .her daughter. Ain't no suicide as far as I'm concerned."

"You're saying you think the KKK was behind Greta Canfield's death? Are you saying the Klan didn't want the truth to come out about Gary Banks' death? But who?" As if a neon sign had lit up, Dana said, "Doctor Hansen."

"You better believe it! And that whole thing about the AMJ—."

"You mean the AMA?"

The sergeant nodded. "Yep, I do. Ya know somebody dun planted a bomb in the AMJ's president's yard and started one of those burnin' crosses in his yard." He picked a small particle of food from his rear tooth and chewed on it. "And the man's daughter's death? Ain't no secret. The KKK was behind that, as well, They're all 'bout revenge no matter how they get it."

Dana's jaw dropped. She didn't know what to say.

McKnight nodded again while he tightened his belt buckle. "Just like Walter Robinski. Don't mean to scare you none, but I'd watch my behind if I wuz you."

"You're trying to say the Klan would target me, are you?" Dana's own words sent goose bumps down her arms. That isn't what he was saying, was it? She didn't come to see the man to have him instill an unfound fear in her. He was not a man who she put much trust in to begin with, even though, his words rang true. All she could think to say was, "No matter what, I intend to get to the bottom of this case."

"Suit yourself. I'm only sayin.'" He wiped his mouth on his sleeve. "I'd say you're one lucky lady to still be alive. . .snoopin' around in that home and all."

Something about the sergeant's warning made her feel as if an icicle were melting down her back. Yet, she responded to the sergeant's cautionary remark with, "Let's just say, at this point, I don't think the brothers are aware of how much I do know."

"Better be sure to keep it that way."

Dana could not believe the man's warning. He had to think she had the intelligence of a lizard! "Sergeant, do you have anything better to tell me?"

The man shook his head and stood up.

Dana didn't bother to shake the man's hand as she left his office. She wished Brenda well and left the station. With Robinski gone, she had no one to intercede for her. Perplexed, she wondered how she might meet with Timothy again. There were still more questions she needed to ask. Feeling as if she was at a dead end, Dana didn't know quite where she was to turn.

As she backed up the truck and drove off, heading to Ellie's house, a sense of deep fear came over her. Was it her nerves, her imagination? She looked into her rearview mirror. "God, no," she said. Dana's hands shook as she tightly gripped the steering wheel. "It can't be. Tell me it's not." A black car like the one that had been parked in front of Ellie's house was behind her. Dana sped up but so, too, did the vehicle. She put her arm out the window in a gesture she intended to turn left and so did the driver of the car behind her. Had the sergeant been right? Was the KKK after her, following her? Or, was it someone else, someone who thought she might know a little too much of what was happening between the walls of the youth home? She tried to weave in with some other drivers, but once again, the black car tailed her. She knew she couldn't take the chance of returning to Ellie's and put her friend's life in danger, but where could she go? Her mind was spinning as quickly as the turns she made in hopes of losing the black car. To her relief, she spotted a Lubbock Police Cruiser parked in an empty lot up ahead. She quickly maneuvered her wheel in its direction. She stopped the truck, shut off the engine, and pulled out the key. As she did so, the black car sped off, squealing its wheels, leaving a wake of gravel while it turned in the opposite direction. Lucky, she thought, as the police cruiser was empty. Had the driver of the black car gotten out and discovered that, Dana was not sure what her fate might have been. Shivering and shaking, she drove back to Ellie's place. She tried to still her heart rate and told herself to breathe deeply. She decided not to worry Ellie by divulging the news that she had been followed.

When Dana arrived, Ellie had all she could do to prevent herself from jumping up-and-down. She held a long, white envelope in her hands. "Got something for you. It's marked personal and confidential."

Dana took the envelope from the woman and noticed the return address.

Theodore Prussia, Esq.
One Liberty Street
Utica, New York

Ellie took one look at Dana. "I had a feeling this would make you happy."

"Let's see what it's about before I make that leap."

Dana carefully opened the envelope and removed the sheet of stationery with the man's name and address blazoned on the front in small red letters. She began to mouth the words as she read to herself:

> Dear Miss Greer:
>
> Recently, it was brought to my attention someone has been inquiring about Douglas Clifford's Will. My secretary, Margaret, informed me that a man named Max Freda called her and inquired about the contents of the document. He said he was representing the boy's biological father, who he felt was the child's closest next of kin. When Margaret tried to set up an appointment to meet with Mr. Freda, the man refused, saying he would find another way to make claim to the Will.
>
> Theodore Prussia, Esq.

Dana's hands began to tremble slightly. As if listening directly to the sergeant, she heard, "Max Freda. . .besides tearin' open bodies in his autopsy business, he's got friends." So, Max Freda knew the biological father of Douglas Clifford? Dana made up her mind. No matter how the attorney Howard Rhodes warned her and now Sergeant McKnight to stay away from the coroner, she had no choice but to speak with him. She would do that first thing tomorrow morning.

In the meantime, she found herself reminiscing again on Nate's sudden death. A young man at the peak of his career shot down while trying to resolve a domestic dispute. It all seemed so unfair, so unexpected. But, then again, wasn't a law officer's life always on the line. Fiona Wharton had told her that police work was similar to the life of a gambler. Some days you might win big; some days you might lose, yet in the end, a gambler only had himself to blame for getting into the game. Police work was like that—a mere gamble. The stakes sometimes high, a life put on the line but all in the interest of a safer society. Sometimes the very citizens an officer tried to protect were the very ones to turn on them. In this case, Nate was only trying to do his best, to restore peace, to prevent an innocent from getting hurt. The best of efforts with the worst results. Maybe that was the reason Dana turned to private investigative work instead. She still came face-to-face with the dark side of life but at least was not in the front-line trenches.

Chapter Thirty-Six

Dana got out of the rusty Chevy pick-up and scanned the building in front of her. If she didn't know better, she would have guessed the building to be abandoned, but then again, why would a coroner's office have to be appealing to the eye. The wooden structure looked more like a shack one might find at the end of a dead-end road. The wood slats begged for paint. Splotches of red, the original coat, peeked through the white. All the windows were boarded up, except for one small one next to the grey, metal door. If the appearance of the place didn't scream, "Stay out," the grounds around it, sure did. Near the curb stood a brittle holly bush; what was left of a dead crepe myrtle minus its usual, vibrant flowers; and a high pile of dead branches. A dirt path wound its way to the front door. With no doorbell, Dana decided to pound with her fist as hard as she could. She saw a reflection of a man's face quickly peer out the small window.

The door opened slightly and a man in a blue, pinstriped suit with a white, linen handkerchief stuffed in his breast pocket appeared. "Yes, who are you?"

Dana stared into the man's watery blue eyes beneath which were large, puffy bags of skin. His bulbous nose was covered with broken red veins. Across his jaw, a jagged scar ended beneath his right ear. Dana found herself staring at the injury wondering what possibly could have caused such a brutal wound.

"Must I repeat myself? Who are you?"

"Perhaps, you heard—. I am –. The name's Dana Greer." Dana could not remember the last time she'd felt so intimidated by a man, but something about his six-foot frame and stern mouth caught Dana in a moment of fright.

Max Freda grilled her with his eyes. "Your purpose in being here?"

"Are you Max Freda by chance?"

The man sarcastically answered, "I am he, not by luck but by choice, I'll have you know."

Dana swallowed hard. "Could we speak, Mr. Freda?"

"You mean inside? Why not?"

Dana entered and the smell of medicinal odors slapped her in the face. The last time she recalled aromas such as these was in her high school biology lab, the frogs, lizards, and eels compactly trapped in their jars of formaldehyde.

Max Freda led her down a dark, narrow hall, the walls covered in a sickening pea green, and turned into a room at the back of the building, his office apparently.

"Seat yourself," he said.

Dana could not help noticing the photographs along the walls. One showed the Klan with a large burning cross in the background. Another was a picture that must have been from the 40s of the Klan's members perched on horses with a large American flag furled high above the crowd. Alongside the members, in a shadow, was a group of uniformed police officers. She couldn't believe the police supported the Klan and immediately began to wonder about Sergeant McKnight. A third photograph exhibited a group of angry men with protest signs reading:

KKK won't take our rights away!
Unite to fight against the right wing!
Stop police officers!

From his desk, the man pulled a pack of Camel's cigarettes, lit one, and took a long, drawn-out puff. "Miss Greer, I do say, you look a bit frightened by my photographs."

By the smirk on Max Freda's face, Dana could tell the man wanted to be seen as a wise guy. She decided not to give him the chance. "No, not at all," she lied. "I am familiar with the KKK and its tactics."

"You are, are you? Maybe, then, you should tell me what *you* know, instead of the other way around." He straightened his navy tie that lay on his highly starched white shirt, his neck red as if a reaction to the product.

"That's not why I'm here, Mr. Freda. I'm not interested in your position in the Klan or its activities." She cleared her throat. Casually, she reached into her bag and fingered her small Bible. She could feel her breathing becoming belabored and hoped she could get her words out without nervously stumbling.

"Well, then—."

"I'm wondering what you might know about the young boy who was found murdered in his cell at the youth home."

"I didn't perform an autopsy if that's what you mean. Waste the time? Not get paid? The boy was nothing more than a varmint."

Dana stiffened her shoulders and clasped her hands in her lap. "That's not what I mean, Mr. Freda." She grasped at the miniature Bible for support. "I'm more interested in what you know about Douglas Clifford and, in particular, if any monies were put aside for the child once his parents passed away."

Max Freda's hands balled into fists. He bit down on his inner lip.

Dana knew the man was concealing something, and she had no intention of leaving until she learned what it was.

"I know of the boy. Heard about him when he committed that horrendous crime against his parents."

"Did you know anything about him before this?"

"No, no, of course not. Why would I?" The man stretched his neck from side to side. His blue eyes narrowed. He wiped the sides of his cheeks as if he could rub off the fuchshia color.

Without a doubt, Dana knew the man was lying. Dana preferred not to mention Theodore Prussia's name. If Max Freda presented as much of a threat to people as the sergeant had said, the last thing she wanted was to put the attorney in a precarious situation. Dana had to figure out how to phrase her words to get the answer she'd come looking for without involving Prussia. Then, the idea came. "From what I understand about Wills if the beneficiary is deceased, the monies often go to the person's caregiver."

The man's face glistened with perspiration as he tugged on his scar as if trying to remove it. "Are you implicating I may know the child's next of kin?"

Dana had him. She never mentioned kin, only caretaker. For a coroner, he had just dug his own grave. "Do you?" she asked.

"Quite frankly, Miss Greer, I do. It's the father of the child who has every right in the world to the contents of the Will." He stood and straightened one of the picture frames on the wall, licking his index finger to dust it off. Before seating himself again, he grabbed the edges of his desk until his purple veins stood rigid in his hands and half his body extended over the desk. "You're not expecting the proceeds of the Will to go to those damn brothers over at the youth home, are you?"

By the sound of his voice and the wrinkles covering his face, Dana knew she had more than touched a nerve. She had gotten used to her white lies working in her favor when she said, "No, no, of course not. From what I've gathered from my investigation, Douglas Clifford was not cared for in the best of ways. Certainly, I see where you're coming from. You believe the monies belong to the child's next of kin, by all means."

"Why, yes, yes." The man sat back down and pretended to brush some dandruff off the lapel of his coat.

"Then, perhaps, you can help me; I need to find this person. Make sure the Will is placed in the right hands before the brothers begin meddling in this. They are, after all, the last caregivers of the boy."

"How dare you say this, Miss Greer. The boy's blood relative certainly deserves whatever is in the Will before those damn hooded animals!"

Dana pushed her hair behind her ears. Had Max Freda even been listening to what she was saying? She repeated, "Agreed. The boy's next of kin certainly deserves whatever is in the Will."

"But, I'm not about to release the man's name if that's what you're asking me."

"Well, until you do, how do you expect the rightful beneficiary to receive the proceeds from the Will?"

"Let's say that'll have to be decided between the attorney and me." He pointed both of his thumbs at himself. The man stood up. "Good day, Miss Greer."

Dana got up, as well, about to say one more thing but decided against it and let herself out.

As soon as she got back to Ellie's, she dialed Theodore Prussia's office.

"God speaks, doesn't he?" the man said.

"What do you mean?"

"I was beginning to call you."

Dana waited, tapping her red nails on the phone.

"A young man stopped by today, saying he was the father of the deceased." Dana almost felt faint. This was the moment she had waited for. "Yes?" She clutched the phone closer to her ear.

"He claimed the nuns over at Holy Angels Adoption Agency confiscated. . .that was the word he used. Can you believe that. . .confiscated his child without his signed permission."

"But how can that be? When I spoke with Sister Raphael, she told me adoptions happen like this one all the time. The father's name is blotted out on the birth certificate because the baby was illegitimate. I was even told when I went to Paramount Studios, where the boy's mother worked, that the father broke off all correspondence with the mother, the star Miss DeBour, once he found out she was pregnant."

"Remember what I told you? Next of kin have a way of working themselves back into the picture whenever money is involved. The young man mentioned he was forced against his will to place the child up for adoption."

"Well, that's an outright lie. From everyone I spoke with, the father left town before the child was even born."

"Not saying what you're telling me isn't the truth. I'm only telling you this man lays claim to the Will, or so he says."

"And?"

"If he can prove what he says is the truth and that the child was illegally taken from him, he stands a better than good chance of moving to the head of the line in terms of inheritance."

"And, if he can't?"

"Money would go to the stated beneficiary of the Will, the caretakers of the child. In this case, I would highly suspect this would be the brothers of the youth home."

"By chance, could you give me the name of the man?"

Mr. Prussia rattled some papers and took a deep breath. "His name is Judas Hudson."

"Judas Hudson…the name doesn't ring a bell."

"What's that?"

"His looks? What did he look like? How old might you say he was?"

"Handsome lad. Looked a lot like Julius La Rosa, about twenty-six, said he operated a small music store somewhere in Niagara Falls."

Dana grabbed one of the wicker chairs from under the kitchen table and sat down. "You say, Julius La Rosa?"

"Yes. Good looking young man, yet something about him concerned me. I could tell he wasn't the best at controlling his anger. Well, the man balled his hands into fists, and a vein pulsated in the side of his neck. I could tell the man meant trouble."

Silence lingered.

"Listen, Miss Greer, don't worry. Unless the man can prove what he is saying is the truth, the Will stays put until the brothers make claim. I wouldn't worry if I were you. I've seen this kind of thing happen more often than you'd guess."

"Sure, sure." She thanked the man and said she'd keep in touch.

Julius La Rosa. . .that's how Candy at Paramount Studios had described him. Twenty-six years old would be exactly right if he impregnated Miss DeBour at sixteen years of age. Could it be she wondered?

* * *

"You what? You know who killed the Clifford kid?" Howard asked.

Dana reached into her bag and found the rubber-banded collection of holy cards. She fanned them out on the kitchen table, stopping when she came to the one of St. Aloysius. "Someone you'd never expect."

"Can't wait! Who?"

"The seminarian at the boys' home."

"Oh, c'mon. You've got to be kidding me. The guy I met at Walter Robinski's funeral?"

"Carl Fenton!"

"That can't be. Thought he had his heart set on the priesthood."

"From what I learned, hardly. Candy, the woman I met at Paramount Studios, told me Miss DeBour's lover resembled a young Julius La Rosa."

"Okay, so the guy's good looking enough."

"Enough to resemble Julius La Rosa," Dana said, glancing at the picture on the holy card one more time. She remembered thinking at the time Carl Fenton gave her the picture that St. Aloysius bore a striking resemblance to the singer. When she'd first met the seminarian, she recalled thinking he reminded her of someone. Was it a singer, she had pondered. Now, she had her answer.

"Add to this, Theodore Prussia, the attorney, told me the man, claiming to be Douglas Clifford's biological father stopped by his office."

"And, let me guess. Mr. Prussia said the man looked like Julius La Rosa?"

"Exactly! Mr. Prussia said the guy was about twenty-six, which would be the right age if he became romantically involved with Miss DeBour at the age of sixteen. I'd say that's probably how old Carl Fenton is."

"Well, when you think about it, working in the home would have given him easy access to the boy plus who would have ever expected him? Heaven forbid, no!" Howard gulped. "What the hell? What about the seminary, the internship—?"

"All made up and all an outright lie, I assume."

"Wait one minute. If you're telling me Douglas Clifford was the product of Carl Fenton and Miss DeBour, then Carl murdered his own son? How can that be?"

"Believe me, Howard, it is."

"The guy betrayed everyone? Are you telling me even the brothers had no idea?"

"I don't believe so, but I'm headed there next."

"This is unbelievable. The guy's a real con man."

"But, there's more. I spoke with Max Freda."

Howard quickly interrupted. "I thought I told you to stay away from the guy."

"I had no choice. After Theodore Prussia told me Freda had spoken to him on behalf of the child's father, I began to add up the results. Freda refused to give me Carl's name. Only said the man deserved whatever Miss DeBour left in her Will," Dana said.

"So, the guy's motive is money."

"There's more. Sounds as if the seminarian's got the support of the KKK behind him. He might even be part of the Klan himself for all we know. It sure would explain Walter's shocking, unexpected death. Walter worked hand in hand with Carl Fenton to get me Douglas Clifford's file from Brother Donald's office. Before I had the chance to return the files, Walter was killed."

"A two-timing traitor! Holy God, no." He stopped for a moment. "But wait a minute! Why would Fenton help Walter get you the files if he's the guilty party?"

"I thought about that, too. Near as I can tell, Fenton gambled the odds. He played the good guy all along to take the suspicion off him. Furthermore, nothing in Douglas's files directly indicted the man." Dana could hear Howard's breathing escalating.

"A cocky you know what! Listen, you go over to the home and find out what you can. In the meantime, let me get ahold of Bill Traynor; he's Chief of Police in Lubbock County."

"But this is Punkerton."

"Punkerton's in Lubbock County. It's part of the reason there's never been any police officer other than Sergeant McKnight. And, everyone knows that fool is in uniform only. He doesn't hold any more authority than a lamppost. On the other hand, Traynor is one straight shooter. He doesn't take guff from anyone. He'd find a judge who'd give the Fenton guy at least life in prison, if not the chair."

"Music to my ears, Howard." She paused for a moment. "What about the murders in LA—Douglas Clifford's parents, Chantel DeBour, her chauffeur?"

"What do you mean?"

"I'm left wondering about Miss DeBour's accident. There's some thought it might have been rigged. And, her chauffeur was driving."

"Without a doubt, it would make sense Fenton would want his former lover out of the way, so the money would go to him."

"Exactly. Any thought on those deaths?"

"Know the Chief of Police there, too. I spoke with him about one of my cases on my last trip. Guy by the name of Lincoln West."

"Okay, your connections make me feel a hundred times better. Where do you suggest we begin?"

"Let's start with Traynor. I'll fill him in on the details. Let's get the Fenton guy indicted in the death of his son first. We'll take it from there."

"Thanks, Howard."

"My pleasure, pretty lady, I'll be back in contact with you."

Dana could feel herself blush. "Be quick!" She sighed with relief. Could this nightmare finally be over?

Chapter Thirty-Seven

Dana realized she had no friends at the youth home now that Walter Robinski was dead. If anything, the brothers would be more than happy to see her gone, too, but not until she spoke with Carl Fenton, the seminarian.

Dana tapped on Brother Donald's office door.

"Come in," he said. His mouth in a *U* shape, the puppet lines defined.

"Might you be able to call for Carl Fenton? I'd like to speak to him briefly."

"Afraid not," he said, his mouth in a straight line.

"What do you mean?"

"Carl Fenton is no longer here with us. His internship period is over. He left yesterday. A fine, young lad, the priesthood will stand to benefit greatly from him once he's ordained."

Dana gulped. "But, where. . .where did he go?" She quickly thought to add, "I had hoped to say goodbye."

"I'm assuming he's gone back East for what remains of the summer. You know, that's where he's from."

"I knew that. The seminary—?"

"Has the summer off. Won't be returning to Dallas until the fall."

Dana prevented herself from asking the obvious: Do you realize there might not even be such a place as the Seminary of the Holy

Spirit? Until she knew for sure whether the brothers were aware of Carl's façade, she decided to let that question go. "Is there a way I can contact him. . .a letter. . .a phone call?"

"Not able to provide you with personal information. You might expect that. We honor the privacy of those who work here."

She said nothing, only looked at the bald-headed, old man, hoping her eyes would arouse some sympathy, but from experience, she knew otherwise. She could tell the man was not about to budge for her.

"Why not wait until the fall, Miss Greer? Contact the seminary then, and I'm sure the young man would be happy to hear from you."

"Say that again, please."

The brother repeated his words.

Her question answered. Either he was involved in the conspiracy and attempting to keep the truth from her, or else he had no idea who the real Carl Fenton was.

* * *

"Oh, hello, Dana? What's up?" Theodore Prussia asked.

Dana wasted no time and got to the point. "You mentioned Douglas Clifford's biological father stopped by."

"Sure did." Without waiting for Dana's next thought, he said, "Man couldn't get out of here quick enough."

"Did he say where he was headed?"

"Like I said, the man appeared to me to have an angry side. He stormed out of here and said he'd be back once he had proof the infant had been taken from him. Would you believe he actually had me by the shirt sleeves?"

A day ago, Dana would have to say that in no way could she believe Carl Fenton had a violent bone in his body. Knowing what she knew now, his burst of anger against Theodore Prussia did not surprise her in the least. "Mr. Prussia, as an attorney, how might someone prove such a thing. . .I mean that his child was deliberately taken from him?"

"A good lawyer, I guess. But, I've got a feeling Judas Hudson has ulterior plans."

"What do you mean?"

"Guess, like the Judas of the Bible, he'll go to whatever means to get his silver." The man chuckled at his own attempt at humor.

"Are you, by chance, referring to his association with Max Freda?"

"Sure am. Got the feeling those two are used to covering each other's—."

"…behinds."

"After seeing the look in the man's eyes, I'd have to say it would not surprise me in the least if he were the murderer you have been trying to track down."

* * *

There were only two places where Carl Fenton might be. Either he was at the City of Angels Adoption Center, or else he was staying with Max Freda. She would try the first possibility and give a call to Sister Raphael.

"Yes, of course, I remember you, Miss Greer. And, yes, two men did stop here inquiring about the adoption of Douglas Clifford only yesterday. The younger man. . .dear, Jesus, Mary, and Joseph. . .had quite the temper. He kept insisting his child had been taken from him without his knowledge. He kept raising his voice, well, screaming. I tried to explain the hospital delivered the child to us when he was only days old. The birth certificate was blackened out where the father's name should have been. He absolutely refused to believe. Kept saying I was keeping the truth from him."

"When did these men see you, Sister?"

"Yesterday afternoon, around three or so. The young man left, mumbling something about, 'This is not going to end here.' Why, I have no idea what he meant. Might you?"

Dana bit down on her lower lip. Who knew for sure what the two men were up to. She had not experienced Carl Fenton's angry side. . .ever. But, if the proceeds from the Will were at stake, who knew how far he might go to prove he was the first in line? "Sister, did they happen to say where they were headed?"

"No, they just left."

"I'm not trying to scare you, Sister, but I'm afraid this man is not stable."

"You mean—?"

"As in, he might try something if for no other reason than to seek revenge against the orphanage. You might want to call the police and explain the situation. They could keep watch to make sure these men don't try anything. They're not to be trusted."

"Miss Greer, do you actually think—?"

"Yes, I do. Please. . .call the police!"

Chapter Thirty-Eight

The following morning Sergeant McKnight paid Dana a call at Ellie's house. Most unexpectedly, Dana knew his visit had to be an omen of bad news.

"Y'all see the paper this morning?" He rattled the "Punkerton Press" in front of Dana. She had never seen the sergeant this serious before.

Ellie invited him in. As he sat down on the couch, adjusting the silver star on his pocket, he pointed to the headline:

Holy Angels Adoption Agency Burns to the Ground

"Oh, my God, no," Dana cried out. "No, just as I thought. I told her; I warned her!" Dana sat down next to the sergeant, her lips and chin trembling.

"Not sure what yer talkin' 'bout, Miss Greer, but here, read this."

Dana took the paper and read out loud:

The Los Angeles Fire Department was called last night to a three-alarm fire at about eleven p.m. to the City of Holy Angels' Orphanage on 429 Broadway. By the time the engines arrived, the building was a blazing inferno. It took the LAFD three hours to put out the fire. Thanks to the heroic efforts of the Mother Superior, Sister Raphael returned to the building one more time to make sure all the children, sisters, and employees were out of the building and, in so doing, died of smoke inhalation. The cause of the fire is still under investigation; however, there is speculation the Ku Klux Klan may have played a part in the disaster. An eyewitness told the police she saw two men dressed in KKK attire shortly before the fire, lingering on the perimeter of the premises. The LAPD are presently investigating the case.

Dana stood up and threw her arms outward. "I told her; I warned her. Maybe, I should have called them myself. . .the police."

"What y'all tryin' to say?"

"Sister Raphael. . .the two men. . .the police—." Dana stopped. "This can't be." Tears ran down her cheeks. She covered her trembling lips with the palm of her hand. "Why take revenge against the good sisters? They had nothing to do with this."

Ellie sat down across from the sergeant and Dana. "Give her time, sergeant. She's obviously upset," Ellie said. She scowled at the man and shook her head.

"The KKK hates Catholics. No surprise there," the sergeant said.

"There's more. There's more to the story," Dana blurted out.

The sergeant stared at Dana waiting for her to gather her composure. He scratched at his left temple. "More to the story—?"

"Douglas Clifford's father and Max Freda are to blame. I'm sure of it!"

With one hand the sergeant rubbed his chin and with the other massaged his neck. "Whoa! Lady Jane. What y'all talkin' 'bout?"

In broken sentences, Dana tried to fill the sergeant in on the Will and the fact that the boy's biological father felt he was entitled to its proceeds. Then, she stopped, chastising herself for even trying to explain the matter to him when he had not displayed any real interest from the start.

"How could he hold the agency responsible for this?" Ellie asked. "It was ten years ago, and the child was legally put up for adoption."

"Not to mention he walked out on Miss DeBour as soon as he learned of her pregnancy. With a possible inheritance to be had, he's trying to claim the child was taken from him without his consent."

"Sheer lunacy," the sergeant said.

"I'm sure when Sister—," Dana could say no more, simply wept into her hands.

"Ain't no way of stoppin' 'em," the sergeant said. "Got too damn much power, and everyone's scared of 'em."

In between her sobs, Dana interjected, "How would I have known? Carl Fenton. . .a KKK member?" Memories flashed before her: the holy card the seminarian had offered her of St. Aloysius; his offers to pray for her; even his willingness to set a false alarm so Dana could retrieve Douglas Clifford's file. How could Carl Fenton have portrayed such an innocent, caring man yet have been a cold-blooded killer. . .and of his own son yet? Dana shivered at the thought. Throughout it all, he never swayed from his priestly identity. Even Walter had praised the man as being like a big brother to the boys, visiting with them, helping them write letters, reading to them, playing board games. All a façade, an act.

"The seminarian?" Ellie asked, her face one of disbelief and confusion. "But, I thought the man wanted to be a priest?"

Dana nodded. When she regained her composure, she went on. "Carl Fenton made it appear as if Douglas Clifford had bludgeoned his adoptive parents to death with his own baseball bat, yet all along, he was the killer."

"Wait one minute," Ellie said. The woman stood up abruptly. "Are you telling us Carl Fenton is the father of Douglas Clifford? But how can that be? You mean, the man murdered his own son?"

"That's correct, Ellie, and most likely he also found a way to tinker around with Miss DeBour's car, forcing her off the road and to her death. I'm almost certain of that. Once Miss DeBour and Douglas's adoptive parents were out of his way, he found a way to enter St. Aloysius Home for Troubled Youth, actually working side by side with the boys, making it possible for him to also do away with Douglas Clifford."

"This all makes total sense. Carl Fenton would have known his son would be sent to the youth home once he was found guilty of murder," Ellie said. "He betrayed us all."

"Exactly! It's the only place in the country where boys eighteen and under who commit felons are sent. He knew quite well where to find his son. He had betrayed everyone into thinking he was someone he was not, all in the name of making claim to Miss DeBour's inheritance. Convoluted, sick, and yes, evil. But, as Sergeant McKnight said, there's no way of stopping the KKK's power; who would want to take them on when they're capable of such hate, violence, and destruction?"

"Better y'all git over to the boys' home and warn those men of the cloth," the sergeant said.

In the event the brothers at the home were unaware of who the true Carl Fenton was, Dana had no choice but to tell them. If they were the recipients of DeBour's Will, it made sense they would be the next targets of Carl Fenton's wrath. She needed to tell the brothers what she knew. The KKK would surely be after them next, and she wanted to be sure she stopped them in time.

On a hunch, Dana dialed the operator to see if, indeed, there was a Seminary of the Holy Spirit in Dallas as Carl had told her. Was there such a place, or had he made this all up? Was this all part of his façade? All along, he had played the part of a future man of the cloth doing an internship at the boys' home. It worked as the perfect disguise. She went to the phone and dialed the operator. "I'm looking for the number of the Seminary of the Holy Spirit in Dallas." She waited.

The operator kept saying, "Still checking." Then, with a huff, she said, "Sorry, but I have no such name in my records."

"But, you must. Maybe, it's under Holy Spirit Seminary."

"Ma'am, there is no such listing," the woman growled and disconnected Dana.

Dana hung up the phone. She had answered her own question. The man had feigned that bit of his background, as well.

* * *

Dana pulled around the circle of the youth home and shut off the rattling engine. Two brothers were sitting on a bench out front. Each read from his black breviary, probably the Morning Hours' prayer. Neither of the men looked up as she rushed into the building. She ran headlong into Brother Victor. "Brother, it's urgent I speak to Brother Donald!"

In a slow, drawn out voice, the man said, "Surely. Follow me." He shuffled his sandal-clad feet along the marble hallway floor, bowing his head slightly in front of the Mother of Sorrows' painting. He knocked on the head master's door.

"Brother Victor, please! Can you not see I am busy?" In an irritated voice, Brother Donald said, "Excuse me, but Miss Mitford and I were finishing our conversation."

Dana's jaw dropped. She stood with Brother Victor at the open office door. Shirley Mitford squinted her eyes and glared at Dana as if she had never seen her before. With a dismissive glance, she said, "Never mind. I was leaving. Bless you, Brother," she said. As Brother Donald stood, Shirley went around his desk and hugged the man. "You brothers have been like angels to me."

"Sorry, brother," Brother Victor said, as Shirley brushed past him and bumped into Dana's shoulder, offering no excuse, only a loud humph.

"Well, come in, come in," Brother Donald said. "You were in such a hurry."

Without waiting to be seated, Dana sat across from the brother, and Brother Victor closed the door and left. "You look worried, Brother."

"You read me like a book, I must say."

"Is there anything you'd like to tell me?"

"Shirley Mitford gave me her resignation, turned it in this morning. Said she plans to move back East. . .Upstate New York to be exact."

The word East jarred Dana. "Isn't that where Carl Fenton is from?"

"Why, yes, I believe you're correct. Strange coincidence, I'm sure."

All of a sudden, Dana blurted out, "Is it?" Her investigative mind began putting the clues together. Candy at Paramount Studios had said Douglas Clifford's biological father was close to his mother. He had actually come out West with her and had plans to make it in the movies. His mother was his supporter. "I don't have much time to tell you this, Brother, but there is something you must know."

"Sounds urgent, to me," the brother said.

"It is. Quite urgent!" Dana started the story from the beginning. She hoped her words weren't sounding like a blur of syllables as she hurried to tell him everything she knew, complete with the fire at City of Holy Angels Orphanage. She ended with, "Carl Fenton is not who you thought. He betrayed us all, and it looks like Shirley Mitford is in on it, too. In fact, it was all a conspiracy. The two are mother and son!"

Brother Donald stood abruptly, his hands on the sides of his head. "But, Brother Calvin checked the man's references. How can this be?"

"There is no Seminary of the Holy Spirit. Don't you see? It was all a sham!"

"And, you're telling me Shirley Mitford might have a part in this, as well? Isn't this a bit absurd? Surely, this can't be. The woman played a supportive part on our board, and Carl. . .well, you couldn't find a more devout young man. Do you have any idea what he did to help the boys here?"

Dana stood up, gritting her teeth. "I am only telling you the truth. I'm afraid the youth home may be Fenton's next target. He's working with the KKK, and who can predict what their plans are?"

The brother stood up and pounded his fist on his desk. "Carl Fenton a KKK member? This is rubbish, rubbish if I ever heard it. How can you expect me to believe such nonsense? You're mad, woman. This is sheer lunacy!"

"I don't know how to make you believe me, Brother, and I understand why this comes as such a shock, but you must. The youth home actually stands in great danger."

At this point, the man's facial expression changed to one of grave concern, and he pulled himself closer to his desk. His chest rose and fell. "What should we do then?" Beads of sweat formed above the man's brow. He fumbled with the mole on his nose, his hands shaking. He reached for the phone on his desk.

Dana yelled, "Alert the others. If anyone sees Carl Fenton or Shirley Mitford near the property, you must call the police at once. In the meantime, I strongly suggest you and the boys be prepared to vacate the building as soon as possible if need be!"

"What? But, that's impossible. Where in heaven's name will we put the boys? Certainly, they'll run for their lives. They'll escape."

"Do as I say. You have no choice!"

* * *

As soon as Dana got back to Ellie's, she called Howard. She needed Traynor, the Chief of Police from Lubbock, involved immediately. The phone rang continuously for two minutes. Howard did not pick up. There was nothing more to do tonight. She would try again first thing in the morning. Unable to keep her eyes open, exhausted from the revelations of the day, Dana immediately went to sleep; that is, until she was startled awake, only minutes later, by the banging on her bedroom door. She peered over at the clock on her night table. . .six a.m. The pounding intensified. She thought she saw a flicker of light through the venetian blinds.

"Dana, hurry," Ellie called out hysterically. "Please come!"

"What's wrong? What's happened?"

"Quick. Come to the door."

Dana followed Ellie.

Ellie opened the front door a small crack. "Look!"

There in the center of the grass, not far from the fountain, stood a large, white cross, its wood ablaze. Orange flames lit the dark sky of morning, the smell of smoke and ash in the air.

"Oh my, God!" Dana said.

"What do we do?"

"A garden hose...do you have a garden hose?"

"It's out here on the porch."

The two women stepped onto the concrete stoop. Ellie bent and lifted the green hose and turned the sprinkler head on full blast.

Dana took the hose from her and walked over to the fire. She sprayed the burning wood, embers flying into the black sky. The heavy smoke caused Dana to cough, her eyes watering.

"My, God, Dana, this is only a warning! You'll be next."

Ellie's words were like an echo of those spoken by the sergeant. Dana could hear the desperation in Ellie's voice. It was much simpler than adding two plus two for her to figure out who had done this and why. Dana continued to hose the flames for at least fifteen minutes until the last of the blaze was finally out. Only the smell of burnt cinders filled the air, and a large patch of black covered the front lawn.

"Hurry, let's get inside," Ellie said, standing in her bare feet and an eyelet nightgown. "Who knows who might be watching us?"

In their haste to put out the fire, the thought had never occurred to Dana. But, Ellie was right. Someone could easily be hiding in the brush. The two women scurried inside.

"We need to call the police. Get the sergeant on the line."

"Forget that, Ellie. Your cat, Patches, will give us better protection. There's no way we're in a position to take on the Klan. We've done what we can do. Let me try Howard again. He'll get the right person involved."

"Hello, Dana, what can I do for you at this hour?" He yawned. His voice sounded groggy and incoherent.

"Traynor. . .the police. . .the KKK has put a cross in Ellie's yard."

Immediately alert, Howard said, "Let me get Traynor on the line. We'll meet you at Sergeant's McKnight's place. In the meantime, keep your door locked. Don't open it for anyone. And, Dana...keep safe."

Dana thanked Howard. She was grateful the man had come into her life.

This time Dana made some tea to calm Ellie's jangled nerves. Then, she told her about her earlier visit with Max Freda.

Chapter Thirty-Nine

Dust blew through the empty field, where once golden stalks of wheat grew. But that was when the land was farmed. Today, nothing remained, a barren field under the hot Texas sun.

Ever since Shirley parked her home, the small, silver AirStream, on the vacant spot in the middle of nowhere, she'd learned to become accustomed to the howling wind, which spoke of isolation and loneliness, the emotions she personally felt. Shirley looked out her kitchen window, squinting to see. She heard a revving engine. . .Judas Hudson, her only son, had arrived in much the same way he had arrived twenty-six years ago. That morning she had driven herself to Community Memorial Hospital, pressing down on the gas pedal, racing her engine to make it on time. Her contractions less than sixty seconds apart, she knew her baby was not going to wait. She had decided to go through with his birth after all, but originally, she wanted to do away with him. She had been impregnated by a married man who paid her to abort the child. Yet, her conscience told her to take the money and have the child. Was that why she felt such a oneness with Judas, such a bond with her son? In the end, he was all she had. She had never married. Never wanted to. She lived and breathed for her son. She had high hopes once Judas met Chantel, the older woman would have given him a break, introduced him to the right people at Paramount, gotten him into some bit parts, and once everyone saw how great the man was, he would be on his way to stardom. But, instead, she enjoyed being romanticized by a younger man until she learned of her pregnancy. What choice did Judas have then? If Miss DeBour's husband had found out Judas was the father, whatever hope he had had for a career in Hollywood would have been over. Judas had no choice but to leave. But, in the end, the joke would be over that hussy's dead body. Judas would gain her inheritance. And, in the end, there was not a thing Shirley wouldn't do for her son even if it meant. . .murder.

The door to the AirStream trailer slammed shut.

"Honey, you're home." Shirley adjusted one of her pink, plastic curlers and realizing her hair was still damp, rerolled it. She placed a big kiss on the man's cheek and lit up a cigarette. "Boy, you've sure been busy going from one coast to another…jetting to New York, California."

Judas Hudson opened the icebox and took out a cold bottle of beer. He poured it down his throat. "Ah," and let out a loud burp. He wore a pair of Wrangler Jeans and a short-sleeved plaid shirt. "Feels great to be out of the gabardine frock. That damn stuff itches like a bitch." He sat down by the kitchen table and propped his legs on one of the chairs.

"You know, son, in the early days of the Church, some of the saints actually wore hair shirts as atonement for their sins." She exhaled into the air.

He winked at his mother. "I sure don't have any of those. . .sins, I mean, do I, mother?"

Shirley did not bother to answer his question but led into another. "What have you been up to, son?" Shirley knew her son too well. He was used to having things go his way or else. Right now, the young man was faced with one of these times. He intended to get the proceeds from Chantel DeBour's Will. He would stop at nothing.

"Max and I been making plans, Mother."

"Let me guess. You want me to iron your whites?" Shirley laughed. She recalled the day Judas was admitted into the Klan and how proud she had been of him. The Jews, the Catholics, the Negroes, and the Queers. . .Judas stood a chance to be rid of them all. What a role he would play. She knew it. He might not have made it to the Hollywood Star of Fame, but she could not be any prouder of her son. She snuffed out her cigarette in the kitchen sink.

Judas wiped the frothy white beer off his lips with the back of his hand and gave his mother a hug. . .no answer to her question forthcoming.

"You know I worry so much about you."

He shoved her aside. "Mother, stop it! I've been in the Klan now for almost a year, and I'm still alive!"

"Oh, it's not I don't support the good you do; it's risky; that's all."

"Let me see. If it weren't for the damn Jews, Catholics, Negroes, and Queers, we'd be out of business." He laughed so hard, it sounded more like a coyote's howl.

Shirley joined in the laughter. She pulled out another curler and felt her hair to see if it was dry. Again, she rolled the lock back into place.

"Where you going today, getting all pretty? Off to work?" Judas asked his mother.

"No, dear. Turned in my resignation yesterday. Free and clear of that damn place."

"Do you think that was smart? I mean, you and I leaving at the same time. Think they suspect anything?" Judas took another swallow of his beer and sat back down.

"No, honey. We carried out our plan with no complications whatsoever. It was such a great idea, wasn't it honey...you being the seminarian and me on the board of directors? What an actor you were. You always had it in your blood. No one suspected you and me of being mother and son. My idea of coming up with the visitation rule was the best yet! Can you imagine if that Greer woman would have been able to ask Timothy Laughton any damn thing she well pleased? If it hadn't been for me, God only knows what that queer might have told her. Getting his tongue snipped was the perfect solution for the kid." Shirley lit up another cigarette.

"Eh, Maw, that kid didn't see or hear a thing anyway. He's just a bag of hot air."

"I'm not so sure about that. After all, he's the one who opened his God damn mouth and squealed to that Stevie queer."

"Now, now, mother. We took care of that, too. Didn't we?"

"You mean the note you stuck to Brenda's door, scaring the wits out of her?"

"Yeah, yeah, and Stevie ran far away with his tail tucked between his legs."

The two laughed.

"And, Timothy got his, too, right?" Shirley chimed in.

"A round of thanks go to Calvin and Hansen for that one." Judas set his empty beer can down on the window ledge and began digging around in the icebox, pulling out a chicken drumstick from last night's meal. He bit down hard and swiped his mouth with his hand. A small bone fell onto the stained brown carpet. Judas picked it up and chomped on what meat remained.

Shirley handed him a napkin. He needed her so, she thought.

"Speaking of Calvin. . .what about the dear ol' brother? He thought, all along, he was getting somewhere with you. Was stupid enough to believe your flirtations, your ass kissing."

"Judas!" his mother scolded. "I must admit the man was a handsome dude. I sure played him for a fool and had fun while I was at it. He actually had talked about leaving the order, if you can believe it." She snickered and gave her son another hug. "Nothing I wouldn't do for you, Judas."

"I know, mother. I know, complete to feigning love for a man of the cloth." He swallowed the last of his chicken and began to pick at a piece stuck in his front tooth.

"Like I said, not a thing I wouldn't do for you." Shirley hummed the lyrics to an old Ginger Roger's song "We're in the Money."

"Not quite yet," Judas said. "Not until I can prove my kid was swiped from under me, confiscated. Yeah, that's what happened. Those damn sisters at Holy Angels. How dare they take my flesh and blood and put him up for adoption."

Shirley looked up at her son admiringly. "Not exactly, honey. You know that bitch DeBour saw to it you'd never see your boy let alone have the inheritance from the Will."

"That's not the story we're telling, Mother! Better keep the facts straight or keep your God damn mouth shut!"

Shirley pulled back like a reprimanded puppy. She could feel the tension in her son's voice. She regretted making him angry. She never could tell how far his madness might go. As a teenager, he had taken a knife to her throat when she refused to lend him her car. On another occasion, he had threatened to strangle the cat they owned if his mother did not give him a buck to attend the corner movie theater. As he got older, so, too, did his volatile behavior escalate. She knew better than to push him to the brink.

"We stick together on this. The nun at City of Holy Angels' Orphanage forced me to sign that adoption form. Plain and simple. That's exactly the way I worded it to Prussia," Judas said.

Shirley attempted to lighten the situation some, chuckling a nervous laugh and snuffing out her Lucky Strike cigarette into an empty glass in the sink. Cigarettes always helped her release her stress. She lit up another, exhaled, and watched the smoke rise to the metal ceiling. "And the nun—."

"Sister Raphael, Judas said."

". . .won't be able to say anything otherwise, boy. Such a smart move getting rid of her."

"Up in flames! Poof! We think alike; like mother, like son, right?"

Shirley kissed her son on the cheek. "How right you are."

Judas carefully removed Shirley's cigarette from between her fingers and took a puff on it. He smiled. He placed the cigarette back into his mother's pursed lips. I've got one more thing up my sleeve and then we can leave this god forsaken place, but I need my whites."

Shirley set up her iron and board in the living room.

Judas got her a spray bottle of water. He sat on the sofa, picking on his cuticle, as he watched his mother spray the garment and press a sharp crease into the white fabric.

"What's up your sleeve? What are you talking about, son?"

"Don't go worrying yourself silly, Mother. Do what I say: Wait here until I come back. When I do, we're off for Utica! My bags are packed and in the car."

Shirley had no idea what her son was talking about. She would have to trust him.

* * *

Max opened the door to the coroner's office. "Oh, hi, Judas. Was there a meeting scheduled?"

Judas pulled his mother's pistol, taken from her bedroom drawer, from beneath his white robe. "Sit down, Max. Have a little something I'd like to discuss with you."

"What are you talking about? Why are you pointing that gun at me?"

"Do as I say."

Max sat down at his desk and began to write.

Chapter Forty

After a few hours of sleep, Dana found herself pacing the kitchen floor, waiting for Howard's call. She needed to know when to meet him and Traynor at McKnight's office. But then her thoughts were interrupted by the ringing of the phone. She picked it up immediately so as not to wake Ellie after their harrowing night's experience.

"When should I meet you at McKnight's office?" she asked Howard.

"In a half hour."

"See you there," Dana said and hung up.

* * *

Dana extended her hand to the officer in the navy-blue uniform, "Pleased to meet you, Mr. Traynor. Howard speaks highly of you," Dana said. Something about Traynor's appearance gave him a presence of authority. He looked to be in his fifties with his grey hair in a buzz cut, resembling William Holden.

"I'd like you to meet my deputy Buck Casey."

Dana shook the man's hand.

"Let me begin by saying you have wrapped up a hell of a case here, Miss Greer," Traynor said. "A man who feigns to be a so-called wanna be priest…this sure isn't the kind of case one sees every day. You deserve a round of applause."

"Well, thank you, Sir, but we're not out of the woods yet. There's more to the case. I believe Shirley Mitford who sat on the board at St. Aloysius was part of it, too. In fact, the two are related...mother and son. Both suspects need to be indicted."

Howard added, "Dana's correct, Bill. From what she tells me, mother and son are no longer at the youth home, and we sure don't need Bonnie and Clyde to get out of our sight."

"Let's get talkin'," Traynor said, in a mild Southern drawl, hardly noticeable. "McKnight, we need your help."

McKnight threw his arms in the air. "Hey, hey, hey. I ain't 'bout to be pinned against no KKK." His face grew pale. His hands turned into shaking fists.

Just the type of response Dana expected from the man. Pointless, worthless.

"We need you to pay Shirley Mitford a call," Traynor said. He looked at McKnight for the idiot he was. "Tell her she's wanted for questioning and bring her into the station," Traynor told the man. "Where do you think our *priest* might be hangin' out?"

"Either with his mother, I suspect, or with Max Freda," Dana said.

"One other thing, McKnight. If the mom's got her son, bring them both out here." He turned to Buck. "You go with the sergeant."

"Will do," the deputy said.

McKnight took the star off his pocket and placed it near his mouth. Once his breath made contact with the metal, McKnight rubbed the sleeve of his shirt until the five points shone.

Dana forced herself not to comment and only hoped the men would hurry. Time was critical.

"In the meantime, Miss Greer, why don't the three of us pay Max Freda a call. It's time he realized he's not above the law. Let's go, Howard."

Chapter Forty-One

Shirley pulled her train case from the upper shelf and threw it on her unmade bed. Then, she grabbed her tweed suitcase from the floor. She moved quickly from her dresser to the small piece of luggage and threw in her toiletries. Next, she yanked clothes out of her dresser drawers and without caring to fold anything, she tossed the belongings into the black and white luggage. It was time for her great escape. She had not expected to stay in Punkerton as long as she had, but she made up her mind she would do whatever Judas asked her. . .even if it meant temporarily falling in love with the brother. She had to be honest with herself, though. It sure was fun being in a clandestine relationship and with a religious no less. And, to think, the man actually took her seriously. Plus, she reminded herself that she had accomplished some legitimate tasks while at the home. She had convinced the brothers to adopt the *Approval to Speak* clause into their board rules. She only had wished the addendum had been added before Timothy Laughton's tongue had to be taken out—poor boy, she laughed out loud to herself.

It still amazed her that her son had been able to get in the home, pretending to be a seminarian and her, as a woman on the board of directors, a much easier ploy than either of them had anticipated. The plan Judas and she had derived allowed her son to get away with the murders of Miss DeBour and her child plus his adoptive parents and opened up the possibility that the inheritance from the Will prepared on Douglas Clifford's behalf would soon be theirs. Shirley had the words to the song "We're in the Money" committed to memory. In time, their only concern would be how to spend the funds that were rightfully theirs. Shirley assumed the amount would be at least enough to buy a new home, travel to Europe, and purchase two new cars.

Shirley tossed two dresses—one a yellow polka-dot number with a ruffled neckline and the other a black silk—onto the floor. "Forget it," she said. "These were fine before I put on ten pounds." Something about fretting over their getaway, worrying they might be caught before they got their hands on the money, caused Shirley's anxiety level to soar. And, whenever it did, she put on a few extra pounds. She took a moment to stare at her figure in the trailer's narrow mirror. "Not bad," she said, "for a forty-six-year old."

All in all, though, Judas and she had carried out the perfect scheme right up to making the murder of Mr. and Mrs. Clifford appear as if their adopted son had done it. Judas felt sure, all along, that Douglas would be sent to the youth home and sure enough he had, as was the case with all juvenile offenders throughout the United States who had committed heinous crimes. With the boy right beneath his nose, Judas had no problem carrying out the perfect crime while the boys were in the lavatory preparing for bed.

Shirley closed her pieces of luggage and placed them next to the door. She knew she would be happy to get out of the AirStream trailer. It gave her and Judas temporary housing, and it gave Brother Calvin and she a perfect place for their romancing. But, she couldn't wait to be back in her home in Utica, New York. She missed the place, where she had raised her only son. She had such fond memories there. She would return to her job as nurse at Community Memorial Hospital. She stopped herself there. Would she? Did she have to?

Once the Will's proceeds were distributed, it might mean she would become a lady of leisure, free to do whatever she wanted. One thing, though, for sure, she and Judas would remain side by side. There was no doubt in her mind about that; that was a given.

She remembered the days they had spent in Los Angeles, where Judas had hoped to land a part in the movies. She had moved with him across the country, so he could pursue an acting career. Thank goodness, she had worked for Doctor Evan's office. There would have been no way Judas could have survived without the support of his mother. As far as Shirley was concerned, it only served to strengthen the bond between herself and Judas. He depended on her solely for everything, and that is just how she liked it. With herself in the control spot, she had been able to get Judas to do whatever she proposed. No wonder she loved the boy so. Her thoughts quickly focused on Chantel DeBour. What a fool, married to one of Paramount's top producers, and she'd fallen head over heels for a minor. For heaven's sake, what did she think the boy could offer her other than young, fresh love; which he did. But, a child? Shirley convinced Judas the only way out would be to convince Chantel to have an abortion in some back alley in Hollywood. Surely, there were plenty of those. But, no, the woman refused. Judas had no choice but to leave the glamour scene.

At that moment, the door to the trailer opened and banged shut. In stepped Judas, no longer in his whites.

"Have you got everything packed, Mother?"

"Been reminiscing about before you were born, son."

"No time for that shit. I say we'd better get the hell out of here!"

"My luggage and my pocketbook are right by the door."

When Shirley's back turned, Judas slipped the pistol into her handbag. He picked up her two pieces and took them out to the trunk of his black car, complete with shiny, new hubcaps. In the rare possibility the Greer woman identified his car, he wanted to make sure he changed its image. On a quick trip to Lubbock, he purchased the spindled covers, and the car looked as if it has come off the assembly line. When he came back inside, he confided in her. "Mother, I can't thank you enough for standing by me."

Shirley hugged her son. "I would not have it any other way, Judas. What are mothers for if they can't be by their son's side?"

"I feel like a failure in your eyes." Tears brimmed in the man's brown eyes.

Shirley hated to see Judas become emotional. It didn't become him. She had raised him to be hard, to believe boys don't cry. Shirley loathed men without self-respect.

"A damn failure," Judas continued.

"What makes you say that, son?"

"How long were we in LA. . .a year, and I never got more than a measly part in a radio commercial. I had hoped for so much more. . .to be a star. . .to see my name on the big screen."

"Well, you've got Chantel DeBour to blame for that, a true bitch. She was a ticket into Paramount, and what did she do for you other than to give you a kid…a kid she, eventually, stole from you! I'm sorry, Judas, but I'm glad you put an end to that woman."

"That's not exactly how it happened, Mother. I was sixteen. How would I have raised a kid? I was a kid myself."

"Need you ask? Douglas Clifford was my grandchild. You should have fought for him right then and there. I told you so. I told you that is what you should have done." Shirley looked down at the floor and then at her son. "You could have demanded support money; you could have blackmailed the fucking starlet. We could have lived quite well." Shirley's voice got louder with each exclamation. It was easy for her to take two sides in an any argument.

"Mother, stop! You know as well as I do that having a kid hanging around would have cramped our style. At least, we stand a better than good chance of reaping the benefits from the Will. What would we have gained raising a child? He would have been a drain on us financially. You know that, Mother."

Shirley looked at her son lovingly. "It's about time we'll be on the receiving end of things."

Judas said, "Don't you worry, mother. Now that DeBour and the Clifford's are out of the way, it shouldn't be hard to prove I'm the boy's biological father and, therefore, entitled to the entire estate. There are plenty of eyewitnesses at Paramount who knew I was the father of Chantel's child including her ex-husband."

"You're right, son. Let's get the hell out of here." Shirley couldn't wait to end the conversation; she hated to see her son so weak, so pathetic, his face flushed, tears streaming down his cheeks.

The two scurried out the door.

Judas started the engine of his car, and he and Shirley sped away from the scene.

"Take the highway to Dallas," Shirley said. "Once there, we'll get bus tickets out of town. C'mon step on it, son."

* * *

Buck and Sergeant McKnight pulled up to the front of the AirStream trailer and noticed the door flapping in the wind. There were no vehicles around. The place looked deserted, but they still entered with guns drawn.

"Well, I'll be a monkey's uncle; the place's been plumb cleaned out. We're too late," McKnight said. He sighed with deep relief.

"Quick, let's head over to Max Freda's and let Traynor know what we've found here," Buck said.

Chapter Forty-Two

Dana, Traynor, and Howard stood on the porch of Max Freda's office. After knocking several times and calling out to the man, Traynor said, "Step back." He shot at the doorknob, a huge hole splintering in the wood. He unlocked the door, and Dana and Howard followed him in as Traynor yelled, "Law enforcement. Mr. Freda, come out with your hands up." After they had made their way into three of the rooms, including Max Freda's office, Traynor opened the door to what appeared to be a storage closet. A straw broom fell out. A metal pail banged down the hallway.

"Jesus, no," Dana said, as she fell to her knees next to the fallen objects. There from the ceiling rafter, Max Freda hung from a thick rope noose. His tongue, thick and swollen, stuck out from his mouth, and his eyes bulged from his face, which looked as if it were covered in flour.

Howard helped Dana up, when she said, "Wait, look here." She found a piece of paper on the tiled floor. She opened it and read:

My time here, I've done the best I could to rid the world of scum and decay.

Wore the white hood with pride and honor

I pass along my role as Grand Wizard today

To a man worthy of my pride and honor: Judas Hudson.

"Guess, the guy must have felt his future was doomed. Rather than risk losing his coveted role in the Klan, he chose to go this way," Traynor said.

"This makes it even more clear the seminarian was part of the KKK all along," Dana said. "Or, maybe, he pretended to be long enough to gain the Klan's support. How ironic. The man wanted to be an actor and sure proved to have the skills."

"That's what I was thinking—at least as long as the role served him," Howard said. "With the KKK's support, the man was guaranteed accomplishing what he set out to do."

"For sure," Dana said, "the murder of Walter Robinski, the destruction of Holy Angels' Orphanage, and—."

"Is there something else?" Traynor asked.

"The youth home. Pray God, the seminarian hasn't taken the place down in flames," Dana said. She ran into Freda's office and called the home.

"Brother Calvin, here."

"Brother, this is Dana. Is everything okay there?"

"What do you mean?"

"No sign of Carl Fenton or Shirley Mitford?" Dana asked.

"Heard they have headed back East. That's what Brother Donald said."

"Thank God," Dana said

At that point, Buck Casey and Sergeant McKnight came down the hall. "We got there too late. Holy smokes, what's happened here?" McKnight said.

"Supposedly a suicide. Found a note, but it's got me wondering. Looks staged to me. I suggest the body go to the Lubbock morgue and see what the county coroner finds after the autopsy," Traynor said.

Howard offered to stay until Max Freda could be taken to a morgue in Lubbock.

Traynor and Dana turned toward Buck and McKnight. "What the hell! What are you doing back here? Where's Shirley and her son?" Traynor asked.

"Afraid we were too late; the trailer's deserted," Buck said.

"You've got to be kidding me. We've got a couple of fugitives on our hands," Traynor said.

"Headed back East," Dana added.

"Not for long. I'll get a call over to my deputies to set up roadblocks. Any idea what vehicle the two might be in?"

Dana was about to say, "no" when she recalled the green Ford truck she had seen Shirley Mitford in only days ago—the one with, what appeared to be, white sheets on the back seat.

"Wait a minute," Dana said. "They might be traveling in a green Ford truck or a black car with missing hubcaps." The former images of the auto played in her mind. The strange vehicle that seemed to show up for unexplained reasons suddenly began to make sense to Dana.

"Got it," said Traynor.

* * *

Several miles outside of Punkerton, Shirley noticed the red stoplights on the cars in front of her. The two-lane road was narrowed to one as a parade of floats, dancing clowns, and student bands marched through. Rows of people sat alongside the curb, clapping. Children were whistling, cheering, and screaming affirmations. A representation of the armed services marched down the street, with four sailors in the lead. And some in the crowd waved small, American flags. A large poster read

Welcome to the Lone Star State

"What the hell is this?" Judas asked.

"Here comes Uncle Sam," Shirley huffed. "Of course, it's a Labor Day celebration."

"Just what we need!"

Shirley tried to take the wheel. "Go around 'em."

Judas did as his mother directed, and the sound of pebbles banging against the tires told them they were on the shoulder, only inches from a deep ditch. "Damn, my new hubcaps!"

A man driving a tractor, pulling a float covered in red, white, and blue carnations, yelled, "Watch what you're doing, you fool! You almost knocked me off the road."

Back on the main road again, Judas felt like a free man; he put his head out the open window and let the muggy breeze blow through his hair. He let out a loud sigh. On the way to the Dallas bus station, Judas and his mother began to sing the lyrics of Tony Bennett's "Rags to Riches." They were singing so loudly, they hardly heard the siren screeching several yards behind them. But once Judas took notice of the flashing lights in his rearview mirror, he screamed, "Mother, Christ no!"

Shirley turned around in her seat and stared out the back window.

"Stop, Judas. They're drawing guns at us."

Judas did as his mother instructed and skidded the black sedan off to the side of the road.

"The gun...my purse...I hope it's in here somewhere!"

He watched in horror as his mother pulled the revolver out.

"Mother, drop it. You don't stand a chance. We'd better do as they say."

Instead, Shirley put her index finger on the trigger ready to do what she felt necessary.

Judas tried to reach over to the passenger's seat. He and his mother fought over the possession of the firearm when the gun went off with a loud blast, the smell of smoke and burning powder in the air. The bullet had plunged into his mother's left temple. A large cavity remained in the side of his mother's head, liquid and bleeding tissues oozing from the burnt hole. "Mother, oh God, no. Mother. . .Mother?" he called, to the bleeding corpse at his side.

Two deputies stepped up to the driver's door and demanded Judas step out. As he did so, they saw the bloody figure of Shirley Mitford. One of the men radioed for help.

Judas stepped out of the car, holding his hands above his head as directed by the deputies, and like an injured animal in the night cried out, "Mother, no. You can't leave me. . .not now. We were so close to our dream." He fell to his knees and beat the pavement with his hands.

"Get your ass up here," one of the deputies said, putting his knee into Judas' back.

Judas struggled and attempted to stand.

The deputy put him in handcuffs and shoved him into the back seat of the cruiser.

An icy chill ran down Judas' back. All he could think about was his mother. He had wanted to run that shop in upstate New York— the music store, but his mother believed he had more potential than that. Whenever people came into the store, they marveled at his handsome looks—some even saying that he looked like a young Julius La Rosa. A silly, young girl had even asked for his autograph once. Mother knew her son was destined for more, more than he would find in Utica. She convinced him to move out West with her where she would provide the source of income, and he could strive to get a contract with Paramount. At first, he landed a meager radio job as a part-time disc jockey, playing the likes of Frank Sinatra and Nat King Cole. From there, he did a commercial for Better Made Potato Chips. Mother badgered him with, "You can do better than this. Who will ever see your handsome face when you're stuck behind a microphone?" She encouraged him to try for bit parts in Hollywood. And, he did but with no success. That is until he met Chantel while he worked as a waiter at the Paramount commissary. She would come in daily decked out in her furs, feathers, and other fineries, obviously a rich and famous woman. Judas never thought he stood a chance with the woman, even though, she always tipped him well. One day while he was bussing her table, he found a handwritten note under the woman's plate:

Looking for some action? Meet me outside my trailer around ten tonight.

Judas had difficulty trying to find Chantel's trailer in the darkness, and it was not until she stepped out glancing at the night's stars that he found her, dressed in a sheer black negligee barefooted. He could feel his heart throbbing as he neared her and introduced himself as Carl Fenton, a name he quickly made up and had kept to this day. Chantel invited him in, and the smell of fine incense wafted through the place. Chantel had a long cigarette, held in place by a monogrammed cigarette holder, dangling from her lips. She giggled over nothing, much like a teenager, as she slipped the straps of her nightgown down from her shoulders. Judas smiled as he recalled the rest—the nights of intoxicating odors, the marijuana highs, and mostly, Chantel's beauty.

"Hey, you, listening to me back there?" one of the deputies called to him. "The woman in the car, your mother? Afraid she died before the ambulance rescued her."

Judas felt as if his stomach fell to the floor. He thrust his head between his knees and vomited onto the carpet of the cruiser. He could not stop his mind from reverberating the endless chant. "Mother. . .how can I go on without you?"

Chapter Forty-Three

Dana knelt in the front pew of St. Rita's, staring into the blue-eyed Clifford boy's photograph, enlarged on an easel positioned on the side of the altar. Before she left Punkerton, she wanted to make sure the Douglas Clifford child had the proper memorial, and Father Neil had graciously agreed. Other than Ellie, Dana was alone in the church, as the first of the invited guests had not yet arrived. This was meant to be an intimate gathering of only a few.

Something about finding herself in the dimly lit sanctuary caused her to ponder on the finality of life, the loneliness and sadness of the living left behind. She contemplated how many lives were taken in a short span of time. As Dana stared at the boy's photo, she could not get herself to believe it was his own birth father who had killed him. He was nothing more than a cold-blooded murderer. And who could ever have imagined Shirley Mitford's demise would be by the hand of her own son, although merely a pure accident.

She turned slightly when Brenda tapped her shoulder. The woman's face was red and puffy. "Life sure ain't fair. Douglas never should have gone this way."

"I hear what you're saying," Dana said.

"But, it's been my pleasure having met you, Ma'am," she said to Dana.

"Likewise. Will you be staying in Punkerton?"

"Afraid not. Stevie wants me with him. And, I miss my boy so much. I'm heading by train to Ohio tomorrow. I'll be staying with my sister."

The city of Punkerton had not been good to her or her son, and Dana was pleased the Brenda chose to relocate. Dana gave her a hug. "I wish you only the best—the same goes for Stevie."

The woman tried to smile and sat next to Dana and Ellie.

Coming up the aisle in a three-piece tan, linen suit was Howard. "This is the end in more ways than one," he said. "Too many innocent souls had to die, unfortunately, before the true evil could be found."

The women slid down the pew, making a space for Howard.

Coming from the vestibule of the church, two altar boys carrying lit candles processed up the aisle. Father Neil, dressed in the purple vestment of mourning, followed them. A small group of women in the choir loft sang, "Guardian Angel from Heaven So Bright." When father got to the front pew, he shook Dana's hand and grasped her arm. "Sorry to meet at yet another service of an innocent," he said.

Dana nodded.

"May these good souls rest in peace."

"Amen."

Father stepped up to the altar and began the Mass. After reading the gospel proclamation from Matthew 19:14 about the little children coming to the Lord for theirs is the kingdom of heaven, he went over to the podium and began his sermon citing what life might have been like had Douglas Clifford not fallen into the arms of one so evil. "The boy's life was blessed with his adoptive parents, who gave him a future he never was able to pursue. Who knows who or what he might have become?" Sniffles could be heard as he concluded his message. When the memorial service finally ended, the altar boys led the way out of the church.

As Ellie, Brenda, Howard, and Dana followed Father Neil toward the front doors of the church, Father Neil stopped Dana. "May I speak privately with you for a moment."

"Excuse me," Dana said, as the others continued down the steps of the church.

"This may not be the best of places for this, Dana," said Father Neil, "but I heard word from a good friend of mine, up in Washington State, a Father Merton. Seems something tragic occurred on the cemetery grounds, behind the Grotto of Lourdes Church."

Dana's eyebrows lowered as she stopped to listen to the rest of Father Neil's account.

"A young postulant's body, a girl a mere thirteen years old, was found behind one of the grottos in the cemetery. When father asked if I might know of any good PIs to investigate the crime, your name, of course, came up. Father is willing to move you up there and get you situated in a guest room in the convent."

"What a tragic story, Father."

"Mary Margaret had joined the Order of Carmelite nuns less than a year ago. She was a mere child."

"Dreadful."

"If you could offer to be of help, father would like you at once. I understand this isn't much no—."

Dana had no hesitation. She did not need time to consider her decision. "Father Neil, I can leave immediately. I would be honored to assist in the case."

"Wonderful. I will contact Father Merton, so he can make arrangements for you at once." He shook Dana's hand. He started to walk away but turned. "Dana, I do have a question for you."

"Certainly."

"There's no doubt you are a competent young lady, but why, might I ask, are you so willing to take on these heart-breaking jobs?"

"I suppose, it's not much different from your profession, Father. We both look at the sins of the world. You hope to bring redemption. I seek to bring about justice."

"Well put," Father said, and know my thoughts go with you. May God bless you."

Dana caught up with the others. She hugged Brenda again and thanked her for coming. When Dana turned toward Howard, he kissed her on the cheek. "A job well done, Dana." A lone tear fell onto her face. As Brenda and Howard walked off, Ellie squeezed Dana's hand. As if having heard the conversation between Dana and the priest, Ellie said, "You go where God sends you," she whispered. The two women hugged.

* * *

As Dana packed her belongings, she reminisced over the many good people she had met while in Punkerton: Ellie, Brenda and Stevie, Timothy Laughton, Walter, Father Neil, and, of course, Howard Rhodes. She sighed deeply. Ellie was right. God found a way to send her where she was most needed. And, who could compete with a boss like that. She knew she was being called. She folded the purple afghan, which Ellie had made for her, and whispered a prayer of thanksgiving.

Epilogue

One Year Later

Thunderstorms crowded out the light of day as Judas Hudson, head hung and his shoulders hunched low, was escorted to his cell on death row. His trial was completed. The news spread throughout the States of Texas and California when Judas Hudson, aka Carl Fenton, was sentenced to death by means of the electric chair for the death of Douglas Clifford. There was no need for extradition to California for the deaths of Harold and Nina Clifford, Chantel DeBour, and her chauffeur due to sentence of death in Texas.

The long walk through the green halls gave Judas time to think, to review his life. He wondered how life would have turned out differently if Chantel and he had married and kept their child. He would be in Hollywood, maybe an up and coming star. Douglas would be on a kid's baseball team. The famous family's names, their photos, would have been blasted all over the covers of star magazines. They would be celebrities. People would stop them for their autographs, and Judas' mother would have been proud of her son. Ever since he had been shoved into his six by eight concrete tomb, Judas longed for the presence of his mother.

Thanks to Dana's intervention, Bishop Lorenzio, from Rome, had come to investigate the St. Aloysius Home for Troubled Youth with a mandate on how best to close its doors forever. Pope Pius the XII ruled the home was no longer suitable to be run by the brothers and stopped all charitable contributions to the home. The boys would be sent to adult facilities in the home states of their crimes. The place would be put on the market and the proceeds would be distributed to the Roman Curia. Brothers Donald and Victor, the administrative arm of the home, were in the process of being investigated for the unexplained deaths of all the boys in the graveyard. In the meantime, they were assigned to a small and secluded monastery in Nogales, Mexico. Chantel DeBour's estate would not be distributed pending the court's decision as to who were the rightful beneficiaries.

* * *

Watertown, Iowa

The remaining brothers in the home were assigned to the Monastery of the Blessed Mother, where they spent their days cultivating the farm lands, working with hoes and rakes until by nightfall, their hands wept blood from the opened blisters on their palms. Although Brother Calvin would have sold his soul to have been assigned to the monastery, instead, thanks to the testimony of the boys and some of the guards at the youth home, he was arrested and prosecuted for his part in the abuse of the boys at the St. Aloysius Gonzaga Home for Troubled Youth. His sentence was reduced by his testimony against Dr. Fritz Hansen in the death of Gary Banks.

* * *

Max Freda's death was not deemed a suicide as originally thought, however, no one was implicated in his death due to lack of evidence.

* * *

As for Timothy Laughton, Dana fulfilled her promise that she would not forget him. After pulling a few strings with Chief Traynor of Lubbock and Howard Rhodes, Dana was able to see to it that Timothy was sent to the Ohio State Prison, where he was only a few miles away from Brenda's sister's house. This meant Stevie would once again be allowed to visit the boy he had become so fond of.

* * *

Dr. Fritz Hansen was sentenced to life without parole at the Texas State Prison for the death of Gary Banks and the cruel and unusual punishment of Timothy. When interviewed by a local newspaper, he was said to comment, "He had no idea what he had done wrong; he was only following orders."

* * *

As was the case, the KKK stayed entrenched in all its glory and power. They assigned the title of Grand Wizard to one Martin Lloyd, a former guard at the St. Aloysius Gonzaga Home for Troubled Youth. The KKK was never implicated in the murder of Greta Canfield, her death was deemed a suicide. Her mother, Louise, the Edgar Allan Poe librarian, relocated to Florida. The KKK was never indicted in the death of Walter Robinski.

* * *

Ellie Banks continued to live in her small home with Patches, her cat, and Maize, her yellow canary. She often thought about Gary but knew he had to finally be at peace, knowing the truth of his death had finally come out. She passed her time working on her crafts, reading her Bible, and sending Dana an occasional note.

* * *

Howard Rhodes, the Lubbock attorney, contacted Father Neil of St. Rita's rectory, asking for the forwarding address of Dana Greer. He sent the following to the private investigator:

Dear Dana,

It was my pleasure working with you during your short stay in Texas. Tragic as the outcome was, with so many deaths, you deserve praise for solving not only Douglas Clifford's murder but the murder of the others, as well.

I wish you only the best and hope one day our paths may, once again, cross. I would like nothing more than to keep in contact with you and to hear about your outstanding work in the field of investigation.

Fondly,

Howard

* * *

The Archbishop had telegrammed Dana with the following note:

My heart is filled with sorrow at the misdeeds of the brothers at the youth home. They were called to the service of God, and yet as men, they have committed the most horrific of sins. There's an old saying: the ship is divine, but the crew is human. May we find some semblance of reassurance in those words.

Many thanks for working on the assigned case of Douglas Clifford. May he and those of the others departed, rest in eternal peace.

May the grace of God continue to surround you in the work you do.

Archbishop Floyd J. Boretti

* * *

And, regrettably, the town of Punkerton remained the same: corrupt, intolerant, and narrow-minded.

Enjoyed reading Silent Betrayal? **Here's a preview of what's to come in Delphine Boswell's third novel in the Dana Greer Mystery Series.**

Bitter Wrath...

When the body of a young nun is found murdered on the cemetery grounds of the Grotto of Lourdes Catholic Church in Winter Willows, Washington, Dana Greer, PI, is brought in to solve the case. As she learns more about the girl's background, Dana finds herself involved in the midst of a possible kidnapping, a mysterious suicide, and the questionable alibis of a growing list of suspects. Bitter Wrath takes you behind the scenes of a cloistered convent, where life in the nunnery is far from what you'd expect. When bitterness festers, it can lead one to commit the most heinous of crimes...even murder. No telling what it might drive one to do the most unlikely of souls can do...even murder!

Prologue

October, 1953

Grotto of Lourdes Cemetery established in 1892, a popular tourist stop, was known for its majestic shrine, where said miracles had taken place, all in view of the archangels, seraphims, and cherubims who looked down upon the people. The crutches, canes, braces, and even soiled bandages of those afflicted with various diseases and ailments lay in a glass case as a reminder of the power of prayer. To this day, pilgrims journeyed from miles away in hopes of a cure.

Charles Fillmore, the groundskeeper, wiped the sweat from his brow. Dusk turned the clouds to a splash of purple, pink, and bright neon orange. One more grave to fill, and he could return to his wife, Tilly, of thirty-seven years. The business had provided him with a constant income, and he found the job of cutting, trimming, and weeding to be rewarding. His least favorite part of the work was digging and filling the grave sites. Something about the finality of it frightened him and sometimes offered him a piercing heartburn in his chest. He figured tonight would be no different. He grabbed his shovel from his rusted 1939 Dodge TD-21, one ton, pick-up and headed toward the opened grave next to the statue of the Archangel Michael. The porcelain figurine bore a chipped nose and a missing hand that formerly gripped a sword. At his feet was a slayed devil. Charles edged closer to the rim of the grave, a pile of moist soil on the blade of his shovel. About to toss the wet dirt into the deep hole that bore the burial vault of a recent deceased parishioner, Charles blinked hard. Nearing nightfall, he assumed his eyes might be playing tricks with him. He pulled his flashlight from his back-overall's pocket. He blinked again and shone the light into the dark abyss.

"God almighty! Jesus Christ, no," he called into the lonely air. Taking his time as his stiff body didn't work quite as well as it did when he was twenty, he got down on his hands and knees. With his shoulders hunched over his humped back and his head as low as it would go, he propped himself up on the palm of his hand. Aiming the shaking flashlight downward, he saw, there, atop the vault, what appeared to be a young woman, lying face-up, dressed in the habit of a postulant, all in white. Her legs and arms splayed in the form of a letter *X*. The position of the body convinced Charles that someone had to have pushed her into the grave. Blood oozed out of her head covering as if it had been crushed against something. It was then that Charles identified the young girl. "Sister Mary Margaret, Sister." He continued to call out her name, an echo reiterating in the cold night air. "God, in Jesus' name, no!" he cried out. The woman never responded. He tried yet one more time although he knew his screams were in vain.

Charles remembered the day Mary Margaret had been granted special permission to join the Order of Carmelites at the mere age of thirteen, the oldest of ten children, when her mother could no longer financially care for the family. Charles sat down on the wet, dew-covered grass, and wept silently into his hands. His chest burned as if he had swallowed a cup of acid. Bile arose in his throat. Who in God's name would do such a thing to the young, beautiful nun?

CPSIA information can be obtained
at www.ICGtesting.com
Printed in the USA
FSHW012308030419
56875FS